The
Fanlight

Michael Llewellyn

For
Lady Evelyn Gilleland
Those were the days, my friend!

The Fanlight is a work of fiction. Names, places and incidents are either products of the author's imagination or are use fictitiously.

©2024 Scaramouche Publishing

"He was born with a gift of laughter and a sense that the world was mad."

Cover design by the author.

The Fanlight

Michael Llewellyn

PART ONE

"I suppose we are all wrongly made up
and have a fallen nature;
else why is it that while the most thrifty
and neat and orderly city only wins our approval...
such a thriftless, battered and stained
and lazy old place as the French Quarter of New Orleans takes our
hearts?"
-Charles Warner, Harper's Magazine, January,1887

1

"If this were hurricane season," Gemma grumbled into the phone, "last night's storm would've had a name."

"Any damage?" Maddie asked.

Gemma took quick inventory through the French doors. The courtyard was littered with palm fronds and tree limbs, and a potted camellia bush was toppled, red blooms strewn like confetti. Her majordomo, Tyrone Miller, struggled to reattach a bower of trumpet vines torn from the high brick wall by fierce winds.

"I'll manage."

"So tonight's still on?"

"Good Lord, girl! You ought to know it'll take more than a winter storm to wreck my Twelfth Night party. Ty's already on clean-up duty, and I'm sure he'll…oh, there's the doorbell. Gotta scoot."

"You need anything?"

"Not a thing, darling. See you at seven!"

Gemma clicked off the phone and hurried to the back door. Her home, an 1848 Creole townhouse occupying half a city block along Esplanade Avenue, was the only one in the French Quarter with a service entrance. She was ushering Sydney Ball, her indispensable caterer, into the kitchen when the phone rang in her hand. She checked caller ID. Who was Philip Brooks?

"Hello."

"Gemma Stafford Clark?"

Gemma frowned. No one had used her maiden name since her first marriage almost thirty years ago. "Who's calling?"

"Your cousin, Philip Brooks."

"My what?" Her confusion came not only from surprise but from the caller's slurred response.

"Cousin," the man repeated. "Our grandfathers were brothers."

Gemma's family tree was a long-standing mystery. Her parents never mentioned it, and she'd been dismissed whenever she asked. She had only a vague recollection of a New Orleans ancestor named Samuel Stafford and knew that her father was an only child. She knew nothing about her mother's people in Savannah.

"Which side of the family?"

"Father." A loud hacking cough made Gemma pull the phone from her ear. A long pause, then, "We need to talk."

"We *are* talking. What do you want and how did you get this number?"

"The house," Brooks blurted. "You gotta buy the house."

"What on earth are you talking about?" Gemma was annoyed by another long pause. "Are you drunk?"

"I've had a couple. So what?"

Gemma had heard enough. "Good-bye, Mr. Brooks."

"No, no! Wait! Wait! We gotta talk."

"You already said that. Look, whoever you are. I've got a crazy busy day, and have no time for drunks claiming to be relatives."

"Okay. Okay. Look, Mama left me the house when she died last spring. I grew up there. So did your daddy, and I'm…I don't…I can't pay the mortgage."

"Money," Gemma muttered. "I should've known."

"No, no. Please listen. The house has been in our family over a hundred years, and if you buy it from me, we can skip the realtor's fee. It's a win-win." Brooks coughed again and cleared his throat. "Not that money's a problem for you."

"Pardon me?"

"I live in Natchez and saw your story last summer in the Democrat. You mentioned our great-grandfather, Samuel Stafford. I saved the article because I thought I might get in touch someday. Good thing I did, huh?

The more Brooks talked, the less Gemma understood. "I'm not following you."

"You live in a mansion, lady. Poor people don't live in mansions."

Gemma recalled her interview about life in one of the few French Quarter townhouses not chopped into apartments or condos. The Natchez writer was polite, if fawning, and she'd been pleased with the story and glamorized photos.

"My finances are none of your business, Mr. Brooks. I know nothing about my family history and see no reason to start now." To Gemma's annoyance, Brooks began to cry. Not soft whimpers, but wracking sobs. "Oh, for God's sake, man. Get a grip."

"You…you don't understand," he moaned. "I'm broke. I got covid right after Mama died and lost my job. I grew up in that house, see, and—"

"You already said that, Mr. Brooks, but I've no proof this isn't a scam."

Gemma heard a rude slurp before Brooks rattled off a chronology that left her reeling. "Our great-grandfather, Samuel Stafford, came to New Orleans from England in eighteen-seventy and married Elizabeth Morgan. He made a fortune as a cotton factor and built a mansion in the Garden District. Chestnut Street. He had two sons, Daniel and John. Daniel was your grandfather and John was mine. They—"

"Whoa!" Gemma cried. "I can't process all that."

"You wanted proof."

"All I'm hearing is a bunch of names and dates that anybody could get off the internet."

"Look, lady. I'm trying to do us both a favor. I need the money really bad, and you'd be getting a super good deal. A little TLC you could see that house for a fortune."

Gemma was intrigued in spite of herself. "You say it's on Chestnut Street?"

"No, no. That's the one Samuel built. The one where your daddy and I grew up is in the Lower Garden District. Eight Baptiste Street. It's two-stories and has a big back yard and was built in eighteen-thirty-eight. If you'd just go over and take a look—"

"I'm going nowhere without proof that you're legit."

"Uh, okay. I get that. How about I send copies of the deed and mortgage?"

For the first time, Gemma thought the caller might be legit. "Alright."

"I'll need your email address."

"You've got my phone number. Just text everything."

"I...I don't know how to do that."

Gemma chided herself for caving, but the guy sounded so pathetic she rattled off her email address. "Got it?"

"Yes. Thanks cuz. You're a godsend."

"I'm not anything until I see some documents."

"Okay. Okay." Brooks coughed again and stopped with some difficulty. "But please hurry. The bank's threatening foreclosure, and I—"

Gemma heard Sydney calling from the kitchen. "I have to go."

"Please, cousin!" Brooks pleaded.

"Good-bye, Mr. Brooks." Gemma clicked off and stared at the caller ID. "What a loon!"

Invitations to Gemma's Twelfth Night party were considered pure gold. Her reputation as a grand hostess was assured by Tyrone and Sydney whose teamwork addressed every detail. The house had a glittering Mardi Gras tree in the parlor and a three-tiered King Cake held court in the dining room. Swathed in purple, green and gold icing, it contained a tiny baby Jesus revealed when the cake was cut and served. Whoever found the precious souvenir would be crowned monarch of Twelfth Night. Chic in vintage black Chanel, blonde bob freshly colored and clipped, Gemma was the epitome of late fortyish glamour as she swanned among her elegant guests, but efforts to lose herself in the revery were undermined by nagging thoughts of Philip Brooks. Deciding she needed to talk about the phone call, she searched out best friend, Maddie Foster. Maddie worked at the WIlkins Research Center, but looked anything but bookish in a snug red cocktail dress, brunette hair piled high. She tried to make sense as Gemma reiterated the bizarre story.

"Think the guy's on the level?"

"Who knows? He sounded drunk as a lord, but he sure had a sharp memory for family names."

"Did you recognize any of them?"

"Only my great-grandfather, Samuel Stafford. Mother mentioned him a few times. I don't remember why. Nor do I know how he got my phone number."

"Maybe he's a computer nerd." Maddie's long-time companion, Henri Chabrol, slipped an arm around her waist. A physics professor and vice chancellor at Tulane University, he had swapped his usual tweed jacket for a tuxedo, but still radiated academia, especially when peering over wire-rimmed glasses. "Those guys can pretty much find anything they want."

"He's way too old to be a computer nerd. In fact, the way he hacked and choked, he sounded like he was on his last leg."

"Maybe an accomplice worked things out for him." Henri took a cellphone from his dinner jacket. "Do you remember the address of the house?"

"Eight Baptiste Street. That's your neck of the woods, isn't it?"

"Not far." Henri entered the info, waited a few seconds and tapped more buttons. "That address isn't on any of the realtor sites, but I was able to pull up number ten. You can see the side of number eight next door. Here." Gemma and Maddie saw a wooden two-story house with deep galleries on both floors, the uppermost swarming with vines. "I remember it now from my walks around the neighborhood."

"Well," Gemma conceded, "It's pretty much as he described it."

"Let me have another look." Henri's avocation as an architectural historian made him a much sought-after speaker and consultant. "It looks like an American version of a Creole townhouse. Probably dates from the eighteen forties."

"Brooks said eighteen thirty-eight."

Henri enlarged the photo. "Definitely a fixer-upper. Is the place empty?"

"He didn't say, but if he was that desperate for money he must've rented it out."

"He said he grew up there?"

"My father too, apparently."

Henri despaired at the picture. "No sane New Orleanian would let an old wooden house sit empty. You know that saying. 'If the mold don't get you, the mildew.'"

"I seriously doubt Mr. Brooks is sane," Gemma sniffed. "C'mon, Henri. Doesn't this whole thing sound crazy to you?"

"Sort of, but on the off-chance that it's not, why don't we head over tomorrow for a look-see? If it's a rental, maybe the tenants can tell us something about your cousin."

"That depends."

"On what?" Maddie asked.

Gemma snagged a glass of champagne from a passing waiter. "On how much fun I have tonight." She took a generous sip and glanced at Maddie's watch. "What time is it?"

"Almost seven."

"Then, here goes!"

Gemma swept into the crowd, raised her hands and called for quiet. "Ladies and gentlemen. In a few minutes, the Phunny Phorty Phellows and the Storyville Stompers will board the St Charles streetcar and officially proclaim the beginning of the carnival season. Everyone raise their glasses and toast Mardi Gras, two thousand twenty-three. *Laissez les bon temps rouler!*"

2

Gemma awoke at eight-thirty and sat up in bed to welcome a clear head. She dressed, grabbed her cellphone and went downstairs to find Tyrone in the kitchen squeezing orange juice. A cup of black coffee, poured when he heard her footsteps, steamed on the breakfast table. Everything, she thought happily, was as it should be.

"Good morning. Ty."

"Good morning. With or without?"

Since Tyrone came to work for Gemma eighteen years ago, they'd long since transcended any traditional employer/employee boundaries and become friends. He knew her habits even better than Maddie, and this was his way of asking if she wanted her orange juice straight or laced with prosecco.

"Without, thank you. I was a good girl last night."

"Coming right up."

Gemma sat and stirred sugar into her coffee. "I thought the party went very well, didn't you?"

"One of your best. People had fun but not too much fun."

"Meaning you didn't have to pour anyone into a cab."

"Or throw anybody out."

Both chuckled at last year's memory of Tyrone slinging an obnoxious and very inebriated state senator over his shoulder and hauling him outside. A black man wearing 270-pounds of muscle, courtesy of eight years as a marine and rigorous gym workouts, Tyrone was well-equipped for handling unruly drunks. Gemma was one of the few who about the sweet soul behind the fearsome façade.

"Will you be needing me this afternoon?" he asked.

Gemma remembered Philip Brooks' promised email. "I don't know yet." She picked up the china cup and saucer and headed for the library. "I'll let you know in a minute."

Gemma opened her laptop and watched the monitor brighten to life. She clicked on email, and there it was. Ptbrooks79. She started to click again, but hesitated, wondering if she was flirting with Pandora's box. Her father Robert had been steadfastly mute about the Staffords and took their secrets to his grave when he died of a stroke thirty-nine years ago. Bewildered by his silence, she had assumed the family history was too terrible or shameful to mention. As she continued to hesitate, fears morphed into exasperation. Gemma Clark was a lot of things, but diffident wasn't one of them.

"Get on with it, woman."

Gemma opened Brooks' email to find his address and phone number along with the name and phone number of his property manager, Canaan Gentry.

"So the place is a rental," she muttered.

A quick scan of the attachments revealed the deed to the Baptiste Street property and a mortgage with Crescent City Bank on Poydras Street downtown. Another attachment held a photocopy of an envelope and letter dated May 6, 1924, addressed to Daniel Stafford at Eight Baptiste Street. Gemma scrolled down to a letter faint and fragile from repeated readings and so riddled with water stains that it was barely legible. The elaborate handwriting didn't help. She read aloud as she deciphered a phrase here and there.

"Dearest Papa…sad good-bye at train station…can harbor no more secrets between us…must vow all my love." It was signed "Sloane."

Gemma remembered Brooks saying that Daniel Stafford was her grandfather, but who was this Sloane person and why had Brooks included her letter along with the legal documents?

"This is maddening!"

Gemma phoned Maddie and left a message when her call went to voice mail. She waited for the beep.

"Guess what, kiddo! I got the documents from the mystery man in Mississippi, so I'm ready for that road trip uptown. Sometime after lunch because you know I love lazy mornings after party nights. It was great fun, eh? Call me when you get this."

Gemma returned to the kitchen for Tyrone's breakfast of juice, mango yogurt and croissants. She was searching the Lagniappe section of the Picayune for Mardi Gras events when Maddie returned her call.

"So you think this guy is for real?"

"Looks like. He also sent a family letter from nineteen twenty-four, from someone named Sloane. Fabulous handwriting, very gushy."

"Typical of the Roaring Twenties, I imagine. Henri and I will scoop you at one. You don't mind if he comes along, do you?"

"Now why wouldn't I want the opinion of the best architectural historian in the city?"

"Lord, Gemma! Promise you won't tell him that. I'll never hear the end of it."

"I promise." Gemma thought a moment. "Tell me something, Maddie."

"What?"

"Am I crazy to go on this wild goose chase?"

"I think you'd be crazy not to, but that's because I'm fascinated by genealogy. I know you couldn't care less, but if I found a long-lost cousin who'd grown up in the same house as my father, I'd definitely want to know more. Which reminds me. Why didn't he contact you when he lived in New Orleans?"

"He said he knew nothing about me until he moved to Natchez and saw that article in the local newspaper."

"Be glad he did."

"I guess I am, but I'm still worried about what I might find."

"You should be, but that's part of the fun. C'mon, Gemma. Finding out where your grandfather lived isn't like learning he was in the KKK."

"God forbid."

"Then put on your big girl pants, and we'll see you at one."

3

The French Quarter fell behind when Henri drove Maddie and Gemma across Canal Street. As they headed uptown on Magazine Street, he began, to no one's surprise, a running commentary on the neighborhood. "The Lower Garden District was carved from five plantations not long after the Louisiana Purchase in 1803 when the Americans took over. The French Creoles barred them from the Quarter, so the newcomers were forced to build across Canal."

"So much for French hospitality," Gemma observed.

"You'd be inhospitable too if you woke up one morning to discover your country had changed flags, languages, customs and governments overnight."

"Without your permission," Maddie added.

"Good point."

Henri crossed Calliope, Clio and Euterpe Streets before turning left onto Thalia. "The guy who designed this neighborhood was a character named Barthelemy Lafon. He had a thing for Greek mythology which is why the streets are named for the nine muses. He also had delusions of grandeur with plans for a coliseum, cathedral, parks, canals and turning basins. He even wanted to build a prytaneum."

"A what?"

"A kind of town hall, another Greek idea. The closest he got was Prytania Street and the Prytania Theater."

"Katrina didn't flood up here, did it?"

"No. It's part of the sliver on the river like the Quarter and the Garden District. The neighborhood was just turning around when the storm hit and everything stagnated. It started another comeback a few years ago with hipsters, artists and young families moving in. Some spots are still rough, but there's charm if you know where to look."

"Like almost every neighborhood in New Orleans."

"True enough." Henri turned right onto Baptiste Street. "Lots of single and double shotgun houses through here. Further uptown, the houses get grander with second stories and generous galleries and Greek Revival facades."

"Like the one we're looking for."

Henri parked and pointed across the street. "Which is right there!"

Gemma peered through the car window. "I didn't see that chain-link fence in the photo."

"Neither did I."

"Let's get a closer look."

The raised cottage was deeper than it appeared in the cell phone photo. It definitely needed work, but Henri said that the fine architectural detailing, though badly weathered, looked intact. One end of the second-story gallery was obscured by cat's claw, a potentially destructive tropical vine. Gemma's eye trailed from the vine to a front door crowned by a fanlight covered with plywood. The yard roiled with towering weeds, and a large No Trespassing sign beside the door warned would-be squatters.

"So much for it being a rental," Maddie remarked.

"Well, it was at some point because Brooks' email included contact info for a property manager." Gemma's disappointment was evident. "He didn't mention a padlock, or that hideous chain-link fence."

"Wonder how long it's been empty."

"Judging from that cat's claw, I'd say several months.

Henri inspected the lock and considered climbing the fence until he saw that the front door was padlocked too. He wandered to the side of the house but found it obscured by a thick grove of banana plants. Their battered fronds, turned brown by the winter, clattered in a breeze from the nearby river.

"See anything?" Gemma called.

"Nothing, but I can't get very far. I'm guessing the whole yard's fenced."

Maddie rattled the padlock. "Surely the property manager's got a key to this thing. Aren't you dying to see inside?"

"I was a second ago, but, oh, I don't know." Gemma scanned the damage, taking inventory of broken windows, hanging shutters and the boarded-up fanlight. "It...well, it looks like way too much work."

"That's not what you were going to say."

"You know me too well."

"Yes, I do. And?"

"The place kinda freaks me out."

"Why? You worried about ghosts?"

"If I worried about ghosts, I wouldn't be living in the Quarter. It's what I said before about looking into the past. Rattling family skeletons and all that. It's fear of the unknown, I guess."

Maddie draped an arm around her shoulders. "You don't have to come back if you don't want to. Henri and I can check it out for you, or we can forget the whole business."

"That's sweet, but I'm not giving up just yet."

They were getting back into the car when someone called Henri's name. A couple of bicyclists waved and pulled over. Henri recognized two of his students from a few years back, but couldn't recall their names. Fortunately, the man volunteered both.

"Hi, Dr. Chabrol. I'm Larry Wilson, and this is my wife, Annette. Remember us?"

"Of course. It's not every day I get a husband and wife in my classroom."

"What're you doing in our neighborhood?" Annette asked.

"Checking out the house across the street. Do you live nearby?"

"That shotgun on the corner. The painted lady."

"Very nice." Henri nodded at Brooks' house. "Do you know the fellow who owned this place?"

"No, but we heard he was a drunk." Gemma and Maddie exchanged looks. "He moved out a while back and rented it. We had problems with his last tenant. The whole neighborhood did."

"What kind of problems?"

"He was a sludge rocker and a druggie. People were always calling the cops about his loud parties. Including us."

"Everyone was glad when he moved out last October," Annette added. "Then, some guy padlocked that chain-link fence and posted that No Trespassing sign, and it's been empty ever since. You looking to buy it, Dr. Chabrol?"

"No, no. Just curious."

"Us too. Everybody around here's hoping it'll go on the market. Real estate's on fire in this neighborhood."

"That's what I hear." Henri opened the car door. "Nice to see you two."

"Thanks. You too."

Gemma watched the two cyclists disappear around the corner. "Thanks for keeping me out of that little chat, Henri."

"I figured you had no comment."

"No, I don't, but if the local real estate's really that hot, I'd better get over myself and look into it."

Maddie brightened. "So you'll call the property manager?"

"Why not?" Gemma fished through her purse for her phone. "I'll get his number from my email and call before I change my mind." She knew Maddie's expression without looking. "Darling, I know changing my mind all the time drives you batty, but I can't help myself."

"Don't be silly. It's one of your most endearing traits."

Gemma grinned. "You're such a sweet liar."

"A label I wear with pride."

Gemma was still chuckling as she punched in Cane Gentry's number. It rang so long she expected it to go to voice mail, but he finally picked up.

"Yeah?"

"Mr. Gentry?"

"Who's this?" The voice was gruff, edgy.

"This is Gemma Clark. I understand you're the property manager for Six Baptiste Street."

"Not anymore."

"I beg your pardon?"

"The owner stopped paying my salary five months ago, so I quit going over there."

"Did you padlock the gate?"

"Yeah. Why?"

"Mr. Brooks is my cousin," Gemma replied, thinking fast. "He asked me to check on the house and make sure everything's alright."

"His cousin, huh?"

"Yes."

"Does that mean you'll be paying my back salary. No offense, but your relative's a deadbeat and a drunk."

"No offense taken. I'm just glad you didn't tell me what you really think." Gentry either ignored the joke, Gemma thought, or didn't get it.

"So you'll pay me what's due?" he pressed, voice louder.

"How much is that?"

"Eight hundred bucks."

"Seriously?"

"I'm a ten percenter, lady. Rent for that house was sixteen hundred a month, and ten percent of that is one hundred sixty bucks. Brooks is five months behind. Do the damned math."

Gemma stiffened. "There's no need to be rude, Mr. Gentry." He muttered something unintelligible. "Suppose we discuss the situation at the house?"

"Sure thing, lady!" he boomed. "I go over there and unlock the place and then you decide you're gonna stiff me too. That's bullshit!"

"I said we'd discuss it," Gemma said, reining her temper. "Look, Mr. Gentry. I never knew my cousin existed until he called yesterday offering to sell the house. I'm not obliged to either of you to do anything, so I hope you can appreciate my situation." There was a long pause while Cane weighed her words. "Are you still there?"

"Yeah," he said slowly. "But I gotta tell you Philip Brooks was a pain in the ass from that first day he came to the batture looking for me, and a red flag went up when you said he was your cousin. I should've quit that job the first time he missed a payment."

"I'm sorry he treated you so unfairly."

"Like you said. Not your problem."

"Thank you."

"You thinking to buy the place?"

"Right now, all I want to do is take a look inside. I know your time's valuable, Mr. Gentry, and I assure you I'll make it worth your while to unlock the house and show me around and answer some questions. Does two hundred dollars sound fair?"

"I guess so."

"Could you meet me tomorrow? Say ten o-clock?"

"Sure."

"Wonderful. I'll see you then."

He clicked off before she could say good-bye. Henri and Maddie were looking at her.

"Did you hear any of that?"

"Most of it," Henri said. "The guy was loud."

"Angry too, but I would be too if I got screwed out of eight hundred bucks."

"Did he say he lives on the batture?" Henri asked.

"Apparently that's where Brooks came looking for him."

25

"I've wanted to see that place for years."

"Those shacks on the river? Why?"

"Because there's no place else like it."

"Why didn't you just go over there and look around?"

"Because I hear those people aren't fond of nosy strangers."

Gemma sniffed. "Not if Canaan Gentry's any indication."

4

"Coffee," Cane muttered.

He rolled out of bed, found the kitchen in the pre-dawn darkness and turned on the coffeemaker. While waiting for it to brew, he stumbled onto the back porch. He was still in sleep shorts, and a thick, unseasonably warm fog hugged his face and chest. In the growing light, steam from his coffee merged with the fog, as though marrying the river's breath. Cane liked the idea and marveled, as always, at a backyard with a million cubic feet of water hurtling by every second. Sometimes more. The Mississippi was at its deepest here in New Orleans, cavernous enough to hide a twenty-story building. It was a sleepy, sluggish half-coiled serpent…until it wasn't.

"Coffee," Cane said again, alerted by escaping steam that the coffee was ready.

He poured a mug, took a tentative sip and went back outside. He settled in his favorite chair and leaned back to enjoy the fog's usual tricks, thickening here, thinning there, vacillating between light and dark until sunlight glowed over the West Bank. He thought of the old joke that, in this corner of the city, the curving Mississippi meant that the sun rose in the west. He sipped his coffee, absorbing a familiar silence until the river reminded him he had company with a deep horn blast and the monstrous shadow of a nine-hundred-foot container ship. Fully laden, she rode low in the water, but as she glided by, her eight-story bulk blotted out the sky. A blurred scattering of Chinese merchant seamen looked down on the tiny riverside enclave but no one waved. They never did, the Chinese, so Cane long ago stopped trying to be friendly. He listened to the ship's wake sloshing ashore in lazy ripples and watched as her captain swung stern to port in anticipation of the wicked curve ahead. Cargo ships, oil tankers and bulk containers this size negotiated the perilous turn well in advance, allying themselves with the fierce current. Cane never tired of this nautical ballet, a daily performance for people living on the batture. That ephemeral stretch of no man's land between the levee and the Mississippi was named for the French *battre*, meaning "to beat," because the river beat the shore. When the French arrived three centuries ago, they called it *flottant*, the floating land. Canaan Alexander Gentry called it home.

Sunlight finally riddled the cloudbank and melted the fog. The nearby tangle of willows and tallow trees sharpened and emerged, along with his neighbors' houses. Called camps, the nineteen structures perched atop stilts, each connected to the levee with meandering catwalks as unique as their occupants. Cane anchored the downriver end, and his good friend Poppy owned the camp next door. They sometimes chatted, porch to porch, over morning coffee. If Poppy had been in a baking mood, she'd stick a slab of orange bread in a plastic baggie and toss it over. On lucky mornings, Cane got chocolate bread pudding. He was salivating at the thought when he heard the whine of a rusty screen door and saw Poppy step outside. Against the gray dawn, she was a tropical bird in a gaudy scarlet robe embroidered with gold dragons, a souvenir his father brought back from Vietnam. Cane had kept it for years after his parents died and gave it to Poppy when they became friends. A pair of fluffy alligator slippers grinned from her feet, and her gray hair was a lopsided mess from sleep. No treats this morning, but she offered a cough and half-hearted wave.

"Up with the birds again, I see."

"Speak of the devil."

Cane nodded when an egret fluttered to earth not twenty feet from Poppy's porch. It grandly ignored her as it stalked the riverbank. It froze for a long moment, then, with a fierce flash, the rapier beak darted into the water, seized a fish and tossed it high. It disappeared into the bird's gullet and triggered a spasm in the huge breast as it was swallowed whole. Mission accomplished, the egret flapped slender, elegant wings and disappeared through the trees.

"Who else gets to see that from their back porch?" Cane called, relishing the moment.

"Nobody, that's who." Poppy eased herself into a plastic chair, registering each of her seventy-nine years. "Can't believe how balmy it is this morning. Wore my long-johns to bed and woke up in a sweat. I reckon that storm day before yesterday brought us a warm front."

"I reckon."

"How long you been up?"

"It was still dark when I came outside."

"You and your damned insomnia. When're you gonna do something about it?"

"I'm okay. My sleep issues are seasonal like the river."

Poppy gave him no further argument. She knew he'd no more act on his insomnia than she'd give up cigarettes. She also knew Cane was a lone wolf, but being his closest neighbor and not a woman to be put off, she eventually eroded his resistance and the result was the unlikeliest of friendships. It thrived, she joked, because it had everything going against it. "How else you gonna explain why an old black saloon singer and hard-headed white man gonna be good buddies?"

"I had a weird phone call yesterday afternoon," he said.

"That crazy drunk on Baptiste Street back in town?"

"Not exactly." Cane shaded his eyes when lofty winds shredded the clouds and shards of blinding sunlight danced on the river. "Some woman saying she was his cousin."

"I'll never forget that time he came down here looking for you, came to my camp instead and knocked one of my plants into the water." Poppy snorted. "That fool was so damned loaded he nearly fell off the catwalk."

"Yeah. If I hadn't needed the money so badly I'd never have gone to work for him."

"What did his cousin want?"

"To get inside the house. Not sure why, but she's paying me a couple hundred to unlock it and show her around." He grunted. "I swear, Poppy, every time I think about Brooks screwing me out of that money, I get pissed off all over again."

"Ain't nothing you can do about it, so why get yourself all worked up? I never knew anybody worries so much."

"Can't help it, Poppy. Never could."

Poppy snorted. "You ask me, worrying's a sorry waste of time." She waved a silencing hand before Cane could respond. "I know. I know. You didn't ask me."

"No, I didn't, but you're right."

She grinned at him over the top of her coffee mug. "'Course, I am."

"Don't gloat."

"Can't help it," she mimicked. "Never could."

5

Gemma was waiting in her Tesla when Cane parked an ancient pickup truck and climbed out. She cringed. Dressed in sweatshirt and dirty jeans, Cane was short and stocky, face browned and weathered early by too much sun. Shaggy brown hair and beard were shot with silver, and Gemma decided he could use a haircut. He looked to be around her age and was probably handsome before he broke his nose. She waited until he unlocked the gate before calling from the car.

"Mr. Gentry!" Cane waved over his should but didn't turn around as he pushed open the gate and strode toward the front porch. Gemma called again and hurried after him. "I'm Gemma Clark, Mr. Gentry, and I truly appreciate you coming over here."

"Said I'd be here."

"I still appreciate it."

"Okay."

Cane popped the padlock, pushed the front door open and finally faced her. Unapologetically vain, Gemma never ventured out without being well-dressed and made-up. Long hair, pulled back and tied with a black ribbon, complimented tailored beige slacks and black blazer. A Chanel purse dangled from one shoulder.

Cane's eyes widened. "Wow!"

Gemma smiled, anticipating a compliment. "Is something wrong, Mr. Gentry?"

"Is that you're idea of what to wear for exploring dirty houses?"

"I wasn't aware of a dress code," she shot back.

Cane noted her designer pumps. "Better watch your step. Got some wonky floors in there."

"They're low heels, Mr. Gentry. I'm sure I can manage."

"Suit yourself."

"I will." Because of his brusqueness, Gemma was surprised when Cane politely stepped aside and steadied her elbow as she crossed the uneven threshold. She forgot about manners when she was hit hard by the smell of must, dust and age. "Good Lord! How long has this place been closed up?"

"Since last fall when I evicted the junkie tenant and your cousin stopped paying me."

"That reminds me." Gemma reached into her purse for a roll of twenties. "Two hundred dollars as promised, Mr. Gentry."

"Thanks." Cane tucked the money in his jeans and began the tour. "This is a typical American townhouse from the eighteen-thirties. Called a double gallery because it's got galleries on both floors. The second story and long, narrow footprint made good use of the land. These houses look pretty fancy from the street, but there weren't that many rooms so people usually added a service wing in the back. There's one here, in fact."

"Slave quarters?"

"Probably."

"I have one on my property too. I converted it into a guest cottage but its history still gives me the willies."

Cane didn't seem to hear. "You're lucky most of the original woodwork's intact. Usually rots or gets stolen. Chandeliers are always the first to disappear, but the ceiling rosettes are still in place." He pointed at the front door. "Had a stained-glass fanlight up there until the last tenant smashed it. Threw him out before he could do more damage. Saved the frame and pieces just in case."

"That was very thoughtful of you." Gemma trailed Cane up the stairs and noted the wobbly banister. "That's an accident waiting to happen."

"Yeah, but it's an easy fix." He paused at the top and looked around. "Lots of little projects. Broken windows and loose shutters. Walls need scraping and fresh paint. I coulda worked wonders with the place if I'd had the money."

"You do restoration work?"

"I do all kinds of construction, lady. Built my own house on the batture." Before Gemma could comment, he said, "That bathroom was redone, probably in the twenties. Maybe thirties. Tile can be saved, but it's otherwise a gut job." Gemma cast a cursory glance before following him into the next room. "Lots of light in here before those bananas got so big. They need to be cut down. Whole yard's a wreck in case you didn't notice."

Gemma peered through filthy glass panes. "You're not kidding." Back downstairs, she explored a kitchen with antiquated appliances and walls streaked and reeking of grease. "Talk about needing work."

"Would look fine with an island. Granite countertops. Some bar stools. Good light in here too."

Gemma considered. "Except for that upstairs bathroom, it seems like it's mostly cosmetic work. Am I right?"

"Well, assuming there's no termite damage or structural issues, yeah."

"A buyer will love that."

"Is that you?"

"I'm here out of curiosity, Mr. Gentry. I already own a house, and have no need for another one. Certainly not in this neighborhood."

"I'm guessing you prefer the Garden District."

Gemma bristled. "Guess again."

"Metairie?"

"God forbid! Do I look like an old soccer mom?"

"I wouldn't know."

Gemma's designer clothes, Gucci watch and Tesla had already cemented Cane's opinion. In his years of restoring houses, he'd had plenty of clients with more money than sense, out to fix and flip houses with no concern for historical provenance. A few were knowledgeable and sincere, but they were the exception.

"Service wing's through there."

The two additions faced a porch extending along the side yard. The first room was bare and nondescript. The second was padlocked. Cane opened it and ushered Gemma inside. It was empty except for a stack of cardboard boxes.

"What's in those?"

"That one has the frame of the fanlight window, and the one on top has the broken glass pieces. Those others have the original hardware. Doorknobs. Hinges. Shutter hooks. Switch plates." He rummaged through them. "When Brooks stopped paying me, I thought about selling this stuff to that salvage place on Felicity Street. It wouldn't cover my loss, but it's better than nothing."

"I apologize again for my cousin's behavior, Mr. Gentry."

"Like you said on the phone, it's not your problem. I blame myself for not being more careful when…good God!"

Cane went to the lone window for a brisk look before rushing outside. Gemma followed, confused until she saw what triggered his behavior. A live oak lay on its side, massive root system facing the window. Luckily, the tree had fallen away from the house and into the back yard and vacant lot beyond. A stretch of chain link fence was twisted and tortured flat.

"Must've come down in that big storm."

Gemma repeated her remark to Maddie. "It would've had a name if this was hurricane season."

"You're right about that. Stirred things up pretty good on the batture, too." He explored the wreckage, dwarfed by a root ball nine-feet high. "Can't believe the size of this thing. I've brought down bigger, but this one's pretty fierce."

"I beg your pardon?"

"Worked as a logger once." Cane peered into the enormous hole beneath the roots. His eyes widened. "Looks like you got a trash pit, lady."

"A what?"

"A trash pit. Some people call them trash piles."

"You mean a privy?"

"No, no. Privies were located much further away from the house and regularly cleaned out by men called honey-dippers."

Gemma made a face. "A poetic term if I ever heard one."

"In the days before garbage collectors, trash pits were how people disposed of stuff. Broken bottles, dishes and jars. Buckles and buttons. Snuff glasses. Old toys. Even clothes. The pits eventually got filled in or covered over and forgotten about."

"What are snuff glasses?"

"Some snuff brands came in glasses with tin lids. They were fluted inside to make them pretty enough for drinking glasses." A flash of white caught his eye and he peered into the pit. "See there? Looks like a piece of crockery."

Gemma was impressed. "Tell me, Mr. Gentry. How'd you come to know so much about old houses?"

"When I started restoring them. It was baptism by fire, but I managed without getting burned. Spent a lot of time at the WIlkins Research Center."

"You said you built your own home?"

"Yeah. Another baptism by fire."

Before Gemma could probe further, Cane disappeared into the tangle of moss-draped limbs. She watched and waited until she heard voices inside the house.

"Anybody home?"

"Out here!"

Maddie and Henri appeared in the back door, jaws dropping when they saw the downed tree. "When did that happen?"

"That storm Thursday night."

Henri looked at the roof. "This was one lucky house. Damn! Look at the size of that root ball. That tree must be a hundred years old."

"Closer to two I'd say," Cane announced, pushing noisily through the branches.

"This is Mr. Gentry," Gemma said.

Henri shook his hand. "I'm Henri Chabrol. Nice to meet somebody who lives on the batture. Place has always fascinated me."

Cane frowned and brushed a wisp of Spanish moss from his shoulder. "How'd you know I lived there?"

"You mentioned it on the phone yesterday," Gemma said. "Something about meeting my cousin there."

"Oh, yeah," Cane grunted. "You need me for anything else, Ms. Clark?"

"I guess not. You've been very helpful. Thank you."

"Sure." He handed her the keys to the locks. "Here you go."

"Why are you giving them to me?"

"When I quit a job, I return keys to the owners, and you're as close as I'm gonna get. I'm done with this place." He jerked his head toward the oak. "Better do something about that tree before you get fined by the city. Trust me, you don't want to mess with those folks."

Gemma shook her head when Cane disappeared back into the house. "Not the politest gent in the world."

"No kidding." Maddie looked at Henri. "You think he's typical of batture folks."

"Don't know. When I learned about the place, I assumed they were loners or oddballs or just people who like being off the grid. Imagine living somewhere that could be wiped out by a passing ship."

"Is it really that dangerous?" Gemma asked.

"Well, they've also got floods and levee collapses to contend with. There used to be hundreds of batture houses but only a handful now." Henri moved closer to the root ball and peered into the hole. He also noticed the flash of white. "Hey, Looks like a trash pit."

"That's what Mr. Gentry said."

"Then I better have a look-see." Henri snapped off a broken limb and scraped around the protruding object. A few carefully aimed thrusts dislodged a large clod of earth, and the three stared at something that stared back.

"Good heavens!" Gemma cried, "Is that a doll!"

6

Maddie took Henri's arm as they crossed the Roosevelt Hotel lobby to the Sazerac Lounge. "Did Gemma say why she wanted to meet us?"

"I was hoping she told you."

"Not a word. She's been out of pocket all week." They settled into a banquette visible from the entrance. "When she disappears that long, she's either traveling or up to something."

"We're about to learn which." Henri stood as Gemma approached and offered her cheek for a kiss.

"You're truly the last of the Southern gentlemen, darling." She slid in beside Maddie and pecked her cheek. "No doubt you're wondering why I wanted to meet here."

"Girlfriend, we wonder about everything you do," Maddie laughed.

"I'm betting it's because it's where cocktails were invented," Henri said.

"Kudos to the historian. Yes, indeed. The Sazerac drink was all the rage before the Civil War. It was served in an egg cup called a *coquitier* which mixology lore says was corrupted into cocktail. Actually, the real reason it's a fave is because my mother Lydia was one of the ladies who stormed the place in nineteen-forty-nine to demand an end to the men-only policy. She was only nineteen at the time, mind you, and if it weren't for her, my dear Maddie, you and I might not be sitting here today." She turned to Henri. "Did you know Huey Long did some of his shady dealings right in this bar? There's bullet hole in the ceiling because one of his bodyguards had an itchy trigger finger."

Henri chuckled. "I thought you'd been vaccinated against the history bug."

"Usually, yes, but I do know a few things about cocktails and corruption." Gemma noted the hovering waiter and continued after everyone ordered drinks. "Fact is, history is what I want to talk to y'all about. You know I hate woo-woo stuff, but I've been getting strange vibes from that house on Baptiste Street."

"Déjà vu?"

"No. But I can't stop wondering if maybe the place came into my life for a reason. I wanted to know more it and the one on Chestnut Street too. Nobody ever told me anything about my family history, and since genealogy is all the rage these days, I decided to hop on the bandwagon."

"Meaning what?" Maddie asked.

"Meaning that I did a little research and rattled some old family skeletons."

"So that's what you've been up to."

Henri beamed. "I'm so proud of you."

"Unfortunately I didn't learn much from those ancestry sites on-line, so I went to the Wilkins Center."

"What?" Maddie looked hurt. "Why didn't you ask for me?"

"It was a spur of the moment thing, darling, and your day off."

"Did you find anything?"

"I did indeed. For starters, what little Philip Brooks said was true. Our great-grandfather was Samuel Stafford. He came here from England and was the second of three sons and, thank you primogeniture, arrived here penniless. The guy must've been a dynamo because twelve years later he built a big house on Chestnut Street which I found on-line. Samuel had two sons, Daniel and John. Daniel was my grandaddy, my father Robert's daddy, and he's the one who bought the house on Baptiste Street. Granddaddy bought it in nineteen sixteen, and somehow it ended up in his brother John's hands. John was Philip Brooks' grandaddy."

"Was your father Robert an only child?"

"As far as I know."

"Why didn't Daniel leave the house to him?"

"No idea. Maybe he and Daddy didn't get along. I don't know anything about my grandmother either. I plan to go to the court house and look into the marriage records."

"What about your mother?" Henri asked.

"She's from Savannah. I never met her people either."

"No. I meant she must know something about your father's family."

"She never said, so I assumed she didn't know anything either."

"How's she doing, by the way?"

"Last time I visited was great. The time before that, she barely knew me."

"Next time you catch her on a good day, you should ask questions," Maddie offered.

"Good idea. Maybe telling her what I know about the Staffords will stir something. Surely Daddy showed her the house where he grew up." Gemma thanked the waiter delivering drinks and instructed him to put everything on her tab. She sipped a Ramos gin fizz and toyed with a bowl of kale chips. "It's worth a shot."

"Sure it is," Henri said. "Now do you mind if I give you a little advice? I did a little sleuthing about the house too."

Gemma brightened. "You did?"

"After we looked around, I checked the real estate comps in the neighborhood. I also talked to my friend Samara Poché, who's one of the city's top realtors. She said that the house is one of the purest examples of American townhouse architecture left in the Lower Garden District, and that unless it's got serious structural issues, you could fix it up and rent it for a lot of money."

"I already thought about that, but I don't know the first thing about being a landlady."

"That's what property managers are for."

"You really think it's a good opportunity?"

"Not just good, Gemma. Golden. The economy's riding a roller coaster these days, and there aren't many guaranteed investments."

"You sound like Gerald O'Hara telling Katy Scarlett that land is the only thing that matters."

"Gerald was right," Maddie said. "New Orleans real estate is booming. Didn't some guy offer you three million for your property?"

"Almost four, but who's counting?" Gemma looked from one to the other. "How come you two are so interested in that house?"

"Because we'd like to be your tenants," Maddie said.

"What?! Seriously?"

"Henri and I have talked about living together for years, but neither wants to give up their place. Choosing a separate one will break the log jam. We both love the neighborhood, and I've lived in the Quarter long enough. I'm sick to death of drunk tourists and ghost and vampire tours. You're insulated from all that behind those high walls."

"Believe me, I see and hear plenty, but I'd hate to see you move uptown."

"Me too, but maybe your old house is sending me a message too."

"Hmmm."

"Will you at least think about it?"

"Nothing to think about, sweetie. I'd love to have y'all as tenants."

"You're the best!" Henri clinked Gemma's glass. "In the meantime, I'd like to start a dig over there. I know it's private property, but Brooks will never know, and I'm dying to see what else is in that trash pit."

"Help yourself. I may even come over to help." Maddie burst out laughing. "What's so funny?"

"The idea of you poking around a mudhole, that's what." Knowing Gemma's penchant for designer clothes, she said, "You don't even own a pair of blue jeans."

"Says you."

"What do you mean?"

"You'll see, smarty pants!"

7

Henri arrived at the Baptiste Street house early the next afternoon, just as the tree removal service tossed the last limbs into a wood chipper. He was arranging his dig equipment on the side porch when the foreman asked if he wanted the hole filled in.

"No, thanks. I'm going to dig further."

"You some kind of archaeologist?"

"You could say that."

The foreman peered into the hole. "What is that? Six feet?"

"Closer to eight. You saw the size of that root ball."

"Took more time getting that damned thing out than cutting up the tree." He noted Henri's sneakers. "Better get yourself some boots, buddy. A few more feet and you're gonna hit water."

Henri pulled waders from a cardboard box. "Ain't my first time at the rodeo."

The guy laughed. "Good luck."

"Thanks."

Left alone, Henri unrolled his canvas tool bag and arranged a selection of hammers, chisels and trowels alongside brushes, gloves, safety goggles, magnifier and spray bottle. He tugged on his waders and lowered an aluminum ladder into the hole. Tool belt in place, he descended to the doll's head. Using a slender trowel, he carefully scraped away the imprisoning dirt until the porcelain head popped into his glove like a ripe plum. Further inspection revealed that the body was long gone. Henri climbed out of the hole and used the spray bottle to clean the head until it gleamed in the wintry sunlight. The face bore delicately painted bee-stung lips and blue, heavily lashed eyes. Its symmetry was marred by an ugly dent on the right cheek. Henri spread a cloth on the porch and left the doll's head to dry before climbing back into the hole and resuming the search. He well knew the importance of patience. Once a discovery was made, one had to resist the temptation to rush the process and damage other artifacts awaiting detection. Instead, the process slowed further, chisels were swapped for brushes as dirt was painstakingly erased. Hours later, Henri was focused on a shard of green glass when he heard Gemma's voice.

"Did someone fall down the rabbit hole?"

Henri looked up and burst into laughter. "Oh, no!"

Gemma planted fists on hips. "What's so funny?"

"That get-up."

She was barely recognizable under a cable knit sweater over a pair of Versace denim overalls. Her hair was tucked inside a New Orleans Saints cap several sizes too large, and she wore loafers and thick socks.

"First, Mr. Gentry and now you. It seems I'm destined to violate one fashion code after another. I'm sorely sorry, my dear, but this is the best I could do."

Henri couldn't stop laughing. "You look like you're dressed for a couturier hayride." Gemma stuck out her tongue. "Is that Tyrone's Saints hat?"

"None of your business. Now stop picking on me or I'll strangle you with my Hermès scarf."

"I'm sorry. Truly. I was surprised, that's all."

"Never mind. I'm here to help so give me a little respect." Gemma leaned over the hole when she heard muck sucking at Henri's boots. "Have you already hit water?"

"Not yet, but soon."

"Wow! It's one thing to know this city is floating and another to see proof."

"It explains why coffins were weighted down in the old days," Henri noted. "A storm like the one that brought this tree down could've unleashed a lot of caskets."

"There's a happy thought." Gemma pretended to shudder. "What have you found so far?"

"It's all laid out on that cloth over there. The doll's head. Some broken crockery. A couple of china pieces." He turned back to the shard. "I think this green thing is a wine bottle."

"Nothing spectacular, eh?"

"Not yet."

"So what can I do?"

"You can be my washerwoman." A final light thrust with his trowel and a wine bottle slipped from the dirt. He held it up. "This will get you started."

Gemma cleaned the bottle and set it in the sun to dry out. "How about some music to dig by?"

"Fine."

Gemma found WWOZ on her phone, and they were enjoying some Dr. John when Henri let out a whoop. She hurried to the edge of the hole. "What did you find?"

Henri brandished a mud-encrusted yellow pot with black lettering on the side. "Clean it off and see if you can read it."

Gemma carefully washed the stoneware pot and triumphantly read the lettering. *"Maille Seul Vinaigrier. Moutard."*

"A French mustard pot!" Henri exclaimed. "Anything from the French period is special."

"Is that right?" Gemma looked over the assortment of small treasures. "Wonder what else is down there."

"Well, whatever it is will have to wait until tomorrow." He climbed the ladder and scraped mud from his boots. "Hand me that roll of Visqueen, will you? I need to protect the site in case we get rain. I don't want any critters messing around down there either."

"Okay." Gemma seemed pleased with herself as she helped Henri secure the tarp. "This was fun."

"Does that mean you'll come back for more?"

"Why not?" When Henri didn't respond, she said, "I'm not frivolous all the time, you know."

"Oh, you know I've never thought of you as frivolous. You're a woman of discriminating taste and great generosity, and Maddie and I love you madly and have you called your broker yet?"

Gemma cackled. "No, and that's the most convoluted sentence I've ever heard."

"Well?"

"I'll call him tomorrow. I meant to call this morning, but I tossed and turned all night and slept late."

"Bad dreams?"

"Not so much bad as unsettling. I woke up more tired than when I went to bed."

"That's odd."

"So's this." She picked up the porcelain doll's head and turned it in her hand. "No body to go along with it?"

"Rotted away long ago."

Gemma touched the dented cheek. "Wonder what happened here?"

"Little Scarlett probably slammed it against the wall when she had a hissy fit."

"I guess we'll never know for sure."

"Nope. Welcome to the wonderful world of archaeology."

PART TWO

"My girl, my girl. Where will you go?
I'm going where the cold winds blow.
In the pines, in the pines,
Where the sun never shines,
I would shiver the whole night through."
-Unknown

8

1911

Sloane O'Rourke covered her doll's head when her mother struck another discordant chord. "You're hurting Riley's ears, Mama!"

Maura smiled at her five-year-old daughter's compassion. "I'm sorry, baby. I want you to hear my new song, but this old piano isn't cooperating."

Sloane smoothed the doll's wild black hair. "Can't you fix it?"

"I wish I could. Seems like every day something else goes wrong with it."

In truth, the ancient upright, bequeathed by her Irish grandmother, Cara Traver, was a fine instrument that needed only tuning and minor repairs, but such things cost money, forever in short supply in the O'Rourke household. The piano was the only thing of value in the furnished two-room duplex Maura shared with her daughter and husband, Ronan. It easily commanded pride of place alongside a threadbare sofa, table and two chairs and a cheap pine chifforobe. Even off-key, its music offered respite from the endless toil of a dirt-poor Mississippi housewife. For Ronan, who despised it, the piano was a constant reminder that his wife's family was superior to his, and that he had failed as a provider. He was right on both counts.

Maura gave up on the piano and retreated to the table, grateful when Sloane continued quietly entertaining herself in the corner. She turned up the coal-oil lamp and made notations on pages torn from a Sears and Roebuck catalogue. She wished the giant company left bigger margins for scribbling musical notes and lyrics. Her household chores and seamstress work left scant time for writing folksongs, a talent inherited from Grandmother Traver, and she cherished every stolen moment. She hummed the fledgling melody in hopes of finding a lyric to rhyme with "heavenly," but nothing came. It was, she decided, too miserably hot to concentrate. She sought a breeze at the open window and fiddled with the cotton wads stuck in the rusted screen holes to block Mississippi's ravenous mosquitoes. Her efforts were interrupted by her neighbor, Frieda Gunther, who occupied the other half of the ramshackle duplex with her husband Karl. Frieda was an older, world-weary sort, but despite the eighteen-year age difference, she and Maura had become friends.

"Thought you folks could do with some of my blackberry jam." Frieda said. "I put some up last fall and realized I have more than I thought."

Maura hugged her. "God love a sweet liar." She knew the jam was only the latest charity from someone who knew her desperate situation. "Will you sit a while?"

"Wish I could, hon, but I gotta get to the market."

"Please stay a bit. Ronan won't be home for another hour or so." Famished for adult conversation, Maura pulled her friend inside and shut the door. Frieda knelt and opened her arms as Sloane rushed to give her a hug.

"Aunt Frieda! Did you bring me a surprise?"

"Sure did. How about some of my delicious blackberry jam?"

Sloane's eyes lit up. "May I have some, Mama?"

"For breakfast, dear. Now you and Riley go play on your pallet while Aunt Frieda and I talk." Sloane pulled a face. "Be a good girl."

When Sloane disappeared into the bedroom, Maura joined Frieda at the table and picked up a worn palmetto fan. She waved it languidly, stirring wisps of red hair escaping her damp headscarf. "I swear I can't remember a June this hot, Frieda." She never stopped fanning as she drew a handkerchief from her apron and dabbed her damp upper lip. "The man on the radio this morning said it was over a hundred in Natchez, and that—"

Frieda reached across the table and took her hand. "This has got to stop, Maura."

Shame and embarrassment burned the Maura's neck as she feigned ignorance. "What has to stop?"

"No use pretending with me, honey. Karl and me are on the other side of those paper-thin walls. We hear what's going on." She squeezed Maura's hand and spoke in earnest. "And we see the bruises."

Maura fussed with a loose button on the front of her twice-turned house dress. "I'd better fix this poor thing before it falls off and—"

"Maura!"

Her feeble protest failed, undone by her friend's compassion. The façade, which fooled no one, collapsed, and she buried her head in her hands. Frieda rushed to her side and held her shoulders as Maura whimpered.

"God help me, Frieda!" she cried. "I…I don't know…what to do."

"There's only one thing you can do, child. You got to take Sloane and get out of here."

"Where would I go?"

"Anywhere. Couldn't you stay with your cousin down in Pascagoula?"

"That's the first place Ronan would look." Maura straightened and wiped her eyes with the back of her hand. "I'd spend every waking moment wondering when he was going to show up and drag me back here. No, no. I'd be too scared."

"More scared than you already are?"

"I...I don't know."

Frieda's heart ached in the face of such desperation. "Maybe you should talk to your preacher."

"I went to Reverend McIntire last Easter." Maura's voice was edged with bitterness. "You know what he said? He said a wife's duty is to stay with her husband."

"Did you tell him what Ronan was doing to you?"

"Some of it. I...I don't think he believed me."

"Shame on him!" Frieda snapped. "Maybe that fool would believe the bruises!"

Maura looked away. "I'm sure the reverend had heard it all before and probably hears it every day. I'm no different from any other poor Mississippi housewife."

Frieda refuted such hideous status quo. "Nonsense! Karl Gunther has never laid a hand on me and never will. But when a man sells his soul to John Barleycorn like Ronan, there are no happy endings. You know I'm speaking the truth." Maura hung her head again, silent. "What about that time Ronan threw you against the piano? If you'd hit your temple, you might've died, and if that happened, who would care for Sloane? You know darn well Ronan doesn't give a hoot about that poor child!"

"I know. I know." Maura looked at the ceiling, water-stained and flaking paint. "Every day I get up and wonder how things got this way. I wish you'd known Ronan when we were first together. He was twenty, and I was barely sixteen, and I thought he was the most beautiful boy I'd ever seen. All that curly black hair and those pale blue eyes. So sweet and gentle, he was. Whenever we were alone, he...oh, I don't know, Frieda. It was like all the righteousness I'd been taught as a preacher's daughter flew out the window, and I couldn't help myself." She cleared her throat and swallowed hard. "Next thing I knew, I was going to have a baby, and when Papa found out, he threw me out of the house."

Frieda had wondered about Maura's past since she moved in last winter and listened with dread as her tragedy unfolded. After eloping to Gulfport, she said, Ronan found work in a hardware store and things were rosy during her pregnancy. He was endlessly helpful and selfless, but when Sloane arrived, a stillborn twin brother sent Ronan into a sharp downward spiral. He barely glanced at his beautiful daughter, and, far worse, refused to hold her. Pleas from Maura that no one was to blame for their son's death went unheard as Ronan spent less time at home and more in the neighborhood taverns. Alternating between bouts of corrosive melancholy and drinking binges, he went from one job to another until the only work he could find was a traveling shoe salesman working out of Oriole. Maura struggled hard to hold their little family together, but her fight began unraveling one night when Ronan, drunk and overflowing with self-pity, slapped her without reason. He immediately begged forgiveness and vowed he'd never strike her again. That promise lasted until his next bender, and afterwards the two fell into a hideous cycle with no prospect of ending.

"I'm telling you, Frieda, when I look back at those six years, I wonder if I ever knew the man I married." Maura's voice sagged with misery when she added, "To be honest, I don't know who I am either. Not anymore."

"Which is exactly why we have to find a way to—"

Both women flinched when the door burst open, and Ronan O'Rourke lurched inside. Short and wiry, he was only twenty-four, but drink was already taking its toll. His face was pocked with gin blossoms, and he'd begun to grizzle. A flinty glare announced his displeasure at seeing Frieda.

"What the devil are you doing here?"

"She brought us some blackberry jam," Maura said in a placating voice. "Isn't that nice?"

Ronan began unbuttoning his sweat-stained shirt. "Be a lot nicer if she minded her own damned business."

"Ronan!" Maura cried.

"Reckon I can buy my wife jam if need be!"

Flushed with anger, Frieda rose to confront him, but reined her temper before making things worse for Maura. She muttered an abrupt good-bye and hurried next door. Ronan shot her a withering look before dropping his shirt onto the floor and flopping onto the sofa.

Maura trod carefully. "Do you want some supper?"

"Too damned hot to eat."

When Ronan turned to face the back of the couch, Maura knew the whiskey would have him snoring soon, and she sat in silence until she heard the familiar sound. She extinguished the oil lamp and tiptoed into the bedroom. Finding Sloane fast asleep on her pallet, Maura undressed and got into bed and prayed that the creaking springs wouldn't wake Ronan. She was drifting toward sleep when he roared to life.

"Who turned out the goddamned light?!"

Maura held her breath, wondering which scenario would play out. She had her answer when she heard fumbling in the dark and saw a match blaze as Ronan relit the lamp. He stood and staggered into the bedroom, saturating the hot, heavy air with the stink of sweat and whiskey.

"Why'd you turn out the lamp, woman? Hoping I'd fall and break my neck, were you?" With no response, he bellowed. "Answer me!"

"I'm sorry, Ronan. You were asleep and I didn't want to wake you."

"No!" he shouted. "You wanted me to pass out, didn't you?" Maura trembled in silence, knowing no words could keep the dam from breaking. "Answer me!"

Thunderous pounding on the wall shared with the Gunthers fueled Ronan's fury, and he pounded back before turning back to Maura. His open palm caught the side of her face and knocked her from the bed.

"Please don't, Ronan!" she wailed. "Please!"

In the corner, Sloane whimpered softly, eyes wide with terror when her mother was hurled into the next the room. Struck again, Maura spun against the piano. Her spine caught fire when the keyboard caught her in the small of her back. She hung motionless for a few long seconds before crumpling to the floor. Sloane burrowed under the sheet and closed her eyes tight, wishing she could make the moment go away. Riley's vacant stare was the sole witness to the horror that followed.

9

Maura stole a rare moment of solitude. Frieda had taken Sloane for the day, leaving her to finish the song she'd struggled with all summer. She played a few bars on the woeful piano, ignoring its sour notes to focus on the melody. She hummed along before finding her voice. She took a breath and her sweet soprano rose into the steamy air and hovered like angels.

"Little girl, little girl, where'd you go last night? Not even your mother can say. Did you have a fine time with that muscadine wine? Or did the gentleman lead you astray?"

It was the latest of a dozen songs written since spring, and although Maura was pleased with the lyrics, they gave scant pleasure. When she straightened her back, searing pain signaled a broken rib, and the ache behind her eyes reminded her of the bruise on her forehead. It had bloomed violet last night and was now dark purple with ugly red edges. Ronan had surprised her by coming home sober, announcing that he was leaving before dawn for a business meeting in Jackson. He had ordered her to keep Sloane quiet because he was going to bed early.

"Do you understand me?"

"Yes, Ronan."

"You and the girl sleep in the front room."

"Yes, Ronan."

Maura fetched Sloane's pallet and closed the bedroom door behind her. She made a game of letting Sloane sleep in the front room if she promised to be very quiet and smiled when daughter whispered to Riley that they were going on a vacation. The heavy torpor soon lulled Sloane to sleep, and the ensuing stillness was broken only by the faint scratch of Maura's pencil as she worked on her sheet music. As she lost herself in the moment, she began to hum. Softly, then carelessly.

The bedroom door burst open. "Goddamn it, woman!" Ronan roared. "Didn't I tell you I wanted quiet?!"

Maura was seized by the arm and flung across the room. Her forehead struck the edge of the ironing board and sent it clattering. Before she could stand, she was picked up and hurled again, this time with enough force to plunge her into darkness. That done, Ronan turned toward Sloane who was screaming for him to stop. When he yelled at her to shut up, she threw the doll at him. He ducked before it crashed into the wall and, after glaring at the terrified child, stormed into the bedroom and slammed the door.

Sometimes during the night, Maura dragged herself to the couch. When she awoke the next morning, Sloane was curled up beside her and, and Ronan was gone. After calming her still-terrified daughter, Maura took her next door to stay with Frieda who, mercifully, said nothing about her new bruises. The horrific night replayed in Maura's mind as she lay down again, struggling for a position that didn't further torment her spine and head. She dozed off and on throughout the day, unable to move and not caring that she lay in a pool of her own sweat. When Frieda checked on her late in the day, she insisted she was fine but asked if Sloane could stay the night. Frieda, although fearful, agreed.

Maura managed to work on her music a few minutes before pain relegated her back to the couch and more fitful sleeping. She knew she must have something on the stove when Ronan returned, but it was dusk before she mustered enough strength to start supper. The larder was empty except for a basket of wilted collards, a bag of grits and some salt pork. She was stirring the simmering grits when she heard shouting in the hall. Ronan was in a heated argument with Karl Gunther and a voice she didn't know. The quarrel escalated, and she heard grunting and shoving sounds before the door burst open and Ronan reeled inside. His face was blood-red and shiny with sweat as he slammed the door and glowered at Maura. He listed to one side and cocked his head, studying his prey.

She shuddered when he looked around the room. She had been in too much pain to clean up last night's wreckage.

"Place is a pig sty!" he growled. He peeled off his wet shirt and threw it at her. "What you been doing all day?" Maura froze, insides turning over when Ronan spied her sheet music on the table. "So that's it! Wasting time on those stupid songs, eh? What a worthless whore!"

Maura retreated, any hope for escape erased when Ronan blocked her path to the front door. A cornered animal, she radiated the acrid odor of fear. She opened her mouth to scream but nothing emerged as she relived the familiar nightmare of being menaced and unable to call for help. Ronan was now close enough to smell. His stink sickened her as he leaned in and looked deep into her eyes, as though searching for something. Her gorge rose and she swallowed bile while continuing to back away, numb now to everything but the heat of the stove.

"Don't, Ronan!" she whispered. "Please, don't!"

Ronan frowned, bleary eyes widening, and he appeared confused as he looked around the room. He retreated a step and looked back at Maura. He resumed studying her until, with painful slowness, his eyes became murderous slits. He lunged, fist raised.

Maura screamed. "No!"

She spun to seize the wooden handle on the pot of bubbling grits and swung with stunning strength. Grits erupted like a geyser when the pot caught the side of Ronan's head. He bellowed in agony and reeled backwards, clawing frantically at the sticky, scalding splatter on his face and bare chest.

"You bitch!"

Maura watched with total dispassion as Ronan dropped to his knees, consumed with blistering pain. Commanded by smoldering inner rage, she swung the iron pot again, crashing this time against Ronan's temple. An explosion of blood stained the grits a grisly pink. Maura was mesmerized by the horror, seeing and unseeing, until her strength fled and the pot tumbled to the floor. She sank down beside it, silently mouthing the edict.

"No more, Ronan. No more. No more."

There was pounding on the door, and Karl, Frieda and someone else crowded into the small room. Maura somehow struggled to her feet before falling into Frieda's arms, breathing raspy and irregular.

"My god, Maura!" Frieda cried. "Are you alright?"

Maura buried her face against Frieda's shoulder. She clung and shook hard. Voices rose and fell around her, but she fathomed none of it until someone asked if Ronan were dead. She looked up to see Karl nudge the body with his boot.

"Sure as hell is."

"Rat bastard's had this coming for years," someone said. "Meanest drunk I ever saw."

Who was speaking? Maura wondered. She fought to sort her thoughts.

"God forgive me!" she gasped. "I couldn't help it. He...Ronan—!"

Frieda gently stroked her forehead. "Hush, honey. We know what happened. We know."

Maura struggled to break free, but Frieda held fast. "I have to get away! I have to take Sloane and get away from here."

"In time." Karl spoke with reassuring calm. "Things need taking care of, Maura. We'll help you."

"Sure, we will."

Maura finally registered the stranger she'd glimpsed in the hall. "Who're you?"

"Lewis Hatcher. Me and Karl work together."

"But I don't understand what—"

"We and some other fellows were having a drink at Connelly's Saloon when Ronan showed up," Karl explained. "He started bullying and baiting us as usual, so we got him thrown out, and when me and Lewis left, he followed us here. I reckon you heard us in the hall."

Maura nodded numbly and offered no resistance as Frieda steered her to the sofa. She settled against the thin cushions, Frieda at her side, while Karl and Hatcher huddled by the stove. Their soft voices were a comforting drone that made Maura drowse. She stirred when she felt Karl take her hand.

"Listen to me, Maura. Can you describe Ronan's condition when he came home tonight?"

She frowned. "I don't understand."

"Answer him, honey," Frieda urged.

"You know I can. It happens all the time."

"Then that's what you'll tell the police," Hatcher said. "Every gory detail."

Maura bolted upright and winced when a cracked rib protested. "The police? No! I can't talk to them!"

"You have to," Karl insisted. "Listen to me, Maura, and listen carefully. Everybody knows Ronan's history of getting drunk and picking fights. He's been thrown out of every bar on the bluff, and no one, especially the Oriole police, will be surprised when his body's found in an alley down there."

"It's a rough area, ladies," Hatcher grunted. "Knife fights and corpses are regular visitors."

Maura paled. "Dear God!"

"But don't you see? That's perfect for what you'll say." Karl squeezed Maura's hand gently and continued in calming tones. "When you're up to it, I want you to go next door and keep Sloane company while we—"

"Sloane!" Maura cried, half rising.

"She's fast asleep in our bed," Frieda said. "We played so hard all day that she wore herself out. I promise she didn't hear what happened. Now you need to listen to Karl."

"You stay next door while me and Frieda clean up. Lewis will come back after midnight to help me dump the body on the bluff. For sure it'll be found in the morning. When the police come here with the news, you tell 'em Ronan didn't come home last night and that you've been worried sick. They'll say that he was killed in a fight and that'll be the end of it."

"They'll never suspect you in a million years," Frieda assured her.

"Why are you people doing this?" Maura's voice shattered as she cried the terrible truth. "I killed my husband!"

"No, you didn't," Karl declared. "What you did was save your life and your daughter's life too. It was only a matter of time before Ronan killed you and turned his rage on Sloane."

"Exactly what I told her yesterday," Frieda said.

"Maybe it ain't my place to say, little lady, but I'd say you done a service to the community," Hatcher added.

"She sure did."

"You know we're right, honey."

"But—"

"Hush now." Frieda pulled Maura back into her arms. "There was only one path out of this living hell, honey, and you took it."

10

The conductor cupped a hand against his mouth and bawled a final alert. "All aboard for Biloxi, Gulfport and New Orleans! All aboard!"

Maura hugged and kissed Sloane one last time before boarding the Louisville & Nashville Railroad's Gulf Wind. She hurried to a window seat so she could wave at Sloane, held up for a closer look by her cousin Peter Byrne. His wife Dora and their daughter Nancy waved too. The tears that threatened all morning finally came when she leaned out the window.

"I love you, baby! I promise I'll send for you soon as I can!"

A shrieking whistle and blast of steam startled Maura, and a sharp lurch threw her back into her seat. It rippled through the cars like tumbling dominoes as the train pulled away from the Pascagoula station. Maura watched until the shrinking figures on the platform became dolls that disappeared when the train veered south toward the Gulf of Mexico. She closed the window, stowed her carpetbag on the overhead rack and sat again. She'd never ventured out of Mississippi, and watched with an unsettling mix of curiosity and trepidation as the flat landscape swept by. She closed her eyes when the train picked up speed and turned the view into a dizzying blur. Her musician's ear easily recognized the rhythm of the rails, an oddly comforting sound. It didn't, however, keep her from considering what brought about her flight.

The Oriole Police interrogated her only once, the morning Ronan's body was found, and had no reason to doubt her story. Owing to his violent history, the death was, as Karl predicted, promptly dismissed by the cops as foreseeable and was forgotten a week later when another bloody corpse appeared on the bluff. After Ronan was buried in potter's field, Maura wrote her cousin Peter Byrne in nearby Pascagoula, saying only that Ronan had died suddenly and asking if she and Sloane could stay there until she found work. Peter, wife Dora and daughter Nancy generously welcomed them, but after a few weeks in their cramped shotgun house, and no jobs in Pascagoula, Maura knew she had to move on.

"You should try New Orleans," Peter advised. "It's a big city, and there's plenty of work down there."

Maura was hesitant. "I suppose, but I don't have enough money to support the two of us for very long."

"Leave Sloane here and she can join you when you're on your feet." Dora nodded toward the side porch where Sloane and Nancy were giggling and playing jacks. "Look at them. They're already thick as thieves, and we'd be happy to keep her."

"I do love seeing her with a playmate," Maura confessed. "She's never had one, you know, but we've never been separated for a single night. I'm not sure how she'd react."

"Why not ask her?"

To Maura's surprise, Sloane was fine with the idea once Maura promised it was a temporary arrangement. It was a devastating decision, but neither she nor the Byrnes could think of alternatives. She resigned herself to the circumstances and agreed to follow Peter's instructions to contact Traveler's Aid Society as soon as she got to New Orleans. It was founded three years earlier to assist young women traveling alone, and he assured her it could get her safely settled in the famously rough city.

"Anyone sitting here, dearie?"

Maura was so lost in thought she hadn't noticed when the train stopped in Biloxi and more passengers boarded. Smiling down at her was an attractive woman in a smart yellow traveling costume with matching fringed reticule. Her wide-brimmed hat flaunted a mountain of egret feathers, and Maura thought the cameo brooch at her throat was the most exquisite thing she'd ever seen. She looked to be in her late twenties.

"No, ma'am."

"Good." The woman stepped aside so the porter could loft an expensive portmanteau onto the luggage rack. She tipped him, settled in beside Maura and extended a gloved hand. "I'm Starla Callahan."

"Maura O'Rourke."

"What a pretty Irish name. I'm part Irish myself." She cocked her head. "Are you going to New Orleans, Maura O'Rourke?"

"Yes, ma'am."

"Then we'll keep each other company, eh?" Starla removed her hat with a great flurry of feathers and set it on the empty seat facing them. She smoothed her hair, dark brown and lustrous. "I've been visiting my daughter. I see her every other week in fact, rain or shine, and every holiday. She's in school in Biloxi. Her papa's dead, so I'm all she's got in this world."

"I'm sorry."

Starla chattered on, much more talker than listener, but her genial intrusion made Maura feel less alone. The woman proved so sociable and engaging that by the time the train rolled into Pass Christian, Maura decided she'd found a new friend. She'd even grown comfortable enough to share her past history, judiciously edited of course.

"I have a daughter too, so after my husband died, I needed to find work."

"That why you're going to New Orleans?"

"Yes, ma'am."

"Where're you from?"

"Oriole. It's above Pascagoula."

"I've never heard of it."

"I suspect few have. It's not much more than a speck on the bluff."

"Mmmm." Starla had already taken inventory and found Maura comely in a country sort of way. She had good skin and teeth, but was too thin. Her long red hair needed cutting, and her cheap clothing, brave little hat and worn shoes bore the stamp of poverty. "You got any skills, Maura?"

"I sing and play the piano, and I'm a pretty fair seamstress."

"A singer you say?"

"Only in the church choir and at socials, but I—"

"You sing more than hymns?"

"I read music so I can sing and play whatever's put in front of me."

"You comfortable with an audience?"

"Yes, ma'am."

Starla considered. "You know what, dearie? It's a long shot, but I may be able to help you find work."

Maura's neck tingled with the first hope she could remember. "Truly?"

"I can't promise anything, but I can at least put you in touch with my friend Tom Anderson. He owns some cabarets and music halls and is always looking for new entertainers. Never hurts to ask. You'd need to fix yourself up of course."

"Oh, thank you!" Maura cried. "Thank you!"

Starla smiled, heart warmed by Maura's youthful optimism. "Don't be thanking me yet, dearie. I haven't heard you sing."

Starla's admonition woke something that Maura later attributed to a kindling of long-buried pride, a rebellion against being brutalized and dismissed as worthless. It had surfaced only once before, in the fatal showdown with Ronan, and it rushed back when she jerked her head toward the rear of the car and boldly ordered Starla to follow her.

"What in the world for?"

"You'll see."

Starla was thoroughly bewildered as Maura scrambled over her, grabbed her arm and pulled her into the aisle. Once they were between cars, Maura opened her mouth and began vocalizing. A few moments later, accompanied only by clacking train wheels, she sang the Star-Spangled Banner to her audience of one. Starla was dumbfounded by the powerful delivery and told Maura so when they were back in their seats.

"How did that a big voice come out of somebody so small?"

"Did you like it?"

"I did indeed, but that kind of fancy singing isn't exactly suited to cabarets. You sounded almost operatic."

"I had to be loud enough for you to hear over the train," Maura explained. "If I'd sung Some of These Days, you wouldn't have heard a word."

"You can sing that Sophie Tucker song? It's my favorite!"

"Like I said, If I have sheet music, I can sing anything. In different ways too."

"Alright then. I'll do what I can, but New Orleans is a tough town. Scads of young girls land there, heads full of dreams, but soon lose their way. Believe me, I know what I'm talking about." Maura waited for further explanation, but Starla nodded toward the window. "There's the lake, dearie. It won't be long now."

A sudden, sharp jolt and the train clattered onto tracks atop pilings sunk deep into the muck of Lake Pontchartrain. The beat of the wheels was different now, louder and uneven as the cars dipped and swayed. A little girl down the aisle squealed when the car was rocked by a powerful gust of wind.

Maura smiled. "It feels like the train's dancing, doesn't it? Like it's happy to be coming home to New Orleans."

"My, my. Aren't you the poet."

"It gives me an idea for a new song."

Starla was taken aback. "You compose too?"

"Close to thirty tunes I suspect." Before Starla could comment, Maura noted the vast expanse of water whipped into whitecaps on both sides of the train. "Or maybe I'll write about a train about to fall off the edge of the world."

"Sure looks that way, but don't worry. We'll be in the *Cypriére* soon."

"The what?"

"The big cypress swamp bordering the city. It wouldn't hurt to learn a little French, by the way. New Orleans has been American for over a hundred years, but you still hear a lot of French words."

Maura expected to be relieved when the train left the lake, but the swamp that swallowed them conjured a different foreboding. Ink-black waters mirrored cypress trees dripping with spectral Spanish moss. Strange wooden knobs called cypress knees surrounded their fat trunks, like children, Maura thought, or worshipful acolytes. Egrets and herons took flight at the approach of the noisy, smoke-spewing locomotive, and she shrank at the sight of a dozing alligator, great jaws agape, warming itself in the summer sun.

"This really is the edge of the world!"

68

Starla patted her hand. "Don't worry, dearie. We're almost there."

Maura remained glued to the window as a scattering of trappers' shacks drifted by, followed by Negro shanties, all resting on stilts. Perched at crazy angles, they trembled and roiled in the soft soil when the train thundered past. They were replaced by small farms which in turn yielded to wooden houses and dirt roads and finally paved streets busy with pedestrians, horses, carriages, farmer's carts, an omnibus and the occasional automobile. Maura was thrilled to be back on solid ground until a passenger across the aisle opened a window and filled the car with the smell of fish, tar, horse manure and stultifying humidity. The conductor reappeared for final announcement.

"New Orleans, ladies and gentlemen! Last stop. Everyone off, please. New Orleans!"

The Gulf Wind slowed to a crawl and exhaled a screech of brakes before coming to a halt. Another blast of steam, and the aisle erupted with passengers scrambling for their belongings and rushing to exit the train. Starla popped her hat in place and retrieved her heavy portmanteau without waiting for the porter. She passed down Maura's small carpetbag.

"Ready, dearie?"

Maura looked through the fly-streaked window at the crush of humanity, people meeting family and friends, tourists gawking, passengers shouting for redcaps in both English and French. The noise was deafening. She shrank a bit but mustered a soft, "I think so."

"Then come along."

As Maura followed Starla into the throng, she noticed half a dozen raggedy urchins darting about like minnows. They were shouting and waving something in their hands.

"Blue books! Get your blue book! New listings right here! Get your blue books!"

Maura wanted to ask what the boys were selling, but Starla had marched out of earshot. Maura hurried after, curiosity taking her gaze everywhere as she was swallowed by the cavernous, chaotic Southern Railway Station. While the majestic Beaux-Arts façade dazzled visitors along Canal Street, New Orleans' famously wide main thoroughfare, the train sheds lining Basin Street afforded arriving passengers a decidedly different sight. It was, depending upon the viewer, shocking, amusing or altogether irresistible. A neighborhood unique in America, it was created in 1897 by Alderman Sidney Story in an effort to control the city's rampant prostitution. Story's legislation, oddly enough, did not make the practice legal inside the specified boundaries, rather illegal outside them. Bordellos bloomed like mushrooms after a summer rain, as did saloons, dance halls, assignation houses, cabarets and restaurants. Erotic emporia catered to every imaginable taste, from lavish mansions charging seventy-five dollars for a bottle of champagne and staffed with ravishingly gowned beauties, to squalid sidewalk "cribs" where customers got quick satisfaction for fifty cents. This at a time when the average workman made two dollars a day. As many as 4000 women, ranging in color from porcelain to obsidian, worked the sixteen square blocks, and another thousand people served as madams, barkeeps, musicians, bouncers, seamstresses, laundresses, cooks, doctors, pharmacists, pimps and drug dealers. The notorious area was officially known as The District, but, much to the hapless alderman's chagrin, locals and wags dubbed it Storyville, and the nickname stuck.

Like all newcomers, Maura gaped at the row of imposing houses lining Basin from Bienville to Conti Streets. There were simple one-story bungalows, a three-story stone structure and a four-story extravaganza boasting a neo-Byzantine cupola. Domes, turrets, and striped awnings added splashes of color, as did the female residents who waved at arriving trains and called raunchy greetings from doorways and windows. Maura watched, dumbstruck, as a woman in a gaudy robe appeared on a balcony and caught the attention of disembarking passengers by exposing her breasts. Starla noted her shock.

"Something wrong, dearie?"

"What in the world is that woman doing?"

Starla grinned. "Advertising."

Maura didn't miss Starla's meaning. She was far from worldly, but not so naïve that she didn't know about prostitution. She had, after all, heard about harlots from an early age. Her Baptist preacher father denounced them often enough, pounding his lectern with one hand while shaking his fist at the heavens and condemning those "wicked Jezebels to eternal hellfire." She grew up believing them despicable human beings, only to find herself labeled as their scarlet sister when she, tearful and terrified, confessed to her father that she was pregnant. Instead of offering compassion, Reverend Traver damned her as a whore and threw her from the house with orders to never return. His ferocious rejection led to her fateful journey with Ronan and, ultimately, the train to New Orleans.

"Isn't that against the law?"

"Not over there. That's a very special neighborhood called Storyville, and it's all about having a good time. You'll find out soon enough."

"What do you mean?"

"I mean that's where my friend Tom Anderson's clubs are. Look over there, that building at the corner of Iberville Street."

Maura shielded her eyes from the fierce glare and spotted a two-story building with a wrap-around gallery and a sign over the corner entrance spelling out ANDERSON.

"I'll give you a card to take over there when you're ready. For now, you need to find a place to stay, and tomorrow you can put on a good dress and—"

"This is the best dress I have." Maura dismissed Peter's instructions to go directly to the Traveler's Aid Society, squared her shoulders and said, "It'll have to do."

Starla chuckled at the girl's resolve and began fishing in her enormous purse. Maura flinched when she spied a small ivory-handled pistol among a jumble of gloves, handkerchiefs and other feminine paraphernalia. After much rummaging about, Starla produced a card.

"Here you are. Show this to Tom and good luck."

Maura pocketed the card. "I can't thank you enough, Starla."

"Don't mention it. You remind me of myself when I first came here. I could've sure used a helping hand. I could also have used your gumption." Starla patted Maura's cheek. "Where in the world did you get it?"

"From my late husband, I guess."

.

11

Maura's brittle confidence wavered when she entered Tom Anderson's saloon, the Arlington Annex. A combination pub and tourist bureau, with a brothel tucked upstairs for favored clientele, it was designed to dazzle visitors. The longest bar in the country, more than thirty feet of lavishly carved cherrywood, fronted five enormous arched mirrors. Brown-and-white tile floors were dotted with gleaming brass cuspidors, and over a hundred lightbulbs in a reflective ceiling ensured perpetual daytime. Despite the extravagance, Maura recoiled from the odors of whiskey and beer, brimming spittoons and stale sweat. It was early afternoon, but the place was jammed with boisterous drinking men. Women were noticeably absent. Maura shied from the electronic blaze and scanned the room, her gaze returned by a middle-aged gentleman leaning against the bar. He sported a huge red moustache and was nattily dressed in a striped vest, spats and bowler hat. When he nodded and politely touched the brim of his hat, she ventured to approach. To her surprise, he met her halfway and shouted over the din.

"You look lost, little lady. Something I can do for you?"

"If you please, sir. I'm looking for Tom Anderson."

"What for?"

"I was told to ask for him by a mutual friend."

"And who might that be?"

"Starla Callahan."

"Starla, eh?" The man doffed his hat and executed a curt bow. She noted that the red moustache was shot with silver. "In that case, Tom Anderson, at your service."

"You're—?"

"In the flesh, miss." He chuckled at her confusion. "I'm the unofficial Mayor of Storyville, you see, and that's earned me a lot of enemies over the years. I've got to be careful when strangers come looking for me, although I must say you don't look very threatening."

Maura set down her carpetbag and passed him Starla's card. "I'm a singer, Mr. Anderson."

"You don't look like a singer either."

She thought fast. "I'm sorry I didn't have time to fix myself up, sir. Starla and I just arrived on the train from Mississippi, and she told me to come over right away. She also said that you're not one to judge on appearances."

"No, I'm not." Maura was relieved when her lie worked. "Being as I owe her a favor or two, I'll send you to Charlotte Townsend's place, the Windsor. Turn right out the door here and go four blocks up Iberville Street. It's on the corner of Villere. She's not open yet, but the bartender will be setting up. Name's Omar Crowley. He more or less runs the joint. Tell him I sent you and he'll take it from there." When Anderson leaned close, his face looked bloodless in the artificial light and instinct warned Maura that a shark lurked behind the bonhomie. "Anything else I can help you with?"

"No, sir, but thank you. Thank you very much!"

Maura grabbed her carpetbag and fled, eager to escape the racket, blinding lights and Tom Anderson. The stifling heat and humidity outside were equally unwelcoming, as were the stink of swampy, poorly drained streets and uncollected horse dung. She pressed a handkerchief to her nose and dodged a tornado of gnats above a mudpuddle iridescent with filth. Already sweating, Maura resisted the urge to hurry lest her dress be sticking to her when she met Mr. Crowley. At the corner of Villere Street, she paused to marvel. The Windsor was an imposing, three-story wooden structure swathed in galleries extending to the street. The second floor wore ornamental ironwork, and the third was lined with gracefully carved colonettes. An enormous fanlight over double doors was emblazoned with the letter W surmounted by a coronet. A mulatto woman in red tignon and calico apron was vigorously scrubbing the doorstep. She barely noticed when Maura lifted her long skirt and stepped around her to enter a narrow vestibule with a forest of potted palms, rubber plants and philodendra. To the left, a parlor with gold silk-upholstered settees sat empty beneath an unlit gasolier. On the right loomed a spacious bar and the bartender named Omar. He was a bear of a man with a bristly brown beard, heavily lidded eyes and muscular arms that didn't come from polishing bar glasses. Maura's heart sank with his response to her inquiry.

"Mr. Anderson's got it wrong, young lady. It was the Crescent City Club needing a singer, and they already hired one."

Maura noticed a piano on a small stage. "What about here, Mr. Crowley? Could you use a singer?"

"He sure as hell could not!"

The growl came from a booth behind Maura and belonged to a frowsy woman in her mid-thirties with unkempt brown hair. As she sauntered to the bar in her bare feet, it was obvious she wore only a chemise under her flimsy green dress. She perched on a bar stool and threw Maura a rapier stare.

"Nellie Marrero don't share billing with nobody," she announced loudly. "Who the hell are you anyway? The Little Match Girl?"

Maura struggled to steady her voice. "I'm Maura O'Rourke, Miss Nellie. I'm a singer, and I need work in the worst way."

"Looks more like you need a dress shop and a hairdresser in the worst way," Nellie cracked. After enjoying the joke at Maura's expense, she turned to Omar. "Sugar Boy's late for rehearsal again. That damned goldbrick better not show up with the jim-jams."

"Five'll get you ten."

"When did you see him last?"

"About four this morning, heading over to the Big Twenty-Five for another jam. Already high as a kite." Omar huffed on a glass, wiped it clean and hung it in an overhead rack. "Raleigh Rye's gonna be his death."

"Not if I get to him first!" Nellie put her hands on her hips and glowered at Omar. "What the hell am I supposed to do if he's gone off the rails again? I got three shows tonight and no piano player."

"Borrow somebody from one of the other houses."

"You know damn well I can't work with them colored professors. All they do is bang out jazz and ragtime. I need somebody who knows my arrangements and—"

"I play the piano," Maura said.

Nellie groaned. "In church, no doubt."

Maura ignored the jibe. "I read music and I'm a very fast learner." Nellie ignored her and continued her harangue. "You'd be doing yourself a favor."

"I don't need favors, girlie. I need a piano player, and you sure as hell don't look the part."

Maura found a strategy and played it. "Nobody's gonna care what I look like, Miss Nellie. Only how I sound."

Nellie snorted. "Get lost."

"Stay where you are, kid," Omar said. "Listen, Nell. If Sugar Boy's a no-show, we're for sure in a fix. Charlotte's expecting a full house tonight, and you know she don't like being disappointed."

"Only too well." Nellie muttered.

He jerked his head toward Maura. "So?"

Nellie tapped the bar with long fingernails before pointing toward the stage. "Okay, girlie. Hit that piano and play Steamer Lament. Music's on the rack."

Maura hurried to take a seat and scanned the sheet music. She'd never heard the song and was relieved to find it had limited chords and a simple melody. She was halfway through when Nellie drifted over and began humming along. When Maura finished the song, Starla told her to start again.

"Pitch it half an octave lower and slow it down."

Maura obliged and Nellie began singing in a low, smoky voice with a wobbly vibrato. Her voice was nowhere near as pure as Maura's soprano, but her delivery was calculated to sell. By the end of the song about a beloved father lost in a steamboat accident, Maura was almost moved to tears.

"Not bad," Nellie said. "Let's try something fun. Play Jimbo Plunket for me, and speed it back up."

Maura breezed through the light-hearted tune about a naive banjo player with an unfaithful girlfriend. Nellie's husky voice made this one even more convincing, and her teamwork with Maura was good enough to earn Omar's applause.

"Whew!" Nellie grabbed a palmetto fan from the top of the piano and waved it vigorously. "You're not half-bad, kid."

"Then you'll give me a job?"

"Only for tonight cause I got no choice with that worthless Sugar Boy." She glanced at Maura's carpetbag. "What's that for?"

"I just got off the train from Mississippi."

"God help me, I shoulda known." Nellie gave her a wry look. "I'm betting that's your best dress."

Maura's heart sank. "Yes, ma-am."

"I'm also betting you got no place to stay."

"No, ma'am. Not yet."

"Sweet Jesus," Nellie grumbled.

"Minnie's old room is empty," Omar said. "Put her in there."

"Alright." Nellie gave Maura another once-over. "I guess we can put that mess of red hair up and borrow an outfit from one of the girls. She and Hattie look about the same size." She shook her head. "I oughta have my head examined for doing this."

"I won't let you down, Miss Nellie."

"Bet your sweet ass you won't, otherwise you'll be out on your hillbilly behind." Nellie riffled through the sheet music and stacked a dozen songs atop the piano. "This is what I'm singing tonight. We'll run through them after we get you settled."

"Yes, ma'am."

"What'd you say your name was?"

"Maura O'Rourke."

"Alright then, Maura O'Rourke. Grab your bag and come on."

Maura followed Nellie up two flights of stairs, then outside to a generous gallery lined with tall shuttered windows. The black woman scouring the doorstep had moved across the street. Nellie called and waved. "How you doing, Zozo?"

"I'm fine, Miss Nellie, but this heat's wearing me down."

"When you gonna start selling that stuff instead of doing all the work yourself?"

"Takes money to make money, I reckon."

"Talk to Tom Anderson."

"Yes, ma'am. Maybe I will."

Maura eyed the blood-red stoop. "What's she's rubbing on the doorsteps?"

"Brick dust."

"Whatever for?"

"To ward off the evil spirits." Seeing Maura's confusion, she said. "This is voodoo territory, girl, and Zozo's a voudouienne. Next thing I know you'll be asking me the difference between a quadroon and an octoroon."

Maura kept further ignorance to herself and took another gulp of thick air. "One thing's for sure. New Orleans is the hottest place I've ever been."

"Hate to tell you, but this ain't nothing. Come August, the heat's gonna hump you like a junkyard dog." Nellie leaned against the wooden railing to catch her breath. "Sometimes we get a breeze off the river, but not today."

"Which way's the river?"

"Over there."

Maura marveled at a commanding view of the domes and steeples of New Orleans, including the triple spires of St. Louis Cathedral. They shimmered and blurred in the blazing July heat, and beyond, gleaming like a silver ribbon, was the Mississippi River, New Orleans raison d'etre. It bristled with the masts of European trading brigs, coasting craft from New England and frigates from the Caribbean. Smokestacks from half a dozen steamboats punctured the flat horizon.

"It's beautiful!"

"Yeah, it is." Nellie pulled a handkerchief from her cleavage and blotted her damp forehead. "I've worked that old river from here to Memphis and back. Natchez. Vicksburg. Baton Rouge. None of 'em compare with New Orleans though. You hear that?" Maura discerned the faint sound of a trumpet wailing the blues. "I swear you can hear music more often than not. Tony Jackson says it oozes from the city's pores, and he's a local boy so he oughta know."

"The city looks like a mirage. Like something out of the Arabian nights."

Nellie cackled. "Oh, it's real alright. Plenty real. In fact, things in Storyville are about as real as they get. Now come along and keep quiet so you don't wake the girls."

"What girls?"

Nellie was exasperated. "Good Lord! I know you're from the sticks, but don't you know where you are?"

"Isn't the Windsor a music hall?"

"Oh, honey!" Nellie roared with laughter. "Me and you ain't nothing but window dressing. This is one of the fanciest whorehouses in the country!"

PART THREE

"The Mississippi River winds past
the City of New Orleans
between enormous levees
and a rim of land and trees.
This is where the water beats against the land
And where the river breathes."
-Oliver A. Houck, *Down on the Batture*

12

2023

"Hey, you!" Gemma peered into the dig. "Ready for some news?"

Henri looked up and grinned. "You going to buy the house, aren't you?"

"Aw, you're no fun."

"I say good for you. I'll bet Mr. Brooks was thrilled."

"Well, I sure wasn't. I swear, it was the most intense, insane fifteen minutes of my life. He was drunk as a coot, of course, and you would've thought I'd found a cure for cancer or created world peace. He whooped and cried and said I'd saved his life and on and on and on before I finally got off the phone. I was so worn out I almost went back to bed."

"Have you told Maddie?"

"We're lunching at Commander's. I'll tell her then."

"So you rushed right over to tell me? I'm flattered."

"Sorry, kiddo. I didn't even know you were going to be here. When I realized I'm now Miss Chatelaine, I had the sudden urge to explore my new chateau."

"Sounds reasonable."

"Actually, I'm a little giddy. Walking through there just now made me feel like…oh, I don't know."

"Like you were coming home?"

"No. More like I'd never left. You know, I've had that sensation a couple of time before. Once in Peru. Another time in Santa Fe. It's so weird how it comes out of the blue."

"I've experienced it a few times myself, and my advice is to relax and enjoy it. Frankly, I like knowing mysterious forces are at work."

"I suppose." Gemma knelt down by the hole, eyes narrowing as he resumed digging. "Find anything interesting this morning?"

"More broken crockery. That pattern is so common I've nicknamed it Creole Melmac. Oh. And this!" He reached into the niche for temporarily stashing his finds and held up a dirt-encrusted disc. "Check it out."

"What is it?"

"The lid of a rouge pot."

Gemma got a brush from Henri's tool kit and cleaned the lid. "It's very sweet. Lots of tiny little flowers and hearts." She turned it over in her hand. "What are you going to do with this stuff?"

"You should put them in a display case, Gemma. They're yours after all, and they make great conversation pieces."

"What a good idea." She scanned the house and noted some badly blistered paint. "The place may not technically be mine, but I'm not waiting to start repairs. That Gentry guy who managed the place does restoration work. You think I should give him a call?"

"Why not? He probably knows the house better than anybody."

"Be right back."

Henri resumed digging while Gemma made her call. The bottom of the hole got ever soupier as he approached New Orleans' freakishly high water table. He was close to ten feet down when he spotted a dull whitish-gray gleam in the dark brown soil. He carefully brushed away the dirt, and as more coloration came to light, a shape began to emerge. Suspicions stirred, and a few more brushstrokes confirmed his dread. When he heard Gemma's voice, he hastily blocked her view.

"Gentry's interested!" she called. "I'm going over there now to see his house. Did I tell you he built it himself?"

"No, but he sounds perfect."

"I think so too." She waved. "Wish me luck!"

"Good luck."

Henri was relieved when Gemma left without knowing a skull was buried in her new back yard.

Cane was never comfortable with potential clients visiting his camp. He was proud of his carpentry, but his little house was cobbled together with mostly found materials and reflected none of the architectural purity of historic homes. His work bore ample evidence of attention to detail and was solidly assembled with nails aligned in neat rows. Still, he thought glumly, this might not be proof enough of his skill, plus his one encounter with Mrs. Clark suggested that she'd be demanding. The money was welcome, but not if it came packaged in headaches.

Cane sank into a chair on his back porch and tried to relax with a glass of iced tea. These moments of solitude, wrapped in pungent river air, were why he loved batture life and rarely sought company. No doubt, he thought irritably, this Clark woman would want to know why he lived there, along with the usual stupid questions he'd heard ad infinitum. Don't you worry about one of those monster tankers wiping you out? What about flooding? How on earth do you live without air-conditioning? Aren't you overrun with rats? Where's your bathroom? Cane had heard them so often, he could differentiate between people who were genuinely interested and those wanting to ridicule his unusual lifestyle. He blew off the latter, but for those who cared, he explained that, yes, the cargo ship Bright Field had sideswiped the Riverwalk in 1996, but no one was killed and he was far more worried about being hit by a car while crossing the street. Yes, the batture got hot, but the river's cool breath created a microclimate along the shore, a natural air-conditioning that insulated him from polluted city air. It was unbearable only on days when the atmosphere was heavy and absolutely still, but even the worst skeptics conceded that it was always cooler and breezier on the moving water. Cane was wondering which of these questions Mrs. Clark would ask when he heard the catwalk creak. He hurried to open the front door as she started to knock. She jerked her hand back, startled.

"Sorry, ma'am. Come on in."

"In a minute, Mr. Gentry. I've never seen anything quite like this." Gemma looked toward Poppy's camp and the row of houses beyond, barely visible through the subtropical overgrowth. She was impressed by the neat row of potted plants lining Cane's catwalk. "Is that butterfly ginger in the blue pot?"

"Yeah."

Gemma backtracked and stooped to smell the delicate white blooms. "One of my favorite scents." Cane said nothing as she continued to explore. "What are those pretty trees, the tall ones there?"

"Chinese tallow trees."

"I've never seen them."

"Nasty things. Very invasive. They create their own forest and trap summer heat like a furnace."

"In that case, I take it all back." He didn't return her smile. "How long have you lived here?"

"Twenty-six years. You want to see inside?"

Annoyed by his abruptness, she quipped, "It's why I'm here, isn't it?"

As Cane showed her through the four small rooms, he said little and let his carpentry skills speak for themselves. Gemma, to his relief, asked no questions until they stepped onto the back porch. Swollen by weeks of rainstorms across the country's midsection, the Mississippi lapped hungrily at the pilings supporting the house. It took a moment for her to grasp that she was literally standing atop the river.

"My goodness! What in the world drew you to this place?"

"It's where I was born."

Gemma was further amazed. "You've always lived here?"

"No, but…it's kind of a long story."

"That's fine." Gemma fluffed the pillow in a nearby chair and sat. "I like long stories, and I love this wonderful view."

"You sure?"

"Yes, Mr. Gentry. Please tell me."

To his great surprise, Cane began to talk.

13

1995

A mix of dread and exhilaration thumped in Cane's chest as he parked his battered '82 Plymouth at the foot of the levee and began the climb. He paused below the top and gulped the thick, river air. Urged on by the familiar metallic taste, he crested the levee and looked down on the bank where he had romped and tumbled as a boy. In September, a dense canopy of sycamores, willows, and tallow trees cloaked most structures, but, sure enough, the little settlement was still there. Cane was at the upriver end, and as he followed the levee spine toward his old homesite, memories swirled like ground fog. A new build winked through the trees where Cap'n McKay had lived with his pretty Chinese wife, Lily, but his playmate JoJo's house was gone, a missing tooth in an otherwise unbroken row of camps. Because the mind forever flits down odd alleys, Cane remembered JoJo's mom had covered the walls of their house with carpet samples and thought about the times he and JoJo had gone hunting for snakes and lizards and once caught a catfish big enough to swallow a toaster. He recalled a summer storm propelling the river over the back porch and into the kitchen so that everyone had to wear boots inside. He and his older brother Luke had scrambled to help their mother get everything off the floor and put empty Luzianne coffee cans under the table and chair legs while waiting for the ripples across the kitchen floor to slow and recede. Cane had thought it a game, never realizing the danger or how much worse things might get.

Flush with memories, he continued to the downriver end of the settlement. The jungle was at its thickest here, but Cane prickled with excitement when he spotted the catwalk to his family's old house. He half-slipped, half-stumbled down the slope to find the entrance to the catwalk swallowed by a tangle of vines, blackberry bushes and poison ivy. He glimpsed bits of wooden wall and roof through the overgrowth, but the lethal sheen of poison ivy held him at bay. Because the river was low, he found access alongside the house next door. He made his way alongside a tidy catwalk sparkling with pots of zinnias and amaryllis. He marveled at the man-made order in nature's chaos until he found what he was looking for.

"Oh, God! No!"

The front two rooms remained, but the back porch, kitchen and his parents' bedroom had collapsed into an unholy mess of pilings, beams and shingles. The culprit was a colossal sycamore stump wedged against the pilings, hurled with enough force to destroy half the house. Punched in the gut, Cane knelt on the damp ground and fought tears, oblivious to a woman's voice. Distant at first, it grew louder.

"You deaf or something?" On the back porch of the adjacent house was a tall black woman in a coolie hat and ratty chenille bathrobe. She dispatched a hard look that was anything but convivial. "Yeah. You." She turned imperious when he still failed to respond. "I asked what the hell you're doing down there."

He stood and rubbed his eyes. "Just looking around."

"You ain't supposed to be looking around. That's private property."

"I didn't think it belonged to anybody."

"You thought wrong."

"Sorry." The woman's harsh dismissal burnished his sadness over the destruction of his childhood home. He paused below her porch and gestured at the wreckage. "When did this happen?"

"Right after I moved here six years ago. Place's been empty ever since."

"I...I used to live there."

"What?! When?"

"I left in nineteen-eighty, after my father died."

She leaned over the railing for a closer look. "You Dean Gentry's boy?"

"How'd you know?"

"Ain't no secrets on the batture, that's how. Heard all about him when I moved here. Man was a local hero. Second generation batture, as I recall." Cane turned away and hunched his shoulders, eyes gleaming again. "What the devil's wrong with you, son?"

"I'm sorry, ma'am. I wasn't…well, I just wasn't expecting this."

"Ain't nothing to be sorry about. You gonna fix it up?"

"What?"

"You heard me."

"Are you kidding?"

Long, hot hours in the un-airconditioned car had left Cane drenched in sweat. A white tee shirt hugged his beefy frame like a second skin. The woman took inventory.

"You look healthy enough. You afraid of hard work?"

"No, but—"

"Then what's keeping you from doing some repairs?"

"Ma'am, I got to New Orleans this morning after driving all night from Tennessee, and, for no special reason, came down here to see where I used to live. I never had any intention of moving back."

The women leaned over the railing and squinted. "You sure about that?"

"Yeah. I'm sure."

"Good thing," she sniffed. "Losers don't last on the batture."

Cane churned inside. Too many times he'd been called that by his bullying older brother Luke. "You know nothing about me, lady," he grunted.

"Maybe not, but if Dean Gentry was your daddy, that means that you come from good stock."

"And this wreckage mean that no Gentrys should be living here."

"Now, don't go thinking what happened was some kinda omen. Your place got hit by a root-ball. That old river's doing its thing, nothing more, nothing less. Come over here." She stuck out her hand. "I'm Polyhymnia Fields but everybody calls me Poppy. Get it? Poppy Fields. You're too young to remember me. I used to be a singer. Headlined for years on Bourbon Street." She fumbled in her robe pocket for a pack of Luckies and an ornate gold lighter. She lit up with a flourish. "You wanna know who gave me this lighter? Bruno Vitelli himself. Popped into the Streetcar Lounge one night and took a fancy to my singing and sent this as a tip." Cane had no idea who this Vitelli character was and dreaded an old woman's digression into boring memories, but he underestimated Poppy. She took a deep draw on her Lucky and puffed a series of smoke rings. "What'd you say your name was?"

"I didn't, but it's Cane."

"Alright, Mr. Cane Gentry. You're gonna be mighty glad I saw you this fine morning because I'm gonna help you get started."

"What are you talking about?"

Poppy studied him, brown eyes dancing. "Your neighbors, that's what. We're gonna ask them for help in rebuilding."

"I told you I'm not moving here."

"You got some place else you need to be?"

"No, but—"

"I didn't think so." She waited for that reality to sink in. "Well?"

"Nah. The whole idea's crazy."

"Sure, it is. If you stop to think about it, the idea of the batture's pretty crazy too." She paused for another drag. "Which is exactly why you shouldn't stop and think about it."

Cane turned away, but Poppy harangued him as he climbed back up the levee. "There's something about the batture gets in your blood, Cane Gentry. Got in your granddaddy's blood and your daddy's too, so it's for sure gonna be in yours. It ain't easy, but it's what we love. I ain't saying your neighbors are gonna do the job for you, but they'll show you how. Truth is, you can find pretty much everything you need to rebuild if you know where to look. Hardly a day goes by that that old river don't throw up something useful."

Cane stopped and turned around. "Why are you doing this?"

"Doing what?"

"Trying to talk me into moving here. Why do you care where I live?"

"I don't."

"Then why are you—?"

"Maybe because I'm looking at a lost soul who needs help." She puffed on the Lucky and reconsidered. "Nah. That's so corny I ain't buying it myself, so I'll tell the truth and shame the devil. I don't like living at the open end of the batture. I want somebody between me and the outside world and I don't care who the hell it is. Why not you?"

"Because I don't want to live here."

"If that were true, you wouldn't have come back."

"I told you I just came to look around."

"No, you didn't." Another drag, "And you know it."

"No, I don't," Cane contended. "I'm twenty-three years old and I don't know what I want. All I know is that I don't have a job or a place to live or time to waste arguing with somebody I don't know from Adam who—"

"That what's bothering you? A place to live?" Poppy waved a dismissive hand. "Shoot, boy. You can sleep on my back porch. I got a hammock back there suit you fine." She squinted. "I'll bet you had a hammock when you lived here, didn't you?"

"So what if I did?"

"Well?"

"I gotta go."

"Suit yourself."

Cane was relieved when Poppy fell silent and left him to climb the levee in peace. He'd never met anyone so meddlesome and pushy. Dealing with her and finding the wreckage of his family home had sapped what was left of his energy, and he was eager to move on. He climbed into his car and turned the ignition. The click was followed by a low grind.

"Aw, shit!" Cane's temper rumbled as he tried again and again, pounding the steering wheel in frustration. Nothing. "Shit! Shit! Shit!"

He got out and raised the hood. He checked the oil and water. Both were fine, so what next? He had no idea what to do about a dead battery or faulty magneto or whatever the hell was wrong. He scanned the street. No gas station. No pay phone either, but even if there were he had no change and didn't know who to call if he did. He got back in the car and cursed a morning worsening by the minute. He was exhausted from the long drive, and a rumbling, empty stomach added insult to injury, as did a pitiless sun turning the old Plymouth into an oven. He wondered what else could go wrong as he looked through the bug-splattered windshield at the great green mound beyond. He got out and slammed the car door and, scarcely realizing why, started back up the gentle slope. He retraced his steps to where he last saw Poppy and, sure enough, she was still there, watching and blowing smoke rings. She grinned as he half-walked, half-stumbled down the levee.

"Back so soon?"

"My car's dead."

"Broke and broke down." Poppy cackled. "Damn, son! If that ain't an omen, I don't know what is!"

14

"Not sure if Wino's up yet," Poppy said, "so we'll have to go and see."

"Wino?"

"Three camps down." She pointed. "Real name's Ken Paulson, but he got that nickname in his merchant marine days. Funny thing is, I ain't never seen him touch a drop of wine, but, bless his soul, the man loves to sleep. He's a real old timer. Knew your family. Name ring a bell?"

"No. Why are we seeing him?"

"Because he fixes everything under the sun. Man's been a mechanic, rodeo clown, surveyor. Think he was even a lighthouse keeper once." Cane trailed Poppy to a tiny, two-room camp at the end of a wonky catwalk. "Hey, Wino! You up?"

"Getting' there!" a raspy voice barked. "What's up, Miss Poppy?"

"Got a customer for you."

"Hang on a minute!" A crash was followed by some colorful cursing before a tall, bare-chested man in khaki shorts stumbled outside. Chest, arms and belly were blanketed with tattoos. He squinted in the bright sunlight.

"Who's this?"

"This is Cane Gentry, Wino. He's Dean's boy, and he's got car trouble."

"I'll be damned!" Wino gave Cane a bone-crushing handshake. "I remember you kids romping all over the place. Knew your Daddy right well. Fine man. Died way too soon. Met your grandaddy too. Man was a glassmaker as I recall." He squinted again. "You sure favor your daddy. I remember your mama too. Alice, was it?"

"Alicia."

"Pretty little thing. How's she doing?"

Cane looked away. "She died last winter."

"Sorry to hear that." He scratched a shark tattoo over his sternum. "She was a good woman. Yes, indeed, she was."

"Cane's gonna rebuild the old Gentry camp," Poppy announced.

Before Cane could respond, Wino said, "Glad to hear it, son. Folks here will be proud to have you back."

"She's wrong," Cane insisted. "I'm not moving back."

"Then what are you doing here?"

"I just wanted to see the old place and—"

Wino have Poppy a knowing look. "He don't know that old river's callin' him back, does he?"

"No yet."

God, Cane thought. What's with these lunatic river rats?!

"He's gonna stay with me awhile," Poppy continued. "I was telling him how we batture folks take care of our own."

"You're right about that." Wino clapped Cane on the shoulder. "Where's your car?"

Cane decided to stop protesting and focus on getting back on the road. "On the other side of the levee. Upriver a ways."

"I'll take a look after I eat something."

"I'd appreciate it."

"Come on." Poppy clapped a hand on Cane's shoulder. "I'll fix you something too. Now, don't give me that hang-dog look. I know you're hungry. I hear your stomach complaining all the way over here."

Cane knew he was being manipulated, but it made him feel less lost and lonely. He wrestled with the unfamiliar sensation as he followed Poppy home.

"I don't understand why you're being so nice."

"You know all you need to know, for now anyway. So say thank you and that you'll return the favor some time, if need be, and trust me it will."

"Thank you."

"You're welcome. Now, first thing you gotta do is call the Levee Board for a building permit."

"I thought we could do anything we wanted with our houses."

Our houses, Cane thought. As soon as he said it, he realized Poppy and Wino were right that he was succumbing to what seeped into his young soul years ago and now laid claim. It was the same river siren that sang to his father and grandfather before him, and he burst out laughing when he realized that his siren was an old black woman in a coolie hat.

"What's so funny?" Poppy demanded.

"This whole thing," Cane said. "You, me, the batture. All of it."

"You're one crazy white boy. You know that?"

"Probably. Now what were you saying about the Levee Board?"

"Well, the city don't ignore us like weeds any more, which is why we've got water and power now. And in case you forgot, they're called camps, not houses. Anyway, a permit's nothing to worry about. They'll send some bureaucrat down here and he'll poke around and say you need to shore things up and—"

"Shore things up? The place needs a lot more than that."

Poppy ignored him. "He'll give you a form to fill out and send in with sketches of your new plans, which has to be the same...what do they call it now? Footprint. Yeah. That's it. Has to be the same footprint as the existing house, and then you'll get a permit in the mail. In the meantime, you can start cleaning the place up. You're up for that, aren't you?"

Cane felt himself succumbing to the inexorable. "I guess so."

"Well, whaddya know? Sounds to me like you've made up your mind."

"No, ma'am. What it sounds like is that you've made up my mind."

Poppy grinned. "You sure ain't the first man to tell me that." She took his arm as they turned onto her catwalk. "Good to know I ain't lost my touch."

15

By the time he curled up in her porch hammock that first night, Poppy had introduced Cane to most everyone on the batture. The next morning, she inundated him with chores, and in the days that followed, he worked harder than he had in his life. Poppy was a benevolent slave driver, pushing him to his limits but knowing when to back off. He took her advice on everything, including the Levee Board. As she predicted, an indifferent inspector gave the site a cursory look, left a form for Cane to fill out and was gone in under fifteen minutes. Cane mailed in the form and a few weeks later, his permit to rebuild arrived in Poppy's mail.

Cane's experience as a short order cook in Tennessee landed him a job in a seafood restaurant near Audubon Park. It was an easy drive from the batture, and despite the mediocre pay he squirreled away a few dollars. Any and all spare time was spent next door, pulling out nails, sorting lumber and salvaging whatever he could from the wrecked house. Like everyone on the batture, Poppy had a stash of tools, and what she didn't have, a neighbor did. Progress was steady, if slow, but the massive tree stump tangled in the wreckage remained Cane's bête noir. The monster was vanquished one day when Sean Cavanaugh showed up with a chainsaw. Short and pot-bellied, face lined by too much sun, wind and cheap beer, Sean laid into the stump with a cowing ferocity. When he took a break, Cane seized the saw and showed off the expertise learned in his brief stint as a timber faller. The two took turns, and it was Cane who delivered the sundering blow, whooping in triumph as the stump shuddered and split with a loud thwack before being swept away by the river.

His camp was free, but exhilaration was short-lived. When they donned face masks and climbed inside the remaining two rooms, Cane saw up-close what subtropical weather did to abandoned camps. Interior walls were bowed and stained, and almost every surface was smothered with grit. Windows and doors were long gone, scavenged along with anything else that could be recycled. Vines invaded throughout, marching deep inside until their tendrils turned albino from lack of sunlight. The entire place reeked of rot and mold, and even with a fresh breeze wafting through the missing windows and doors, the air was putrid.

Cane recoiled. "Goddamn!"

"Could be a lot worse, son. Looks like your daddy knew how to build solid." Sean tested the floors with a light bounce. "Floor's in pretty good shape. Level too, which tells me the pilings are still doing their job. Gonna need to replace the roof though. I'll help."

Cane took off his cap and scratched his head. "You really think we can do this?"

"C'mon, kid. The batture's not like other places. You gotta see what's there instead of what's not there. You learn about that half-full, half-empty glass business in school?"

"Yes, sir."

"Good. You keep that in mind, and things are gonna look a whole lot better." Sean yanked a vine from the wall and tossed it out the window. "While I'm giving out advice, here's something else. Your other neighbors will help out too, but the biggest and best provider is right out your back door." He chuckled. "If you had a back door, that is."

"You mean the river?"

"Sure do. It coughs up enough treasure to please Jean Lafitte."

"That's what Daddy used to say." Cane was encouraged by the memory. "Thanks for the advice, Mr. Cavanaugh. And for getting rid of that root ball."

"You bet. Now, c'mon. Let's get outta this pesthole. You better get rid of that mold before it gets rid of you."

Like Poppy, Sean took Cane under his wing. After helping with the hazmat equipment needed to scour the toxic mold, he gave scavenging lessons. One morning he loaded Cane into his truck and took him to a dumping ground for cast-off telephone poles. Chain saw in hand, Cane deftly sliced the poles into manageable lengths for loading into the truck. Later that night, they visited a utility yard and helped themselves to a recycle bin overflowing with nuts, bolts and washers. Another scavenging party led by Wino, who had a nose for newly demolished houses, produced an interior door, a back door, a kitchen counter and three double sash windows. Still another search yielded a bonanza of cast-off plywood sheets, and the river contributed by belching a creosote log onto Poppy's beach. Wino's post-hole digger was pressed into service and, with Sean's help, Cane sank the sawed-off phone poles into the soft earth and, with pilings firmly in place, began framing the rear addition. Plywood walls went up, holes were cut for doors and windows, and by late November, the camp boasted a gleaming tin roof that made Cane happy whenever he saw it. For some reason, the roof more than anything else confirmed that he would have his first home.

Then the rains came. An unnamed tropical depression lurked in the Gulf of Mexico for days before deciding to whip ashore at Grand Isle. Wino smelled it before anyone else and helped Cane and Sean wrap the half-finished house in blue tarps. They were stapling the last sheet in place when the rains arrived in huge, playful drops that hit the tarp in noisy splatters. The three men, shirtless and sweaty from the killer Louisiana heat, welcomed the cold rain until a bolt of lightning bleached the batture and sent them scurrying for shelter. Sean and Wino ran to their camps while Cane watched warily from Poppy's roofed porch. He remained outside until the rain began coming sideways and watched, helpless, as wind snatched at the tarps.

Poppy yelled through the screen door. "Get inside and close the door, fool! Rain's comin' in!"

Cane and Poppy spent the next hour huddled at her kitchen table. The winds made conversation difficult, so they sat quietly with their coffee and private thoughts. Cane jumped up when an especially strong gust rocked the camp and, fearing torn tarps, he rushed to the window. His work remained protected, but his tension was tangible in the small, hot room.

Poppy eyed him over the rim of her mug. "The storm will pass, you know."

"I know."

"And if that tarp rips, it rips. Everything's fixable." She rolled her eyes when he hurried back to the window. "I never knew such a worry wart."

"My daddy used to call me Pessimistic Pete."

"Your daddy was right. Now, me? I take things as they come and don't waste time on that coulda-shoulda-woulda business. Sure, I'd like to have been the next Ella or Etta, but fate didn't see it that way. Don't matter. I've done alright for myself. I reckon others might see things different, what with me ending up alone in a shack by the river, but that's their deal. I've had one helluva ride, kiddo, and if there's anything I truly cherish now, it's the strength I draw from living alone. Ain't nothing like it."

"I've liked being by myself as long as I can remember."

"That's fine, but don't lock yourself up before seeing the world."

"Don't worry about me, Poppy. I've seen what I need to see."

"Is that so?"

"Yup."

"Well, I'd sure like to hear about it." Since his sudden appearance on the batture, Cane had been maddeningly mute about his past. Poppy had been generous with stories about surviving childhood in the fierce St. Thomas Projects and colorful anecdotes about her life as a French Quarter singer, but he never responded in kind. She hoped this intimate circumstance might be the moment. "No time like the present."

"Not that much to tell."

Realizing he wasn't going to talk, Poppy left him alone with his fears and retreated to the front room to play an old keyboard and lose herself in her music. She was halfway through Ain't Nobody's Business when the wind slowed and stopped. The scrape of a kitchen chair followed by a slammed door announced Cane was gone. Poppy nodded to herself and began singing, Alone Again, Naturally.

16

2023

"That's quite a saga," Gemma said a bit breathlessly. "Obviously, your friend Poppy has phenomenal powers of persuasion."

"You've no idea."

"When did you finally finish the house?"

"Thanksgiving."

"You did all that work in three months? Very impressive."

"Like I said, I had a lot of help."

"It's still very impressive." She watched the Algiers ferry dart across the path of a tanker flying the Liberian flag. "The river traffic is fascinating. It's an ongoing show right in your own back yard, isn't it?"

"Mmmm."

Cane's noncommittal response and the ensuing silence announced he was finished talking about himself, so Gemma ended the interview. "If I hire you, Mr. Gentry, how soon can you start work?"

"Whenever."

"You don't sound very enthusiastic."

"Sorry, Mrs. Clark. After that long story, you probably think I'm a big talker. Truth is, I'm not, and I apologize for rambling on like that."

"Please don't. It told me exactly what I needed to know about your work ethic. The job is yours."

"I appreciate it. You won't be disappointed."

"I'm sure I won't be." Gemma checked her cellphone calendar. "Can you meet me at the house tomorrow at three for another walk-through?"

"Sure thing."

Gemma followed Cane back outside and down the catwalk. Once again, she paused to smell the butterfly ginger and noted the profusion of potted plants. "You've got quite the green thumb."

"Poppy gave them to me."

"Oh?"

"See you tomorrow, Mrs. Clark."

The mask, so briefly raised, glided back into place.

Commander's Palace was oddly quiet as the waiter ushered Gemma to her regular table in the Garden Room. Maddie was waiting.

"Sorry I'm late, darling! You won't mind when I tell you why." She bussed Maddie's cheek and glanced at the hovering waiter. "Champagne cocktail, please."

Maddie noted the red flag. "You only drink those when you're celebrating."

"Right you are, kiddo. Guess what?"

"You bought the house on Baptiste Street!"

Gemma scowled. "Did Henri call you?"

"No, but I know you like a book. Plus, I can't think of anything else that would have you so jazzed right now."

"Am I really so transparent?"

"Only to those who love you." Maddie smiled. "When did you tell Henri?"

"Earlier this morning when I went to look at the house. He was digging away in the back yard. I swear, he's like a little boy playing in a sandbox."

"Did he find anything interesting?"

"The lid of a rouge pot. Very fancy. Engraved with little flowers and things. Henri suggested I showcase his relics, so after lunch I'm going to scour Magazine Street for a display case. Want to play hooky from the research center and come with?"

"Wish I could, but I've got a staff meeting at two. Plus, the center's been swamped lately."

"Something special going on?"

"Busloads of foreign tourists, with half of them asking where they can catch the streetcar named desire and where they can find Storyville and the House of the Rising Sun. They drive me nuts, but it's my job."

Gemma thanked the waiter and sipped her drink. "I do have a bit more news."

"Oh?"

"After I saw Henri, I visited Cane Gentry, that property manager guy, and contracted him to renovate the house."

"Seriously? You went to the batture?"

"Yes, indeedy."

"What's it like?"

"A bunch of wonky houses propped up on stilts, waiting to be gobbled up by the Mississippi River."

"That's a little harsh."

"Actually, it's a lot harsh. Shame on me." She sipped. "The folks who live there are like modern-day homesteaders. Gutsy, independent types. Their houses are called camps, and Mr. Gentry's little place is very well-built. Something he put together almost completely with scavenged materials."

"Scavenged? You mean, like stolen?"

"Not the way he described it. Anyway, half his camp had been wrecked by a floating tree, but he and some neighbors rebuilt the thing in three months. His carpentry skills are excellent. He's even hooked up to electricity and water."

"So there's a toilet?"

"Some kind of portable thingie. At least I think that's what it was. I only caught a glimpse and was too embarrassed to ask."

"The batture isn't as primitive as I thought."

"Me either, but I'm sure it was pretty crude when he was a boy. No power or water."

"He grew up there?"

"Yes, but left at some point and came back twenty-some years ago. I was dying to know more, but Cane Gentry's not the sort to give up secrets easily."

"He struck me as the strong, silent type."

"In spades. Then again, even though he's brusque, when he talked about the batture, his voice softened and he got almost reverential."

"Maybe he has a feminine side."

"If he does, it's buried halfway to China. I never expected us to get chummy, but the guy's got some kind of personality blocker in place."

"Then maybe he's reserved."

"He's too rough-edged to be reserved. More like cautious, or on the defensive." She shrugged. "Probably comes from living on the batture. People there must be constantly looking over their shoulder. Have to, I guess."

Maddie toyed with the menu. "Maybe you should run a background check before you sign anything."

"I thought about it, but, oh, I don't think it's necessary. I saw for myself that the guy does good work and that's what matters." She drained her glass and flagged the waiter for a refill. "And, what's more, darling, I'm tired of talking about Cane Gentry. I don't know about you, but I'm splurging on bread pudding."

17

"A little to the left, Ty. Thank you." Gemma was pleased when he repositioned the display case in a corner of the library. "It's perfect there, don't you think?"

"I guess so." Tyrone stepped back for a better look. "Where'd you find that old cabinet?"

"Magazine Street of course. The woman told me it belonged to Anne Rice, said she kept part of her doll collection in it."

"Did you believe her?"

"Of course not. Funny how when famous people die, their possessions instantly appear in shops everywhere. I once had a guy try to sell me a typewriter he claimed belonged to Tennessee Williams."

Tyrone drew a dust cloth across the top of the case. "What're you going to put in here?"

"Things in that box there. They're from a trash pit. Did I tell you I'm buying an old house on Baptiste Street?"

"Three or four times."

"Damn! I hate when I do that. I'm not ready to be losing my marbles."

"I wouldn't worry about it, Miss Gemma.

"That's another thing. How many times must I tell you not to call me that? I'm not Scarlett O'Hara, you know. Or did I forget to tell you that too?"

Tyrone chuckled. "You're on a tear this morning, aren't you?"

Gemma laughed too. "Truth is, I'm in very good spirits. I had some delicious dreams last night and am looking forward to organizing things in that display case."

"Anything else I can help you with?"

"No, thanks. I want to do this by myself."

Left alone, Gemma removed items from the dig and arranged them on a tea towel spread on the library desk. There was more Creole Melmac than anything else, enough for Henri to piece together almost a complete plate. Gemma decided to make it the centerpiece of the collection, flanked by the porcelain doll's head, rouge pot, mustard jar and a perfume stopper. There were no snuff glasses, but Henri had unearthed a broken shot glass and half dozen wine bottles in as many colors. She positioned them on the bottom shelf and stepped back to admire her handiwork. As her eyes went from one item to another, she pondered their stories. Who was the woman who used the rouge pot? Were the meals served on that plate cooked by slaves? Who played with the doll and how did it get that dented cheek? Touching these relics stirred the sentience experienced when she first entered the house and occupied the same space as her ancestors. Coupled with what she uncovered about Samuel Stafford, it morphed into a desire to know more. She had exhausted the resources at the research center and doubted she'd get more information from Philip Brooks. There was the source Maddie suggested, but it was far from promising.

"Mama."

Three years ago, Gemma had convinced her mother, Lydia, to move into an assisted living facility uptown. Physically she was fine, but occasional bouts of dementia meant she couldn't be left alone. She had the usual good days and bad, and Gemma knew if Lydia didn't answer her phone that she was off in her own private world. Happily, she picked up on the second ring.

"Hello, dear."

Good, Gemma thought. She'd even read caller ID. "How are you, Mama?"

"Having a lovely day. Are you coming to visit?"

"Tomorrow, if that's alright."

"That's fine."

"I have a favor to ask, and it might be a little difficult."

"I'm listening."

"It's about the family. Daddy's side."

After a long pause, "Oh."

"I don't want to upset you, so if you'd rather we talk in person or don't want to talk about it, that's okay too." Silence. "Mama?"

"What do you want to know, Gemma?"

"Anything and everything. You and Daddy never talked about our relatives."

"Why now?"

Gemma explained about Philip Brooks and the house on Baptiste Street and what she'd unearthed with research. "All this has made me want to find out more."

Another long pause. "I see."

"Did you meet Daddy's parents?"

"They died before I was born."

"Did he talk about them?"

Lydia cleared her throat. "Are you sure you want to dig into the past, dear?"

"How can I answer that when it's a total mystery?"

"I'll be right back."

"Where are you going?"

"To get my coffee." Fearing that her mother was drifting into personal oblivion, Gemma was relieved when rustling sounds announced she was back on the phone. "You were only eleven when your father died. How much do you remember about him?"

"Very little. I remember the day he died because I was sent home from school early. I also remember that he wasn't very affectionate and wasn't home much."

"Your father traveled a great deal for his business, but maybe—"

"But maybe what?"

"Maybe it's time I stopped putting a pretty spin on things."

Because they had never been close, Gemma hadn't expected the intimate admission. She encouraged it. "Please do, Mama."

"I married Robert because I wanted to save him from himself. In a way, deep down, I may have felt sorry for him."

"Why?"

"Your father is a difficult man to explain, Gemma. He was much older. Twenty-three years in fact. Except for those beautiful blue eyes, he wasn't especially good-looking. Rather average actually. On the surface, he was distant and willful, defiant sometimes, but I later learned it was a façade. He had a...oh, I don't know. A sort of hidden landscape inside."

"That's a strange way to put it."

"Your father was very private, Gemma, and I found that appealing because, as you know, so am I. He never asked about my family so I never asked about his. That probably sounds peculiar, but that's how it was. We both loved to read, so we were content to

111

stay home with our books and each other and rarely socialized. When you were born, things changed. He suddenly started traveling for work when I needed him most. It was almost as if you frightened him, that he was afraid of being a father. I…I suppose I should've asked why, but I had my hands full with you and was resigned to never understanding him. Then, one afternoon, when Robert was away on one of those trips, the past fell in my lap when his cousin Anne came calling." Another long silence as Lydia sipped her coffee and sorted her thoughts. "She's the mother of this Philip Brooks you mentioned."

Gemma was floored. "No!"

"In fact, she sat in the chair where I'm sitting right now."

Gemma had a chill. "What did she want?"

"Her father John had just died. John was your great uncle, your grandfather Daniel's brother. His death had sort of freed her and she'd come to apologize and explain why she was estranged from your father."

"Hold on a second." Gemma sorted this out loud. "So Anne was Dad's first cousin and Daniel's niece?"

"Correct. Anyway, guilt does peculiar things to people, and…oh, Gemma. Why not let the ghosts stay hidden?"

"Please, Mama. I need to know."

"Alright then." Lydia sighed. "Robert's parents, your grandparents, died when he was eleven. His Uncle John gave him a home and raised him and Anne whose mother died early on."

"That was kind."

"Not according to Anne. She said your father's childhood was miserable. His Uncle John mistreated him terribly, which explains why your father was so emotionally stunted. I'm sure I was the first person who ever loved him."

"Why was John so abusive?"

"All Anne knew was that it had something to do with Robert's father, John's brother, Daniel. John hated Daniel and his wife too."

"What was her name?"

"Maureen or Moira or something. I don't remember. Anyway, John took his hatred for her and Daniel out on your dad. He was so vengeful that…oh, dear. This is so hard to recall."

"Please try, Mama."

"John was such a poor businessman that Daniel was constantly bailing him out, but, according to Anne, John was smart enough to do your dad out of his considerable inheritance. But he gambled it all away except the house on Baptiste Street, which he left it to Anne."

"How did he manage that?"

"Either your grandfather Daniel's will wasn't ironclad or John paid a judge to break it. It's the old story, darling. Corruption has been in Louisiana since the French came."

"Is that why Anne apologized? For taking Daddy's inheritance?

"Partly. She was six years older than Robert, and even though they grew up together, they were never close. She got very emotional when she described how badly Robert was abused, not beaten but locked in his closet and sent to bed without supper. Her childhood was a nightmare too. She was scared to death of her father. Anyway, I never saw her again."

"This is incredible, Mama. Why didn't you tell me about meeting her?"

"I didn't even tell your father, Gemma. I knew he would've been terribly upset, maybe even angry, so I buried the incident and forgot about it. Until now."

Gemma struggled to piece the puzzle together. "Are you sure Anne didn't say anything more why John hated grandaddy Daniel and his wife?"

"No, but you know what? As soon as I get out of here, I'm going to cut down that sweet olive tree. It's gotten so big that it shades the swimming pool. I better go check on it."

Gemma listened, helpless and frustrated, as her mother's dementia launched her onto a nonsensical tangent. She heard fumbling before the phone clicked off. "Dammit! I've lost her!"

18

The mud sucked hard at Henri's waders when he slogged across the bottom of the pit. The hole was now a nine-foot oval, and although he believed more artifacts lurked, the thick muck had defeated him.

"Hey, Mr. Chabrol!"

Henri shaded his eyes to identify the silhouette overhead. "That you, Mr. Gentry?"

"Yeah." Cane leaned over the hole. "Looks like you've hit bottom."

"Yeah. I was taking a last look before climbing out. Mother Nature wins again." Henri lurched forward, lost his balance and caught the ladder before sliding into the mud. "See what I mean?"

"You stuck?"

"I'm alright." Using the ladder for leverage, Henri worked his feet loose and climbed out. "It's one thing to know about New Orleans high water table and something else to stand in it."

"Did you know it fluctuates with the river?"

"In fact, I did, and I'm sure that's something you batture folks know plenty about."

"We have to." Cane gestured at the dirt piled beside the hole. "You want some help filling that back in?"

"I can't ask you to do that. I know you're here to work on the house."

"You didn't ask. I offered."

While Henri struggled out of his waders, Cane took off his jacket, grabbed a shovel and got busy. Dirt flew with impressive speed, and by the time Henri joined him, the mud had vanished under a layer of dry soil. The two worked together until Henri's back began to ache.

"Time for a break." He sat on the side porch and opened a bottle of water while Cane kept shoveling. He watched with a bit of envy when he saw the biceps straining against Cane's work-shirt as the hole was filled and tamped. "You're a good man, Mr. Gentry. Thanks."

"Sure."

"May I ask you something?"

"I guess."

"How old are you?"

"Fifty-one next birthday."

"Damn! Seriously?"

"Yeah. Why?"

"Because I'm two years younger, and I'm already worn out."

"Want me to pull up those stakes and tarps?'

Henri burst out laughing and passed Cane a bottle of water. "No, my friend. I want you to drink this and tell me why you're in such good shape. No doubt life on the batture helps."

"It does." Cane sat down and gulped some water. "I like being outside, so I've always looked for physical jobs."

"Such as?"

"You-name-it. My dad died when I was a kid, and I've been on my own since I was sixteen. My first gig was circus roustabout."

Henri smiled. "Aw, c'mon. Don't tell me you ran away to join the circus."

"Nah. I just kinda ended up there. It made me grow up fast, but I left when I saw how badly the animals were treated."

"Speaking of animals, I want to show you something." Henri rummaged through his cardboard box of cleaned artifacts and retrieved something a bit larger than a man's fist. He carefully peeled back the protective cloth. "This thing scared the hell out of me when I first uncovered the top. I thought it was a baby's skull."

"Looks like a good-sized cat. A Maine coon, maybe."

"I thought so too, but I did some googling and figured out it belonged to an ocelot."

"You're kidding."

"Not at all." He turned the skull over to show the jaws. "See this extra molar. Bobcats and lynxes and ordinary house cats don't have one."

"So somebody in this house had a pet ocelot."

"I researched that too. Found out ocelots can be domesticated if you get them as kittens. They demand a lot of attention though and can be destructive because they're very strong and love leaping around like housecats. They're also very inquisitive and have a tendency to swallow the wrong things. Like tennis balls."

"Wow."

"Liabilities aside, ocelot owners say they're very affectionate and highly entertaining. Salvador Dali had one. He took it everywhere, even into restaurants. When people got freaked out, he claimed it was an oversized housecat that he'd painted with an op-art design." Henri chuckled and rewrapped the skull. "I found some parrot bones too. Plus the usual wine bottles and broken dishes, the lid of a rouge pot, a perfume stopper, and a French mustard jar."

"That's quite a haul." Cane thought a minute. "I just remembered something. A friend of mine did a dig in the Marigny a few years back and found pretty much the same stuff. She talked to someone in the research center, and they said the animal bones meant her house could've been a bordello."

"Why's that?"

"Apparently prostitutes were fond of exotic pets, at least those on the high end. Rouge pots, perfume stoppers and wine bottles complete the picture. You know. Women. Make-up. Entertaining."

"I've suspected that for some time. A friend of mine, Paige Carter, found the same things in her back yard when she was digging a lotus pool." Henri looked up at the house. "So it's finally revealing its secrets, eh."

"Could be."

Henri chuckled. "I wonder what Gemma will say when I tell her this was probably a whorehouse and ask if she wants to add these bones to her collection. She's putting my discoveries in a display case in her library."

"She has a library?"

"A big one. She makes it available to anybody who asks and is big on supporting local artists. I went to one of her parties once and she was wearing a tin necklace made by some kid from the projects."

"She doesn't strike me as the type."

"What do you mean?"

"Some kind of Lady Bountiful."

"I grant you Gemma can come off as entitled, but don't be fooled. She's constantly hosting benefits in that house. One of the biggest in the French Quarter, in fact. Been in all sorts of books and magazines."

So that's what she meant about not being a suburbanite, Cane thought. "I'd no idea."

"She told me you're interested in historic homes. You should ask her for a tour."

"No way. I'd never invite myself to someone's home."

"Don't stand on ceremony, man. Gemma is very proud of the place and what she's done with it and she loves showing it off. At least to people who appreciate such things."

"No, thanks." Cane grabbed his knees, pushed himself up and stretched. "I gotta get to work. Thanks for the water."

"I should be thanking you filling up that hole and helping to decipher these artifacts."

"You bet."

Cane waved over his shoulder before disappearing inside house. That, Henri decided, is one strange individual.

PART FOUR

"In 1897, New Orleans city officials,
acknowledging their belief that
the sins of the flesh were inevitable,
looked Satan in the eye, cut a deal
and gave him his own address."
-Alecia P. Long, *The Great Southern Babylon*

19

1911

Maura's first week at the Windsor was a juggernaut of shocks and revelations. Her initial instinct upon learning it was a brothel was to grab her bag and flee to Traveler's Aid, but finding another job and place to stay was too daunting. She steeled herself instead and drew strength from the years of navigating adversity with Ronan.

Her small room contained only a single bed draped in mosquito netting, a chair, a small dresser and washstand, but it was hers alone and a river-facing window admitted the occasional, much-needed breeze. She felt better still when Nellie introduced her to the girls sharing the third floor. With only one exception, an icy number named Chloe, they were friendly and welcoming, and she was especially fond of Hattie, a petite blonde who let her borrow a frilly white blouse and navy skirt for her debut performance. Maura fretted that the neckline was immodest, but understood that it was part of the business. Hattie helped her put her hair up and get dressed before steering her toward a full-length mirror for a final primp.

"Don't you love getting gussied up? I sure do."

Maura barely recognized her reflection. "I can't remember when I wore something pretty."

"Shoot! There's plenty more where that came from. Here." She handed Maura a pair of dangling garnet earrings. "For luck."

Maura held them up to her ears but swiftly returned them. "Thanks, but Miss Nellie might not like me gilding the lily."

"Oh, I wouldn't worry about her. Underneath that tough talk, she's a pussycat."

"Maybe so, but tonight I have to do everything right, or else."

Hattie grabbed her rouge pot. "At least let me give you a little color."

"You think I should? I've never worn make-up in my life."

"Girl, where did you grow up? A convent?"

"A Baptist parsonage."

"Same thing," Hattie snorted. "Hold still." Maura watched herself in the mirror as Hattie nimbly applied rouge to lips and cheeks. She was astonished by the transformation. "Much better."

"I don't look like the same person!"

"Ain't nothing wrong with that, honey!" Hattie laughed and stepped back to admire her handiwork. "I'm sure everything will be jake. Me and some of the other girls are coming downstairs to cheer you on." Maura was surprised when Hattie hugged her. "Good luck and don't get anything on my new blouse. Haven't even had a chance to wear it!"

Maura's second shock came when Nellie sashayed onto the stage in a beaded red gown with a neckline exposing half a full bosom and a strawberry blonde wig adorned with scarlet ostrich feathers. Maura had barely registered Nellie's outlandish appearance when she was cued to play, "Oh, You Beautiful Doll." The popular new song began sweetly enough, but halfway through Nellie switched to bawdy lyrics that had the crowd roaring with laughter. Things got even cruder with "By the Light of the Silvery Moon," and when Nellie finished "Come, Josephine, in My Flying Machine," Maura's cheeks were as scarlet as Nellie's dress. As the evening wore on, however, she was too swept up in the excitement of performing and keeping pace with Nellie's rapid-fire repertoire to worry about naughty words. She was much relieved when Nellie tossed her an approving nod before exiting the small stage. Before she could follow, Maura was surrounded by Charlotte's girls, all dressed to the nines.

"You played even better than Sugar Boy!" Hattie gushed.

"Look at you!" Maura cried. "Look at all of you!"

She was happily overwhelmed by hugs and good wishes, along with a clashing mélange of perfumes and the most sumptuous evening dresses she'd ever seen. Each woman wore a costly gown and fine jewelry, something she later learned was a trademark of Charlotte Townsend's house, along with the best entertainment, wines and amber fluids, Storyville slang for beer. Maura was also impressed with the Windsor's wealthy clientele, all dressed in tuxedos and waistcoats dripping gold chains. An older gentleman who swept Hattie into his arms sported a diamond fob that was near-blinding when it caught the light. Maura was so awed by the glamorous spectacle that she ignored the reality that each of these lovely young women would, before the evening was out, retreat to a second-floor bedroom to ply her trade. She knew that harsh truth would undo her unless she brought it to heel, so she reminded herself of the dark circumstances directing her there and that she was in no position to judge or condemn. Life at the Windsor was, for her and the other girls, a matter of survival.

Maura waded into the jubilant throng, gamely ignoring overly familiar pats and squeezes from the men as she made her way to the exit. She found Nellie in conversation with a slender, handsomely dressed older woman leaning on a gold-knobbed cane. Skillful maquillage of rice powder and cochineal on lips and cheeks buoyed plain features and covered what Maura suspected were smallpox scars.

"This is Charlotte Townsend," Nellie said. "She's the madam, and she has good news."

"I was very pleased with your performance, young lady." Charlotte's deep, throaty voice belonged to a long-time smoker. "You do my house proud."

"Thank you, ma'am."

Nellie squeezed Maura's shoulder. "I'm done with that worthless Sugar Boy. I want you to stay on."

Maura was about to burst with joy. "Thank you!" she cried again and again. "Thank you."

"That's enough now." Charlotte stepped closer to dispense a cold appraisal of Maura's face and figure. Her hand quivered a little as she fluffed the frills showcasing Maura's cleavage and tucked a wayward wisp of red hair back into place. "You'll do fine, my dear. All in good time." She patted Maura's cheek and exited with the aid of the cane and Omar, who appeared from nowhere to tuck her arm in his.

Maura gave Nellie a quizzical look. "What did Madam Charlotte mean by 'all in good time'?"

"That's her way of saying you'd make a good whore. That old gal sees dollar signs on any woman who's pretty enough, and I gotta admit you clean up just fine."

The idea would have horrified Maura when she got off the train that morning. Now she shrugged it off. "I better stick with my music."

"I used to say the same thing. Oh, don't look so surprised, girlie. A little extra money never hurt anybody." Nellie gave her corset a tug before adding, "You did alright tonight, Maura, but you fell behind too many times. Rehearsal will take care of that and getting used to my routine of course."

"I promise I'll work hard."

"See that you do. We have another show in an hour. Have you eaten?"

"Hattie brought me some figs and peaches this afternoon."

"You need more than that." She pointed. "Kitchen's out back, through that door. Bricktop will fix you right up."

"Bricktop?"

"Madam Charlotte's cook. Take my advice. Get on her good side and stay there. Cooks are an indispensable part of the operation, like police protection and a tough houseman." She patted Maura's cheek when she saw her confusion. "You'll figure out the rules soon enough, honey, now run along now and don't be late or you'll be out on your bumpkin behind!"

"No, ma'am! I mean, yes, ma'am!"

Maura scurried outside and found the kitchen inside a walled courtyard, a homey, one-room structure with tables for a dozen people. It was empty except for a tall colored woman with brightly hennaed hair bound in a tignon. She was stirring an iron pot emitting rich smells that made Maura's mouth water. She glanced up when she heard the screen door.

"What you want?"

"Miss Nellie said I could get something to eat."

She nodded at a sideboard. "Grab one of them bowls."

Maura's stomach rumbled when the woman ladled a fragrant bowl of redfish soup laced with Creole spices. "It smells wonderful."

"It is." A broad smile revealed two gold teeth. "I'm Bricktop. You one of the new girls?"

"I play the piano for Miss Nellie. My name's Maura."

"Alright, Miss Maura. Now go sit yourself down. Baguettes and butter's on the table."

Maura had been so consumed with getting her fractured life in order that she'd ignored her hunger. The soup was so delicious that she broke off a chunk of crusty bread and scaped up every drop before going back for more. She hummed to herself as she devoured the second bowl, revitalized now and eager to get back to the piano.

"That's a catchy tune," someone said. "I've never heard it before."

Maura looked up at a slender brunette clad only in a chemise. She was pretty except for an ugly purple blotch under her left eye. Bad memories made Maura shudder inside.

"That's because I haven't written it yet."

"You write songs?"

"When I find the time."

"I know what you mean. I write poetry when I get a chance." She smiled sweetly. "I'm Fancy Rose Higgins."

Maura introduced herself. "Goodness! What happened to your eye?"

"One of my regulars gave me a shiner."

"That's terrible!"

"First time for everything I guess."

"So this doesn't happen often?"

"No, indeed. Miss Charlotte's house rules don't allow nobody to hit us girls." She frowned. "I gotta say it was a real surprise coming from Gustav. He's usually sweet as a lamb, but last night he got into the absinthe and it does strange things to men, you know. I was sorry when Omar threw him out, but...oh, never mind. I gotta get something to eat."

Over more redfish soup, Maura heard Fancy's life story about growing up in a shack in Le Cypriére. After her father abandoned the family and her mother died, she was on her own. Unskilled and uneducated, she used her only assets and began the inexorable drift. Within a week of coming into the city, Fancy was swallowed by Storyville.

"I was lucky," she insisted. "I could've ended up one of those crib gals if Mr. Dupree hadn't seen me wandering around Basin Street and asked if I needed work."

"Mr. Dupree?"

"One of Mr. Anderson's men. They keep an eye out for girls they think could work here, usually at the train station and places like that. Anyway, he introduced me to Madam Charlotte and things worked out pretty good." She laughed edgily. "Until last night."

"How long have you been here, Fancy?"

"Almost a year I guess."

Maura frowned. "How old are you?"

"I turned sixteen last month."

20

For the first time in her life, Maura slept until noon. Exhausted and excited by her exotic new world, she had plunged into a deep dreamless sleep and awakened to find the shutters aglow and the mosquito net streaked with sunlight. She sat up and stretched, triggering a pleasant ache in arms and legs. Hattie's blouse and skirt, folded neatly atop the dresser, brought warm memories of last night's performance and praise heaped by the girls, Madam Charlotte and especially Nellie. Maura's Dutch courage had not failed her, and she was grateful for her good luck in meeting Starla. What, she wondered, had become of that frightened little Mississippi girl who got off the train yesterday?

Maura pushed back the mosquitaire and was pleased to find a full pitcher on the washstand. She splashed water on her face, dressed and went downstairs. Because it was Sunday, the house was eerily quiet until she reached the kitchen where pungent smells of frying bacon and fresh-brewed coffee made her stomach rumble. A handful of girls were laughing and talking at the tables. Hattie waved her over.

"Looky here! If it ain't the new piano man!"

"Good morning." Maura sat and poured a cup of coffee. She took a sip and made a face.

"What's wrong?"

"This coffee tastes funny. Kinda bitter."

"It's chicory," Winifred said. She was a willowy thing with big hazel eyes. "Weak coffee in New Orleans is a mortal sin."

"You'll get used to it." Hattie slid over a sugar bowl and creamer. "This helps."

Maura thanked Bricktop when she delivered a plate of bacon, eggs, grits, sliced tomatoes and hot biscuits. She ate hungrily while the girls gossiped and rehashed the night before. One of them, a chestnut-haired girl named Carol Ann was leafing through a blue booklet like the ones hawked at the train station.

"What's that you're reading?" Maura asked.

Carol Ann and the others swapped disbelieving looks. "I'll tell you on one condition."

"Alright."

"You tell us how you got into in a whorehouse without reading the whore's bible."

The girls shrieked with laughter at Maura's bewilderment until Hattie took pity. "It's called the Blue Book, honey. It lists all the houses and most of the girls in Storyville. There are pictures, and advertisements too. Even a map." She took the book from Carol Ann. "Look here."

The cover bore the illustration of a woman in a ballgown with the title BLUE BOOK at the top and TENDERLOIN 400 at the bottom. The book only hinted at Storyville's vast scale which included 786 women - 425 white, 352 colored and 9 octoroons - along with 72 white and 17 "colored entertainers, accompanied by a typical Southern darky orchestra playing all the latest musical selections nightly." Maura flipped back to the front and read the introduction.

"This is the only district of its kind in the States set aside for fast women by law. It puts the stranger on a proper grade as to where to go and be secure from hold-ups, brace games and other illegal practices worked on the unwise in Red Light Districts. When you go on a 'lark,' you'll know 'who is who' and the best place to spend your time and money. Read all the ads as all the best houses are advertised, and are known as the 'Cream of Society.' Names in capitals are Landladies. W=White. C=Colored. O=Octoroon."

Nellie mentioned octoroons yesterday, Maura thought. Not wanting to show more ignorance, she decided to ask Hattie about it when they were alone. She turned more pages, pausing to read about the different houses, their women and their specialties. There were French houses and Greek houses and English houses and a "circus" hinting at taboo things that gave her the willies. She was astonished by the variety of available services, but then her new life was one revelation after another.

"Is the Windsor House listed?"

"Toward the back," Carol Ann said. "Read it aloud, Maura. It's fun hearing about us."

"'Windsor, proprietress Miss Charlotte Townsend, two-hundred-one Villere, corner Iberville. Without doubt one of the most gorgeously fitted-out establishments in Storyville. Bon vivants and connoisseurs pronounce Miss Townsend's mansion the Acme of Perfection. Many of the articles in her domicile came from Paris and Italy and the late St. Louis Exposition. There is always first-class entertainment, and the girls are among the most beautiful and intelligent you'll find anywhere. 'Good times always afoot' is the motto here, and if you have the blues, Charlotte's girls can cure 'em.'"

"Hear that?" Carol Ann preened and tossed a head of brown curls. "We're beautiful and intelligent."

"Some more than others, I'd say." Winifred's quip earned more laughter and a playful swat from Carol Ann. "You know that's all hogwash. We don't even use our real names."

"Like Josie's fake baroness. Remember her, girls?" Hattie leaned toward Maura as though making a confidence. "Last year, the Blue Book made a big noise about some Russian baroness staying incognito at Josie Arlington's house. Baroness, my foot! That phony broad was a kooch dancer who'd worked the midway at the Chicago World's Fair!" More howls of laughter. "People believe what they want though, and Mr. Anderson knows what sells."

"What's he got to do with it?" Maura asked.

"He publishes the Blue Book."

Maura set the book aside and sipped her coffee. "Mr. Anderson seems to have his hand in all sorts of pies. Mine included." When she saw the raised eyebrows, she hastily corrected her innocent mistake. "I meant that he's the reason I got this job."

"How'd you meet him?" Hattie asked. Maura reiterated her encounter with Starla on the train. "Her name's familiar."

"Maybe because it's so unusual."

"It's not that," Winifred said. "She used to work at Lulu White's."

"That's right. One of Lulu's top draws as I recall."

"Wasn't she was one of Anderson's girls?"

"Yeah. She had a trick baby, and everybody said it was his."

Maura was reeling. She had thought Starla a fine lady and could hardly believe this was the Good Samaritan she met on the train. "When did all this happen?"

"Years ago," Carol Ann replied.

"And people are still talking about it?"

"People love gossiping about Tom Anderson," Winifred said. "Nothing happens here that he doesn't know about. If politicians have problems or questions about Storyville, he's the man they talk to. Even the police come to him for help."

"If you haven't already figured it out," Hattie added, "gossip's the most popular pastime in Storyville. After screwing of course."

There was more laughter and naughty banter before the girls dispersed, leaving Maura and Hattie alone at the table. Maura grabbed the opportunity for some answers. "I need to ask you some things."

"Fire away."

"What's an octoroon? And what's a trick baby?" Maura was grateful when Hattie explained without chiding her ignorance.

"An octoroon is one-eighth colored. A quadroon is one quarter colored and mulattoes are half, but you don't hear much about them. A trick baby is fathered by a trick. You know. A john." When Maura looked blank, Hattie said, "The customer."

"Oh." Maura thought a moment. "There was a sign behind Tom Anderson's bar I didn't understand either. It said 'Treat, trade or travel.'"

"Those signs are all over Storyville. Madam Charlotte thinks they're tacky, so we don't have one. It means the johns should either buy drinks for the girls and hire one or get the hell out."

"Oh." Maura picked at her food. "I know you and the others think I'm stupid but I can't help it. Everything here is so different. All these peculiar words, and even day is switched for night. If I were back home in Mississippi, I would've been up for hours and already—"

"I understand, Maura. All us girls do. We're all from someplace else and the sooner you forget about it, the better."

Maura thought of Sloane. "Maybe not all of it."

"Suit yourself, but don't let it drag you down or give you the blues. Storyville is its own little world with special rules and regulations, and you'll figure it out like the rest of us. Oh, and there's another thing."

"What's that?"

"I'm sure you've never been around whores before, but you better never act superior."

"Oh, Hattie! I didn't mean to—"

"Let me finish. I know you're trying to fit in, and I appreciate that, but don't ever think you're better than us girls because you're only a piano player. I suppose it's only natural since you were probably brought up believing we're nothing but jezebels."

"You're right," Maura admitted. "I told you my father's a Baptist minister."

"Yeah, and I heard the same thing because my daddy was the goddamned mayor of Meander, Tennessee, and some kinda pillar of the community." While Maura absorbed this latest shock, Hattie said, "Winifred and Grace came out of the orphanage together. Carol Ann's a sharecropper's daughter from Texas, one of thirteen children. Mary was in a convent school up north and can be downright ornery. She was turning into a snowbird until—"

"Snowbird?"

"A cocaine addict. She straightened out after Madam Charlotte threatened to put her back on the streets. Chloe's mother's a whore, too, so she's second generation. We all have our stories, honey. Each and every one of us."

"I guess so." After a moment, she cried, "Oh, my!"

"What is it?"

"Did you say that Starla Callahan worked for Lulu White?"

"Yes. Why?"

Maura grabbed the Blue Book and thumbed to the section on Lulu White's Mahogany Hall. There it was, plain as day. "Miss White has assembled the most beautiful and cultivated collection of octoroons in America. You simply must see these gems for yourself to believe them."

"I'll be damned!"

"Well, whaddya know?!" Hattie grinned. "So the Baptist minister's daughter knows how to swear after all."

Maura shrugged. "There's a first time for everything, dearie."

21

1914

The Windsor proved to be Maura's salvation, but not without drawbacks. What she initially considered a fine salary for a piano player dwindled considerably once Madam Charlotte deducted for meals, rent and costumes. Nor did she get tips like the professors, the Negro piano men who played when Nellie wasn't performing. House rules dictated that the girls urge their johns to tip the professors who, if their music was hot, pulled down twenty dollars a week. Maura's take was considerably less, so she augmented her income by altering and mending gowns for the girls, extra money that paid Peter for Sloane's room and board. She wrote her daughter every week, promising she would visit as soon as she could, but train fares were expensive and her visits were infrequent. It broke her heart to see Sloane growing up without her, a pain that deepened immeasurably when she told her daughter, yet again, that she couldn't take her to New Orleans.

"Mommy can afford only a tiny room, baby, and there's no school nearby or other children for you to play with." The truth, of course, was that Maura vowed that her family must never learn that she was working in a brothel, even if only as a musician. "We'll have to wait until I can get a bigger place. I promise you'll love New Orleans, darling. It's a big city with plenty to do and see. There's a zoo in Audubon Park that I can't wait to show you and—"

The rest of Maura's words were lost beneath the girl's sobs and Soane's insistence that she hated New Orleans because it took her mother away. She promised Sloane that she'd work harder than ever and would visit more often, but how much the girl actually believed was something Maura couldn't think about. The sad scenario repeatedly played itself out as the years slipped by. Maura struggled not to lose hope, but her dream of an apartment outside Storyville and bringing her daughter, now eight-years-old, to New Orleans, remained elusive.

As she stepped off the train at the Southern Station, Maura's heart was leaden from another disheartening visit to Pascagoula. She was so immersed in melancholy that she didn't hear the newsboys waving their papers in the air and screaming the headlines.

"Austria-Hungary Declares War on Serbia!"

"Europe in Turmoil. Germany Mobilizing for war! Read all about it!"

She waded through the crowds scrambling to buy papers and crossed Basin Street, so eager to get home that she didn't notice Tom Anderson and his cronies discussing the war news in front of his saloon. He called and tipped his hat.

"Good afternoon, Miss Maura."

"Afternoon, Mr. Anderson."

As she walked on, Maura reflected on how far she'd come from the timid country mouse asking Anderson for work to being personally addressed by the Mayor of Storyville himself. She was usually happy to chat with Anderson, whom she had come to trust, but, depressed by the lonely train ride home, she wanted to be alone. This was not to be. She was hanging up her hat and jacket when Fancy knocked on the door.

"Madam Charlotte wants to see you."

"Oh?"

"Yes. In her apartment. Right away."

Maura was wary as she hurried downstairs. She'd visited Charlotte's quarters only once, three years ago when she first arrived, but had never forgotten the place. It was dimly lit and quiet as a tomb, and while Charlotte publicly presented herself as a woman of distinction and elegance, her taste in furnishings ran to the garish. The parlor was crowded with sofas and chairs gaudily upholstered in red and gold. Beaded fringe dripped from lamps, and knickknacks, mostly erotic, covered every surface. As before, Maura found her employer in a far corner, barely visible through a forest of potted palms. She reclined on a chaise lounge, heavy perfume mingling with an odd, acrid odor.

"Come in, dear." Charlotte's colored maid, Katy, set out a silver tea service and disappeared on silent cat feet. "Will you have tea?"

"Yes, please."

As Charlotte poured with an unsteady hand, Maura settled into a chair and wondered why she'd been summoned to the inner sanctum. She wasn't curious for long, as Charlotte was not one for small talk.

"You already know Nellie and I are quite pleased with your work and that you're an asset to the house. Some might say a drawing card. Those times you filled in for Nellie and sang as well as played were crowd-pleasers, even when you don't sing the naughty lyrics. Most of my girls are under twenty, but the fact that you're a bit older is clearly no deterrent. So much so that some very wealthy gentlemen have made inquiries."

Maura instantly intuited where this was going. "Oh?"

"I'm sure I don't need to spell it out, my dear. Your salary will skyrocket, and your hours will, to a large degree, be your own." She studied Maura over the rim of her cup. "Well?"

Charlotte had a reputation for fairness, but Maura knew she was also notorious for forging her will. Tread carefully, she thought. "I'm flattered, Madam Charlotte, but I prefer confining my work to the piano."

Charlotte was undaunted. "You know of course that I run the most refined house in Storyville. I grant you that Lulu White's Mahogany Hall is grander and Josie Arlington's place is bigger with its Mirror Hall and Turkish Room and all that folderol, but neither woman has my reputation for class. My girls are meticulously groomed and well-mannered and greet guests in the Gold Parlor as though welcoming someone into their home. Our famous hospitality attracts the crème de la crème, and once a gentleman's credit is established, he's discreetly billed each month. No other houses offer that, nor do they offer special privileges to their best girls." Maura was wondering why she was hearing the familiar litany of Windsor policies when Charlotte set aside her cup and delivered her coup de grâce.

"These girls choose their clients, not the other way around."

Brothels were like sieves when it came to secrets, and Maura knew Winifred and Carol Ann held that exalted status. She admitted to herself that she was intrigued, envious even, when she saw gifts from their affluent clients. Both received expensive clothes and jewelry, and Winifred even scored a cruise to Cuba, but, glamourous trappings aside, Maura's Baptist guilt ran too deep to reconcile the life of a prostitute. Charlotte continued before she said as much.

"So, Maura. Because you've proven yourself worthy, I'm making you this rare offer, but it's not solely for you. You see, I know all about your daughter in Mississippi and how desperately you want to bring her to New Orleans. This considerable pay increase will enable you to rent a nice apartment in the Quarter and send Sloane to a private school. It will be a much better life for both of you." She took Maura's hand. "Shakespeare himself said the difference between a whore and a courtesan is discipline, and quite obviously you have that quality in abundance." Charlotte released Maura's hand and leaned back. "Will you consider it, my dear?"

The moment she mentioned Sloane, Charlotte's calculated arrow found its target. Maura immediately saw her daughter's sweet face, lower lip bravely thrust out as she tried not to cry when her mother boarded the train for New Orleans yet again. That image unleashed a powerful, painful admission.

"There's nothing to consider."

"Oh?"

Maura's gaze wandered to the table lamp beside her, a bronze female nude holding a crimson shade trimmed in gold fringe. She ran a finger through the fringe and made it shimmer and sway before delivering her answer.

"Nine years ago, I found myself pregnant and alone. The boy wanted to marry me, but my minister father forbade it. He dragged me from the house and shoved me onto the sidewalk." She absently touched her knee. "I still have a scar where I fell. My mother and brothers and sisters watched from the porch, and all the neighbors came outside to watch in silent condemnation while he called me a harlot and screamed that I would burn in hell for my sins." She drew herself up and sought Charlotte's face in the dimness. "From that day forward, my parents considered me dead and wanted nothing to do with their granddaughter. "Since my family and everyone else in my hometown already believes me a whore—"

Maura's shoulders rose and fell with painful fatalism. There were no tears, only resignation as she embraced her fate.

22

Maura took advantage of a quiet Sunday morning to work on a new song. With the girls still asleep and the downstairs deserted, she had the bar to herself. She was scribbling lyrics when she heard the front door swing open. A muffled conversation with George Perry, the weekend bouncer, was followed by footsteps

"Looks like Storyville agrees with you."

"Starla!" Maura jumped to her feet at the familiar voice. "What a wonderful surprise!"

Starla welcomed the hug. "It's good to see you too, dearie."

"It's been…what? Three years? How in the world did you find me?"

"Tom Anderson, of course. Nothing goes on in Storyville that he doesn't know about."

"That's the Lord's truth."

"And you've made quite a name for yourself as an entertainer." She patted Maura's cheek. "Got time for a visit?"

"With you? Always." She took Starla's arm and ushered her into the parlor. "I've never forgotten your kindness on the train, and I apologize for not tracking you down to tell you how things worked out. And to thank you again."

"No apology needed."

"But I might not have survived without you."

"Oh, I don't know. I've met a lot of girls like you over the years. New to the city. Naïve and hungry. Frightened. Most of them fall by the wayside, but I knew you'd be alright when you dragged me between those train cars and sang the national anthem at the top of your lungs!"

Maura looked sheepish. "I'll never know where I got the nerve to do that."

"Pure instinct, dearie. It's worth its weight in gold, and you can't buy it at any price. I know. I was blessed with it too."

"Would you like coffee?"

"No, thanks. I already had some with Tom. She joined Maura on the couch and gave her a peculiar look. "I may as well get right to the point. I didn't come here to catch up. I came to clear my conscience. I wasn't very honest on the train."

Maura guessed what was coming and was pleased when Starla revealed her past without being asked. "Oh?"

"I worked in Storyville too, but not as an entertainer."

"I know."

Starla's eyebrows rose. "But how could you?"

"There was talk when I first got here. Some of the girls remembered you."

"Because of Tom and the baby?" Maura nodded. "Then I suppose you know I was one of Lulu White's girls." Another nod. "And that I'm part colored."

"Yes, I know. I also know that the woman I met on the train was a kind and generous soul and that your color doesn't change a thing."

"I'm glad to hear you say that," Starla said, relief evident. "It was that damned train that made me lie. If the conductor had found who I was, he would've sent me back to the colored car. Or maybe arrested me and had me thrown off at the next stop. That's why I sat beside you. I hoped he wouldn't be suspicious if I was sitting next to 'another' white woman."

When she was growing up, Maura gave little thought to race. She knew only that Negroes were supposed to keep their place and had separate facilities. She was therefore appalled when Starla described the train cars set aside for colored people. "There's no upholstery on the seats and no overhead luggage racks so everything's jammed at your feet. The floor's never swept, and the ladies room's so filthy you wouldn't go near it." She looked disgusted. "No, ma'am. I've ridden those colored cars and promised myself never again. I also vowed that my little girl would never set foot in them. Tom has friends who forge documents, and he came with me when I enrolled her in school up in Jackson. Those people saw a white couple with a white child, and with her pale skin and blue eyes and a name like Katharine Callahan, she had no trouble passé blanc."

Maura recalled the first time she heard the French phrase. She was outside the gold parlor and overheard Charlotte rejecting a new girl when she saw through her racial charade. "No passé blanc in my house," Charlotte declared. "Only white girls. Try your luck with Lulu White or Josie Arlington. They're always looking for pretty colored girls." Uncomfortable with the conversation, Maura was glad when Starla changed the subject.

"There's another reason I came over this morning. When I was in Tom's office, he showed me a copy of the new Blue Book."

Maura knew her photo was in that edition, introducing her as the latest addition to Charlotte Townsend's stable of "highly cultured, world-famous" lovelies."

"There's a girl in there who sure looks a lot like you. Her name is—"

"Désirée Lamballe."

Starla chuckled. "I remember telling you it would help to learn French, but I never imagined you'd change your name."

Maura laughed too. "I think it's ridiculous, but it was Charlotte's idea, and she's not someone to contradict."

"No, she's not. So tell me, dearie. How things are working out for Miss Désirée?"

"She hasn't made an appearance yet. Charlotte's keeping me on the piano until October and is planning some big hoopla to announce my debut."

"She's just like Tom. Ever the promoter."

An awkward silence descended when the women simultaneously acknowledged the unspoken.

"Starla, I—"

"May I—?"

"You first," Maura said, voice an uneasy whisper.

"May I speak frankly?"

"Please do."

"What does that golden instinct tell you about this Désirée business? Are you honestly prepared to switch from piano playing to fucking?" When she saw Maura's reaction, she said, "If my coarse language offends you, then your answer should be no."

"It's not that, Starla. I hear the word so often it barely registers. You've reminded me that I'm cornered, that's all. It happened once before and was a terrible thing to escape." She closed her eyes until the memory of Ronan's corpse played out. "My decision to become Désirée is strictly financial. When I left Mississippi, I planned to bring my daughter here as soon as I found work. Obviously I couldn't move her into The Windsor, but I've never been able to afford a place in a respectable part of town. I'd almost resigned myself to not seeing Sloane grow up, so when Charlotte made that offer—"

She held out her hands, palms up.

"Believe me, dearie. It's a familiar story." Starla sighed. "Few things are more tiresome than an old bawd advising a young one, but here goes. All girls tell themselves that whoring's only temporary, that they'll marry a rich john or make enough money to open their own house. That almost never happens because they become drinkers or snowbirds. Or maybe they die from gleet or a back-alley abortion or get beaten up by their pimp or murdered by a crazy john. Now, I know you're starting at the top in the finest, most elegant bagnio in Storyville but, harsh as it is, here's the truth. Glamorous trappings aside, you're a crib girl with fancy digs." Starla paused. "The way you're shaking your head tells me you've heard this before."

"I lost my naivete the day I walked into this place, Starla, and I've heard the girls talk about all those things. It made me sad because it always sounded like they were trying to convince themselves and each other with their dreams of escape."

"It should also tell you that, deep down, they're not happy, but if you ask them, they'll joke and pretend otherwise. That's because all whores are actresses. They just don't play on conventional stages."

"True enough."

"I would've suffered too had it not been for Tom. Other men would've left me to my fate as a pregnant whore, but he and Lulu saw to my care. After Katharine arrived, he set me up in a cottage on North Rampart Street, and I've done alright over the years, running it as a boarding house. But!" she said with emphasis, "As I said before, I was one of the very few lucky ones to leave the life without getting sucked back into it."

"I'm sure you were, and everything you've said makes perfect sense." Maura glanced around the parlor, eyes resting on the door. "But even if I walked away right now, where would I go and what would I do to support my child? For now, my only hope for escape is Désirée."

"I understand."

"Thank you, Starla. I truly need to believe someone does."

23

Maura sat on the third-floor gallery, eyes closed, mind adrift as she enjoyed the late afternoon quiet. She hoped the autumn sun would penetrate deep and melt the last of her dread. Her hands rested atop sheet music for an unfinished song. Ideas had courted her for days, but inspiration was stalled by an unholy mix of hope and fear of the coming night. She considered a shot of Raleigh Rye to steady her nerves, but reconsidered when Starla's warning against drink flooded back.

"How can you be a million miles away and sitting there at the same time?" Maura opened her eyes to see Hattie leaning against a wooden colonette. "I've been talking to you for a full minute, girl."

"I'm sorry. My mind's on the moon these days."

"There'd be something wrong if it wasn't."

"What do you mean?"

"I mean that I know exactly what you're going through. I remember the first time I turned a trick. I was barely sixteen and I must've experienced every emotion in the book. All at the same time. I might add!"

"I don't know what I'm feeling anymore."

"Well, whatever it is, it'll be gone tomorrow, and, believe me, your next time with a john will be a lot easier. You're lucky, you know."

"How so?"

"I mean that the Windsor clientele is top drawer, and that you're first time's guaranteed to be with a gentleman." She snorted. "Beats the hell out of screwing a blacksmith behind a smelly stable. Bent over a hay bale, for God's sake!"

Maura burst into laughter and jumped up to hug her friend. "Darling, Hattie! What would I do without you?!"

"Have a lot less fun, that's what." Hattie wrapped her arm around Maura's waist as they walked along the gallery, refreshed by a woozy breeze off the Mississippi. "Did Madam Charlotte tell you what she's got planned for tonight?"

"She had me fitted for a new gown at Countess Piazza's house, but aside from that, not a word."

"That reminds me. Did you see the countess herself?"

"No, just her seamstress. She's not an actual countess, is she?"

"An octoroon with a name like Willie Piazza? What do you think?" Hattie hooted. "But never mind about that. Madam Charlotte sent you to the right place because, alias or not, Willie's one of New Orleans' most fashionable women. When she takes her girls to opening day at the Fairgrounds Race Track, the uptown white ladies bring their dressmakers so they can copy what Willie's girls are wearing. I understand she's quite something herself. Wears a monocle and an enormous diamond choker and carries a Russian cigarette holder half as long as your arm."

"Good heavens!"

"She also likes taking her octoroons to Lincoln Park on Monday nights. The other madams go there too. Karla Lawson brings her mulattoes, and Pearl Thomas has her high browns, all of them dressed fit to kill. That must be some sight, but not all those gals are colored, you know. A few are white girls who make more money as Creoles of color. Some of them even darken their skin with make-up." Maura was trying to digest another bizarre facet of Storyville life when Hattie said, "Madam Charlotte's done more than spend a pretty penny on your dress."

"What more have you heard?"

"For starters, she's given Nellie the night off and hired Tony Jackson to play. You're the only star tonight."

Maura's heart clutched. "Oh, my!"

While Tom Anderson was considered the Mayor of Storyville, Tony Jackson was its undisputed King of the Professors. He could write a song in two minutes and had a repertoire numbering into the hundreds. His most recent composition, Pretty Baby, was far and away the most popular song in Storyville.

"And that's not all. You haven't been downstairs today, but there are so many flowers the place looks like a funeral home. And Bricktop has been baking savories and pastries since dawn."

"This is not calming my nerves," Maura lamented. "All that attention says I have a lot to live up to."

"It also says that Madam Charlotte has a lot of confidence in you. She's been in the business a long time, Maura. She's a shrewd old bird who knows a good investment when she sees it."

"An investment, eh?" Maura managed a wry smile. "That sure puts things in perspective."

"Truth is best." Hattie scanned the street below. "You know what'll make us both feel better?"

"What?"

"See those three sailors down there?"

"What about them?"

"Those poor boys could never afford a place like this, so let's give them a peek at what they're missing." Hattie chuckled and began unbuttoning her bodice. "What do you say, Désirée?"

Maura recognized the challenge for what it was and, without hesitation, opened her robe and exposed her breasts. Hattie followed suit, waving and calling to the men down below. The sight of two half-naked women had the sailors whooping and dancing in the street. Two of them threw their hats into the air, while the third rushed to the front door. He rejoined his companions when he discovered the house was closed, and yelled that they would be back. Maura, to Hattie's delight, blew a kiss and waved good-bye.

"That wasn't so bad, was it?"

"No. it wasn't." Maura laughed and pointed to more sailors up the block who had seen the display and rushed over in hopes of seeing more. "I guess you could call it my dress rehearsal."

Hattie whistled and waved at the sailors. "I think you mean undress rehearsal!"

At nine o'clock that evening, Charlotte made a rare appearance in the third floor sitting room to inspect Maura's toilette. The other girls gathered as well and watched enviously as Katy helped Maura into her new gown, hooking and buttoning and smoothing any wrinkles. It was a diaphanous creation of creamy silk reminding Maura of Louisiana moonlight. In keeping with modern trends, boning was minimal and used to support the shape rather than change it. A daring neckline revealed abundant bosom, but Charlotte teased the viewer by nestling a sapphire necklace in Maura's cleavage. Matching earrings added more sparkle. Like most Irish girls, Maura was short, but her five-foot-two-height was augmented with heels and a high, upswept hair-do. She stood motionless while Katy tucked white ostrich plumes in her red hair, only to have Charlotte snatch them away.

"Gilding the lily," she snapped. She aimed her cane at Maura's skirts. "Turn around, girl."

Maura obeyed and caught her breath when she saw her reflection in the tall pier mirror. She scarcely recognized the image, and her husky voice belonged to someone else, too.

"Oh, my goodness!"

Charlotte easily read her thoughts. "Surprised?"

"Very."

"I'm not. I saw something special the night we met, and so will the gentlemen downstairs."

"I hope so."

"I know so. Now then. You'll stay put until ten o'clock. That's when I'll announce you and open the doors to the gold parlor so you can make your entrance. Don't eat or drink anything. I don't want any spills on that new gown."

"No, ma'am."

"One more thing." Charlotte gave her a bottle of perfume with tiny hearts and flowers etched into the stopper. "For luck, but don't use too much. I don't want you smelling like Lulu White." The girls laughed at the dig at a rival madam. "Don't disappoint me, Désirée."

"I won't, Madam Charlotte. I promise."

Left alone, Maura ventured back onto the gallery where a gibbous moon was mounting the Mississippi. Cool night air felt good on her bare shoulders as she registered the familiar Storyville sounds. Music blew from dozens of competing cabarets and music halls, a discordant mix of jazz, blues and ragtime, punctuated somewhere by a plaintive trumpet that tore at the heartstrings. The cries of bawdyhouse hawkers merged with those of carriage vendors selling food, drink and naughty souvenirs alongside a fat Negress peddling voodoo love potions. Maura also heard the rat-a-tat of pellet guns in shooting galleries, and, five houses down, the raucous cries of crib girls luring customers to their wretched cubbyholes. The bizarre, urban cacophony existed nowhere else in the world, and Maura took a deep breath, as though she could swallow the magic and carry it with her. Then it was ten o'clock.

Maura was waiting at the foot of the stairs when the double doors of the bar swung open and she heard Charlotte announce her new name. She gave long gloves a final tug, raised her head and strode inside, instantly engulfed by the heat of two dozen bodies and the smell of tobacco smoke, whiskey and musky colognes. She heard applause and, from the small stage, the sound of a piano and Tony Jackson's rich tenor.

"Everybody loves a baby, that's why I'm in love with you. Pretty baby. Pretty baby."

Overwhelmed at being the center of attention, Maura fairly floated across the room. A quick glance revealed that she and Charlotte were the only women present, and she beamed when the crowd of mostly older gentleman parted, opening a path to the stage. Handpicked by Charlotte, the formally dressed gathering included bankers, brokers, lawyers, cotton factors, sugar planters and even a state senator. Each hoisted his glass when she passed. Their admiring gazes were anything but chaste, and, to Maura's shock, awakened something she thought long dead. She embraced it and moved on, nodding politely to this man and that until she reached the small stage. Before she could mount the two steps, a gloved hand gently cupped her gloved elbow.

"May I?"

Maura turned to thank the man and froze when she faced translucent blue eyes identical to Ronan's. The resemblance ended there, but the shock made her loose her footing and she seized the tall stranger's arm to steady herself. She held tight and willed the awkward moment to pass.

"Are you alright, Mademoiselle Lamballe?"

"Yes, thank you. I'm...I'm fine now."

"I'm so relieved." He bowed low. "Daniel Stafford at your service."

24

It was nearly dawn. Maura was drowsing when she noticed movement overhead. A lightning bug had strayed through the shutters and trapped itself in the gauzy mosquito net. Its tail glowed and dimmed, a silent cry for help. Maura wanted to free the tiny creature but feared waking Daniel Stafford who lay snoring softly beside her. She remained still and offered only pity when the glow paled and grew dark.

"Poor thing," she whispered.

Maura closed her eyes and drifted with last night's memories. After being introduced to each potential client and hearing their stories and propositions, some truly outlandish, she found herself drawn to Daniel. He wasn't the handsomest man present, but he had strong features and a disarming manner, and his gentility erased any further resemblance to Ronan. She recalled with perverse pride the crowd's collective groan of disappointment when she invited Daniel upstairs. As Charlotte had instructed, she reminded the remaining gentlemen that this was only her first night and more were forthcoming. There were other welcome memories. Daniel had proven to be a gentle, considerate lover, the polar opposite of Ronan. Fulfilling her obligation had transpired with remarkable ease and, most importantly, without guilt. She initially tried taking Hattie's advice to remain detached, but Daniel's provocative touch unraveled that notion and she responded in kind. That warm reminiscence prompted Maura to snuggle closer and rest a hand on his bare chest. The creaking bedsprings woke him.

"Ah!"

Maura looked into his eyes and smiled. "Good morning."

"Good morning, Désirée."

Maura recoiled inside at the phony name. "It's early still. Will you sleep longer or would you like coffee?"

"Coffee, please."

Maura tugged the bell pull, then gave him a fleeting cheek kiss before slipping from bed and donning a silky wrapper. "Bricktop makes wonderful breakfasts. Would you like—?"

"Coffee and crullers are all I require."

"Nothing more?"

"Only this." Daniel patted the empty space beside him. Maura, to her embarrassment, blushed.

"I'll only be a moment." After a quick hall conference with Soona, the kitchen maid, Maura returned to bed. Daniel draped an arm around her shoulders and pulled her close. They lay in silence until she remembered Hattie's advice to flatter the john and get him talking about himself.

"Forgive me, Daniel, but I met so many fine gentlemen last night I don't recall the details. You are from New Orleans?"

"Born and bred. I work in the Cotton Exchange. A cotton factor like my father."

"Forgive my ignorance in not knowing what that is."

"I'm a planter's agent. I take cotton on consignment and either find local buyers or ship it to agents up north for sale overseas. I also buy supplies for planters and provide loans during the growing season." A finger stroked her shoulder. "All for a percentage of course."

"I walked by the Cotton Exchange one afternoon. It's very grand. On Carondelet Street I believe."

"Yes. At the corner of Gravier. It's grand alright, but a mishmash of styles. I don't think the architect could settle on Renaissance, Second Empire or Italian, so he used all three."

Maura feigned fascination despite not knowing one architectural style from another. "How daring!"

"The inside's even gaudier with a gilded ceiling thirty feet high and garish murals. There's even a fountain in the middle of the Exchange Room, but not many notice with all the shouting and men on ladders, clambering around like monkeys."

"Why would they do that?"

"Recording the latest market information on blackboards."

"It sounds very confusing."

"I'll show you sometime if you like."

Maura liked the idea of seeing him again. "By all means." She turned toward a soft knocking. "Come in, Soona!"

The servant girl delivered a silver tray with a steaming china coffee pot and, beneath cloth napkins, a plate of crullers still warm from the oven. She refilled the wash basin and replaced the chamber pots before quietly withdrawing. Maura called a thank-you and sat up so she could pour the coffee. She laughed softly.

"What's so funny?"

"I started to tuck the napkin inside your collar but there isn't one."

"Which I plan to keep that way the rest of the morning."

"Aren't you the one!" Maura smiled, pleased with her boldness.

"I try to spend Sunday mornings with my brother and his wife. Our parents died of yellow jack three years ago, and we're all the family we have."

Maura immediately thought of Sloane. "Your devotion is touching."

"Have you family?" he asked.

"All dead," she lied. "From yellow fever, like yours."

Daniel took a bite of cruller and washed it down with black coffee. He sighed, satisfied. "This is much nicer than Mahogany Hall." He chided himself. "My apologies. That was indiscreet of me."

"So you're no stranger to Storyville, eh?"

"My father brought me here eleven years ago, when I was sixteen."

Maura fixed his age at twenty-seven, only two years older than herself. The notion was somehow reassuring.

"I've heard so much about Lulu and her famous diamonds. Did you meet her?"

"She was an…acquaintance of my father so we were ushered into a private parlor where she personally welcomed us. She was pleasant enough, but I was horrified by a huge red wig and so much perfume I could hardly breathe. She tried to appear cultured, and I think all those diamonds were an attempt to seem feminine, but her voice was rough and deep as a man's."

"What was the house like?"

"Jam-packed with overstuffed, overcarved furniture and imitation tapestries and sculptures of naked women. And of course the famous mahogany staircase."

"And the girls?"

"Most were pretty and a few were beauties, but—"

"But?"

"It wasn't a pleasant experience."

"I shouldn't have pried," Maura apologized. "Now I'm the one being indiscreet."

They laughed together but it was an awkward moment. Something unspoken hung over them like the dead insect in the mosquitaire. Maura suspected it was the aftermath of intimacy between strangers, a primal coupling devoid of emotion. It was, she knew, something she must reconcile as it was destined to continue.

"More coffee?"

"No, thank you." He settled against the pillows. "Désirée isn't your real name, is it?"

Maura's face grew hot. "Why would you ask that?"

"Because several times last evening, you didn't respond when your name was called and because you have a heavy Southern drawl and not a French Creole accent." He toyed with the mane tumbling over her shoulders. "And because this red hair and your pale skin scream Irish. As do those green eyes."

Maura sat up, intending to refute his claim, but instead made a face. "I told Madam Charlotte that it wouldn't work. She insisted that French Creole girls were in high demand and that tourists paid handsomely for them." The heat in her cheeks deepened. "Oh, dear. Am I blushing again?"

"Charmingly so. Will you tell me your real name?"

"Maura Aileen Traver O'Rourke." She looked him in the eye and imitated her grandmother's thick brogue. "And right you are, laddy. I'm as Irish as the Blarney Stone."

Daniel laughed. "Well, now. Since we're both being honest, I'll confess that I've admired you for some time. I'm a devotee of jazz and ragtime music, and Storyville is the best place to hear both. I've even gone to the Big Twenty-Five over on Franklin Street where the musicians gather after hours to play for themselves. Tony Jackson and Sidney Bechet and Kid Ory. I once sat so close to Jelly

Roll Morton I could see his gold tooth with the diamond in it. When I heard those fellows talking about Nellie Marrero's talented piano player, I decided to see her for myself. I was here the night you went on for Nellie and realized there was a voice to go with the piano playing. I was delighted to learn that your praise was no exaggeration."

Maura toyed with the lacy pillowslip. "You're very kind."

"I also was here the night Omar announced that you were to become one of Madam Charlotte's girls. I made certain I was invited to your, uh, debut, but, in all honesty, I wasn't sure why. Of course I found you attractive but I didn't dare imagine I would be the one you chose." He turned her to face him. "Why me, Maura?"

"Perhaps because I was nervous and you helped me when I stumbled at the stage. Perhaps you reminded me of someone I once knew. Perhaps not."

"That's not very comforting," he lamented.

"I'm sorry I don't have a better answer." Maura was uneasy with personal conversation. "Would you like another cruller?" Daniel's response was to slip away her wrapper and gather her in his arms. "Oh!"

"Stay with me, Maura. Not just the rest of the morning. I want you all day."

"I'm sorry, but the house closes at noon on Sundays."

"Then we'll go someplace else."

"You're sweet, but some of us girls are taking the electric car out to the old Spanish Fort."

Daniel brightened. "Then I'll drive you in my touring car."

"That's very tempting since I've never ridden in an automobile, but I'm afraid today is ladies only, plus Omar for protection."

157

He held her tighter. "Then we must make the most of our morning."

"As you wish."

25

Omar stepped onto the platform first and dutifully helped his four charges off the electric train. When they saw the fashionably dressed crowd heading for the entrance to Old Spanish Fort, Maura, Hattie, Fancy and Winifred were glad they took his advice to wear their best clothes. He did the same, and would've given Tom Anderson competition with his mustard jacket, red and white checkered vest and snazzy porkpie hat.

"Come along, ladies," he said, eliciting giggles when he doffed his hat and executed a theatrical bow. "Don't dawdle."

Maura took Hattie's arm as they passed through the gates. "Am I imagining things, or are people staring at us?"

"They're staring alright." Hattie reaped whistles when she tossed a saucy grin to a clutch of Greek merchant marines. "And it's not because they're wondering why one man has four beautiful women in tow."

"What do you mean?"

"I mean, Naïve Nancy, that some of these folks might guess that we're not convent girls."

She got a crusty rebuke from Omar. "Behave yourself, Hattie. The Fort is a place to play, not work."

"Sorry, boss man." Hattie whispered something to Maura that made them both giggle.

"I mean it," Omar grunted.

Hattie donned her serious face and walked on. Mischief was forgotten as Omar pointed out the abandoned fort, built in 1808, and explained that most of the amusement park was new after a mysterious fire eight years ago. The Ferris wheel and roller coaster were recent additions.

"How do you know so much about the place?" Winifred asked.

"Because George and I come out here every Sunday to get away from you noisy wenches."

The girls hissed and booed, but it was all in good fun. Spirits remained high as they explored the park, playing arcade games and riding the Ferris wheel for a sweeping view of Lake Pontchartrain and the distant city church spires. While Omar and Winifred tended to Fancy, queasy after riding the roller coaster, Maura and Hattie sought a cool lake breeze along the shore. They bought cones of praline ice cream and took an empty bench beside the ruined fort.

"You hear that?" Hattie said. "When the wind is right, there's jazz from the pavilion.

Maura savored a generous bite of ice cream. "What a perfect day."

"And a perfect place to hear about last night. Girl, I've been dying to get away from the others and hear about your first john."

"His name is Daniel Stafford."

"And?" Hattie pressed.

"He was alright."

"Handsome?"

"Not especially, but he's sweet and gentle and has pretty blue eyes."

Hattie groaned with frustration when Maura turned her attention back to the ice cream. "For God's sake! Getting information from you is like pulling teeth. Did you like him or not?"

"I guess so and I guess he liked me too. This morning he asked if I'd spend the day with him."

"Why didn't you?"

"Because we were coming out here."

"Honey, you got a lot to learn about this business. You don't ever turn down that kind of deal. Better not let Madam Charlotte find out. She charges a bundle for a full night and day. She charged Joel Fletcher a fortune when he took Winifred to Cuba."

"I'm sure there will be other times."

"Then you'd go with him again?"

Maura shrugged. "I don't know. Maybe. Probably. I almost chose Senator Harvey last night. The man has charm to burn."

"Money to burn, too. Carol Ann's been with him a few times. Says he's a big tipper."

"I think Mr. Stafford must be rich too. He left a very generous tip."

"What's his line of work?"

"He said he's a cotton broker like his father."

"Sounds like old money to me."

"Does that matter?"

"It sure doesn't hurt. Either way, keep this gent on your dance card. You'll learn soon enough who to choose and who to avoid, although there aren't any real cheapskates in the Windsor crowd."

Maura demurred. "Let's talk about something else."

"Okay. I just wanted to know about your debut."

"I know, and you're sweet to care." Maura chuckled. "It's pretty funny when you think about it."

"What?"

"Me being a debutante."

Hattie howled. "Take the name any way you can get it, honey. That reminds me. Do you know the story about Josie Arlington and the debutantes? I mean real debutantes." Maura shook her head. "Remember Tom Anderson's Ball of the Two Well-Known Gentlemen?"

"I ought to. It was my first Mardi Gras ball."

"He created it especially for us Storyville folks, you know. It was his answer to those fancy society balls which everyone says are dull as dishwater. Anyway, when those uptown debutantes heard about it, they wanted see what all the fuss was about. They got their menfolk to buy tickets to the ball, and since everyone was masked, no one would know who they were. Well, honey child, it didn't take Miss Josie long to figure out their little scheme. She was mad as hell that they expected some kind of carnival side show, so she decided to get even. Boy, did she ever!" Hattie licked away the last bit of ice cream before it dripped onto her dress. "Delicious!"

"What did she do?"

"She contacted someone in the police department and arranged to have the ball raided."

Maura knew what was coming. "Uh-oh."

"That's right. The cops announced that, since the ball was held by and for the people of Storyville, all females had to show identification proving they were prostitutes in good standing." Hattie chuckled. "I heard there was all sorts of screaming and scuffling when the debutantes tried to escape, but police were waiting outside with Black Marias. I also heard those snooty slummers were packed in like sardines and taken to the police station There were plenty of tears and embarrassment when the masks came off."

"Were they arrested?"

"Of course not. Their rich daddies got them off and kept their names out of the newspapers, but by the next day everyone in town knew what had happened. That night is known as Josie's Revenge."

"Good for Josie!" Maura said.

"One thing I'll say for Storyville. It's never dull."

"I'm finding that out, Hattie, and you know what? I'm starting to like it a little."

"I'm glad. I know it takes a while, and what I've learned is that whoring is pretty much what you make it. At least for us gals on the top tier. My philosophy is easy come, easy go, and so far, it's worked out okay."

"I admire your optimism, Hattie. It's helped me more than you know."

"I'm glad."

"In fact, it's inspired me to make a phone call when we get back."

"You gonna call that Mr. Stafford?"

"No, no. I'm gonna call the Senator. I've been thinking about his generosity."

"Girl, now you're getting it!"

PART FIVE

"The nature of the city is one of contrasts, beautiful as sin and ugly
as hell,
one as damaging as the other
to the innocent far from home.
She'll give you anything you want
as long as you can pay.
She'll kill you with kindness,
then pray over your corpse.
That more than anything marks New Orleans,
the curious contiguity of good and evil,
life and death."
-R. Wright Campbell, *Fat Tuesday*

"If sex was the meat of Storyville, then greed was its leaven."
Al Rose, *Storyville*

26

1915

"You hear that?" Maura grabbed Hattie's arm as they came downstairs. "That's Tony Jackson playing. What's he doing here so early in the day?"

"Madam Charlotte's doing some special entertaining tonight. I guess he's rehearsing."

Maura was enraptured. "I've never heard anyone play like that, like his fingers take on a life of their own. I'm so jealous."

"Get in line, honey child. He's the envy of every professor in Storyville. Even Jelly Roll Morton admires him, and he never says nothing nice about nobody. People say that whenever Tony walks into the Big Twenty Five, whoever's on the piano gives up his seat or gets accused of hurting the piano's feelings. You know what else they say? If you can't play like Tony, you can at least dress like him. The guy is one sharp dresser."

"That's for sure."

They took seats at the bar where Maura had a good view of Tony's extravagant arm garters, checkered vest, pearl gray derby and trademark ascot with diamond stickpin. Those most jealous of his prodigious talent claimed Tony overdressed to compensate for his homeliness. He knew people joked about his looks and was very public in saying that he didn't give a good goddamn what anybody thought.

"I wonder where he learned how to play," Maura whispered.

"In his back yard." Omar stopped washing glasses, leaned close and propped his elbows on the bar. "He was born over on Amelia Street. His daddy was a fisherman who died when Tony was little, and it was such a rough neighborhood that his mama kept him home most of the time. He didn't have any playmates so he figured out that he liked music. When he was seven, he built some kind of musical contraption and taught himself to play it. A neighbor let him practice on her reed organ, and somebody else let him play a real piano in a saloon before it opened for business. Everyone who heard him was knocked out, and by the time he was sixteen, he was playing all over Storyville."

"How do you know so much about him?"

"Because me and Tony have had some long talks with him sitting where you are now. That there's a man who loves his bourbon." He nodded at the glass perched atop the piano. "That ain't iced tea, ladies."

"I knew he was a drinker," Hattie said, "but I've never seen him drunk."

"Because Tony Jackson plays better drunk than other men play sober, and that's not all. He's a master at improvisation and has a beautiful tenor voice. He sings everything from coon songs and folk tunes to blues and opera. I've seen him get down and dirty with the best of them. The man's an honest-to-God genius."

Omar's admiration was contagious. "He sure is." Maura listened to a dazzling glissando as Tony swung from Maple Leaf Rag to The Entertainer. "I've never heard him play ragtime."

"I told you he does it all. Guy has a repertoire in the hundreds."

"I'm going to talk to him. I might even to ask him to sing a duet."

"Are you crazy?!" Omar asked. "Madam Charlotte would have a fit."

"Why?"

"Honest to Pete, Maura." Hattie rolled her eyes, exasperated. "You know damned well that professors can't sing with white girls. Never ever!"

"Maybe not in public, but we're the only ones here right now. Who's gonna know?"

Hattie looked at Omar. "Any chance of Madam Charlotte coming down here?"

"Not this time of day, but I still don't think it's a good idea to—"

"Save your breath," Hattie said as Maura headed for the stage. "I swear that gal gets more headstrong by the day."

"You got that right."

Tony smiled as Maura approached. They weren't more than nodding acquaintances, but he, like Daniel Stafford, admired Maura's talent. "So the mountain comes to Muhammed, eh?"

"I beg your pardon."

"I was here on St. Patrick's Day when Miss Nellie let you sing Where the River Shannon Flows. It ain't easy to hold Storyville audiences if you skip the raunchy lyrics and sing straight, but you sure did." He sipped his bourbon. "You play a mean piano too."

"Nothing like you," she insisted. "Did you really build a musical instrument when you were seven?

"You've been talking to Omar, eh? Well, yes, I did. Made a sort of harpsicord from pieces of junk I picked up around the neighborhood. It was one rickety mess but it made music." He flashed a pearly smile. "Kinda."

"But how did you know how to…what did…how could you—?"

Tony laughed heartily. "Good God, lady. I sure hope you're a lot smoother when you talk to them johns!"

Maura laughed too. "I guess I'm a little awestruck."

"I'm flattered."

"Do you think we could continue our conversation with music?"

Tony frowned. "You talking a duet?"

"Why not?"

He glanced around the room and, seeing only Tony and Hattie at the bar, scooted over and patted the piano bench. "What's your pleasure?"

Hattie and Omar were an enthusiastic audience of two as Maura and Tony began singing Let Me Call You Sweetheart. When the girls upstairs heard the popular duet, they drifted down in ones and twos, and by the time the impromptu performance ended, a crowd erupted with applause and whistles.

"You're wonderful!" Maura gushed. "You make me sound much better than I am."

Tony beamed and sipped his drink. "Ain't my place to say, Miss Maura, but…well, I know you're Madam Charlotte's top gal, but it seems to me you're in the wrong end of the business."

"Not if I want to make good money. Female singers don't make anything like you professors."

"I reckon that's the truth, but it's too bad people don't get to hear you sing anymore."

"It's alright. I'm a lot happier writing music in private than appearing in public."

"You a composer too?"

"Since I first learned to read music. Nothing like you though. Pretty Baby is famous."

"I got lucky with that one. Sorta lucky that is. I've sold a bunch of songs but never got more than four or five dollars. The people what buys them publish them under their own name, so they make the money and I get no credit. I got two hundred and fifty dollars for Pretty Baby, but then the guys changed the lyrics."

"That's awful!"

"Yeah, but that's how things are for colored songwriters. Always has been. Most of us don't never get to…uh-oh."

Tony watched, resigned, as Omar dragged an ornate three-paneled screen to the stage and propped it against the side of the piano. Maura remembered the first time she saw this ugly reminder of Storyville's racist policies. White men had access everywhere in the District, but colored men were allowed in the brothels only as musicians or laborers and were forbidden to patronize all bagnios, even those staffed by Negro women. Nor were black and white prostitutes permitted to work in the same house. The screens were designed to prevent black musicians from seeing provocative performances involving unclad white women, even those wearing flesh-colored body stockings.

"Sorry, maestro," Omar said. "Got a special show tonight."

"Hell, man. Screens don't bother me none."

"I know, but I still gotta put one up."

Tony leaned close enough for Maura to smell the whiskey on his breath. "What those white gals gonna be showing may not be for a black man's eyes, but tell you what. They ain't got nothing I wants to see." He winked. "If you know what I mean."

"I do. And that's nobody's business but yours."

More than once, Maura had overheard men refer to him as Lady Jackson, and his whispered aside confirmed what she suspected about his sexual preferences. She didn't know why she was prompted to pat his hand but decided it was something her pious father would condemn. Tony was surprised by the intimacy.

"Gal, you keep breaking the rules, you gonna get us both in a heap of trouble."

"Some rules are made to be broken."

"I know that's the truth, but sometimes when I see myself in the mirror, I wonder what God was thinking."

"So do I, Tony. So do I."

27

Seeking relief from the heat, Maura and Hattie stripped to their shifts and retreated to the courtyard. A pair of sweet olive trees provided welcome shade and a rich fragrance diluting the odor of nearby privies. The wind was another ally, carrying the smell of the sea as it gusted off the Gulf of Mexico. There was, alas, no escaping the noise. Like the rest of New Orleans, Storyville was immersed in the thunder of pounding nails and the smell of plywood as windows, doors and carriageways were boarded up. Along the riverfront, the shores of Lake Pontchartrain and throughout the bayous, everything from rowboats and Cajun pirogues to heavy coal barges and high-masted schooners, was being hurriedly secured. A few blocks away, on Chartres Street, the tiny chapel of the old Ursuline Convent overflowed with pilgrims praying to Our Lady of Prompt Succor, patron saint of the city. She had, after all, twice exerted divine intervention, saving the convent from a city-wide conflagration in 1812 and destruction by the British army three years later during the War of 1812. When news arrived that a hurricane had set its sights on New Orleans, hopes were high that Our Lady would again rush to the town's defense.

Hattie settled a chair. "You been through a hurricane before, Maura?"

"Never. You?"

"Once when I was a kid. It was very, very loud. Scary too. The rain came sideways and hit me in the face like buckshot. I can still feel the sting."

"What're we supposed to do?"

"Nothing for now. When things start getting bad, Omar wants us to gather in the bar 'cause there are no windows to explode."

"Now I'm really frightened!"

"Only a fool wouldn't be." Hattie scanned the unsettled heavens. "I remembered something else. The air starts getting heavy and close, but it makes you light-headed at the same time."

"How can it do that?" Hattie's answer was drowned by shouts from the kitchen. "Is that Zozo?"

"She and Bricktop were having some kinda powwow when I came down for coffee. Sounds like it's turned ugly."

"Mark my word, woman!" Zozo shouted. "Storyville's goin' down, and it'll take her with it!" She burst into the courtyard like an erupting volcano, face a study in pure African fury as she stormed through the gate. Neither girl had seen her so angry.

"Good Lord!" Maura cried. "What do you suppose that was about?"

"No idea. The storm maybe. Zozo was predicting it before anybody else." Hattie shifted into a more comfortable position. "Wouldn't be the first time she saw the future. Carol Ann says she ought to take a crystal ball over to Jackson Square and set up shop. I used to think she was crazy. Now I'm not so sure."

"Do you think she has powers?"

"You know a voodoo queen who doesn't? You've heard the stories, Maura. Can't all of them be made up."

"No, I guess not."

Hattie closed her eyes and began to doze, leaving Maura to her thoughts. She spent a few minutes watching the ominous skies before something tickled her bare foot. A lone black ant had strayed from the army swarming over a piece of biscuit she dropped earlier, tumbling over each other to reach the marmalade on top. She brushed her foot and leaned down for a closer look. In a matter of minutes, they dismantled their enormous prize and bore it away, paralleling a line marching in the other direction. Maura was so fascinated by their military precision that she didn't notice the drop in temperature until fat raindrops splatted on the flagstones. Their icy bite woke Hattie who leapt up and, with Maura in tow, scurried inside the house. Fierce lightning bleached the courtyard, partnered with window-rattling thunder that had Bricktop running after them. They joined everyone in the bar where Soona and Katy were setting out candles, and Omar was cleaning glasses as though it was business as usual. Only one person was missing.

"Where's Madam Charlotte?" Maura asked.

"She won't leave her room," Omar replied. "George and I boarded up her windows and hooked the shutters, so we can only hope for the best."

"What've you heard about the storm?"

All eyes were on Omar as he looked from one anxious face to another. "I'm not gonna sugar-coat it, ladies. This thing's mean, and it's heading our way. Tom Anderson said it might be as bad as the one that hit Grand Isle six years ago."

"Have mercy!" Bricktop wailed. "That thing killed hundreds of folks and tore up every plantation between here and Baton Rouge!"

Seeking to calm his frightened charges, Omar shouted toward the stage where Tony and Winifred were chattering like magpies. "Hey, professor! How about tickling those ivories!"

Maura's fears eased a bit when Tony, dressed to the nines as usual with the omnipresent whiskey atop the piano, began to play. His music provided a much-needed sense of normalcy, especially when he encouraged the girls to dance and sing along. Everyone caught the spirit, even the usually taciturn George who surprised everyone with his dancing skills by whirling Fancy around the room. As the hours passed, the little gathering struggled to remain brave despite the drone of ever-louder winds. Tony continued to sing until he was drowned out by the howling storm. He got another drink from Tony and took a seat beside Maura. When he leaned close to shout something in her ear, the Windsor rocked so hard that it seemed to lift off its foundation.

"Hang on, boys!" Omar shouted. "It's here!"

The house trembled erratically and then shuddered hard. The girls whimpered and hugged each other when the chandeliers blinked and flickered out. Bricktop and Carol Ann moved like wraiths, lighting candles until the room glowed with haloes of light. While the women cowered, Omar and George wandered the building to check doors and windows. The wind's deafening drone was punctuated with the crash of objects hurled against the building. Poor Winifred retreated to a far corner where she intoned the rosary, beads flowing through her fingers like water. Another hour passed. Two, then three. The air grew ponderous with the pungent zing of ozone and palpable fear as the hurricane bore down on the foundering city. Had they known what was unfolding outside their cocoon, those huddled inside the Windsor would have been terrified a hundredfold.

Shrieking winds scythed through the streets, fierce as a dragon's breath. Small steamers and coal barges were overturned and swallowed by the Mississippi River, now a churning froth of whitecaps, and smaller craft were blown ashore. Lake Pontchartrain blasted over its banks, engulfing the rides at Spanish Fort. Most of the town's spires and steeples toppled. The First Presbyterian Church on Lafayette Square lost its 219-foot bell tower, tallest structure in the city, before collapsing onto itself, as did St. Anne's Episcopal on Esplanade. In the French Quarter, roofs were torn off, including that atop the old French Market, and the Presbytère on Jackson Square lost its cupola. The clock on neighboring St. Louis Cathedral froze at 5:50 P. M. under the hurricane's fury. Flooding was mercifully minimal, but felled trees, collapsed buildings and tons of debris made most streets and sidewalk impassable. The municipal power station, which failed early on, kept the city in darkness, and downed telephone poles cut service to thousands. The eye of the storm passed sometime after midnight, but the winds didn't fade until dawn, replaced by an unnerving calm. Omar and George opened the front doors and hammered down the protective plywood sheets installed the morning before. An uprooted palm tree partly blocked the entrance. Omar clambered over the fronds and extended a helping hand to George.

"Keep the women inside!" he barked. "We need to see what—!"

Omar's words were lost when a chunk of the second-floor gallery creaked, crackled and collapsed. Heavy boards struck his head and shoulders and knocked him unconscious. Tony helped George carry him into the parlor and lay him on the settee where Soona and Carol Ann tended to his injuries. Strong and sturdily built, Omar soon regained his senses and touched his throbbing temple. He frowned at the sea of hovering faces.

"Somebody check on Madam Charlotte."

Winifred and Fancy bustled off and returned in a state. "She's gone, Omar! We looked everywhere."

"Crazy old fool. She must've sneaked off to Hop Alley."

"Want me to go find her?" George asked.

"You need to check the upstairs for damage, and I don't want the girls left alone. Looters will be out soon. And worse."

"I'll go," Maura offered.

"Girl, you can't go out there alone and, besides, you don't know what the devil's between here and Hop Alley. Trees will be down and—"

"I'll take her!" Tony announced. "C'mon, Miss Maura."

Before Omar could protest, Maura and Tony fled the parlor and scrambled over the wreckage at the front door and onto Villere Street. Along with other dazed survivors, they proceeded cautiously through the debris. Maura fought a rush of nausea when they turned

175

onto Bienville and stumbled over the corpse of a mule. They encountered worse at the end of the block where a man lay dead, skull stove in by a wooden wagon wheel. Tony caught her arm when Maura's knees buckled.

"Ain't you never seen a dead man?"

She clung to his shoulder until the ugly memory passed. "Yes, I have."

"Come on then. It's only a couple more blocks."

Hop Alley was in Chinatown, a compact quarter along two blocks of Rampart Street. Maura had been there only once, last June with Hattie. They had marveled at the tiny shops stacked one atop the other, chockablock with oriental novelties. They browsed paper dragons, whirligigs, tasseled lanterns, and fans, along with silk robes and slippers in eye-popping colors. Everyone wore black pajamas, white stockings and black slippers, and the men braided their hair into queues trailing down their backs like snakes. There were a few richly dressed merchants, but it was mostly a sea of drab expressions on saffron faces. Over all hung heavy odors, sweet, sour and putrid. The storm had turned that shard of Orientalia inside out and upside down. Every shop sustained damage except their destination, the Lin Lee Laundry at the far end of the enclave. It was not only unscathed but open for business. A bell tinkled when they entered to find walls lined with neat stacks of paper-wrapped laundry, miraculously intact. When no one responded to the bell, Tony pointed to a door at the rear of the shop.

"Back there."

Maura trailed him through a curtained archway to a door with a Judas hole. Tony knocked and, knowing a black face might get no response, positioned Maura in front of the peephole. After a moment it opened to reveal a small, lanceolate eye. The voice behind it was nasal and high-pitched.

"You want?"

Maura threw Tony a desperate look. He mouthed instructions. "Smoke," she replied.

The door opened a crack. Tony pushed it, and they stepped into blackness and the sharp stink of opium. When their eyes adjusted, they followed a tiny Chinese girl weaving through eight wooden beds with thin mattresses, all empty. Behind them were two lacquered cubicles with curtains parted. One was occupied.

"Madam Charlotte!" Maura cried.

Charlotte lay in the opium coffin and smiled dreamily while the girl stuck a long, curved fingernail into a pot on her lap and scooped a chunk of sticky gum. It was nimbly rolled it into a pill and dropped it into the bowl of a long pipe which she held out to Charlotte.

"We gotta get her outta here before she starts another pipe!" Tony pushed the bewildered girl aside. "Help me, Maura!"

Madam Charlotte languished in such a profound opium haze that she scarcely recognized her rescuers. Having not seen her in months, both were shocked by her frailty. She was almost weightless as they got her to her feet and positioned her between them. They half-walked, half carried her outside where she was oblivious to the chaos as they made their way back to the Windsor. A fragile lady shuffling between a white woman and black man drew no attention among storm-stunned townspeople picking through wreckage and searching for survivors. Maura was aghast at Charlotte's unearthly pallor and a face resembling a death mask. She turned to Tony.

"You've known her a long time, haven't you?"

"Almost long's I can remember."

"Then tell me how this happened."

His response shocked her.

"Zozo."

"But why would she—?"

Tony pretended to lock his lips and toss away the key.

28

1916

The great, hoary oaks lining Esplanade Avenue filtered pale January sunlight, dappling Maura and Daniel as they strolled. With the exception of some sawed-off limbs and a few missing chimneys, little evidence remained of the hurricane devastation of two months ago. These grand houses, after all, had been built to last by wealthy French Creoles, and were now owned by rich Americans who haughtily maintained them as monuments to a vanished culture. A light breeze embellished the pleasant afternoon and inspired Maura to hum.

Daniel smiled. "Is that a new tune you're writing?"

"Could be." She smiled back. "Time will tell."

He patted the gloved hand inside his elbow. "You're certainly in good spirits today."

"Why shouldn't I be? Senator Harvey was very generous last night." She tossed her head to make dangling emerald earrings dance. "These match the necklace he gave me last week and the bracelet from the week before that. Aren't they pretty?"

"You know I don't like hearing that."

"There's nothing wrong with being grateful, Daniel."

"You know what I mean."

"Too well," she said, mood souring.

"If you'd only let me take care of you, the subject would never come up again."

Maura stopped, withdrew her hand and faced him. "The subject of my being a whore?"

"You know I hate that word."

"So do I, Daniel, but you have to face the truth. I've faced it and made peace with it. Madam Charlotte offered me a rare opportunity, and I can't just walk away after she's been so good to me."

"All you mean to her are dollar signs."

Maura sniffed. "Must you be so cynical?"

"When it involves the woman I love, yes. Please, Maura. I've told you a thousand times that you don't have to work, for Madam Charlotte or anyone else. I'll buy you a place wherever you like, and give you everything you need. You can put all this behind you."

"And I've told you a thousand times that I can't be beholden to one man. I was once a prisoner in my own home, the property of someone who did terrible things. Freedom is something I dearly cherish and I am not prepared to give it up." Seeing Daniel's pain, she stood on tiptoes and kissed his cheek. "I know you love me, darling, and I wish I could love you in return, but I can't."

"You mean you won't."

"Alright then. I won't. I won't because it will complicate matters, and I can't allow that when I'm so close to—" She stopped short of mentioning Sloane, a secret fiercely kept from all but a few. "Isn't it enough that we can be together from time to time and enjoy beautiful days like this?"

"No, Maura, it's not. And it never will be."

"What does that mean?"

"It means that you've relegated me to an emotional purgatory."

Maura was weary of the old argument. "I'm not relegating you anywhere, Mr. Stafford. If you're not happy with our relationship, then—"

"Don't, Maura!"

"Then you're free to go."

"You know I can't."

"Then you must make the best of this so-called purgatory and get on with your life." Such suffering, she reminded herself, had been her lot until she put her two grievous sins behind her. "God knows, I have."

They walked in silence, each lost in thought as they turned onto Royal Street and ventured into the French Quarter. The name was a misnomer as the neighborhood was now the domain of Italians, the aromas of charcuteries, boulangeries and pâtisseries vanquished by the equally enticing scents of Sicilian sausages and baking ciabatta. Maura was grateful when fragrant clouds overwhelmed the stench of stagnant water and gutter garbage. The streets and sidewalks grew thick with people bustling about their days. Maura never tired of the spectacle, especially in Jackson Square where she forgot the ugly interchange with Daniel and lost herself in a kaleidoscope of lively humanity. A fez-wearing organ grinder's monkey danced for pennies, competing with the shills of medicine pitchmen and the thump of Haitian drums. Acadian women sold beautiful blankets of coton jaune, Choctaw women from across Lake Pontchartrain offered woven baskets, and wagons sold calas, those sugar-laden rice cakes dear to Creole hearts. Maura especially admired the Negresses balancing baskets on heads wrapped in colorful tignons. It was all so exotic she imagined herself in a foreign country.

"Listen!" She stopped abruptly. "Do you hear that voice?"

"I hear only noise," Daniel replied.

"Over there." Maura pointed toward St. Louis Cathedral where dozens of vendors offered fresh fruits and fall vegetables. "It's the praline woman. I love how she sing-sells her wares."

They moved closer as the woman's deep voice pierced the din and soared to soprano. People turned toward the sound. "Praw-leens! I got New Orleans best praw-leens! Getcha praw-leens!"

"She has quite a voice," Daniel admitted.

"Yes, she does, and I love hearing it. The crab woman and mirliton man too. I memorized some of their tunes and put lyrics to them. My French Market melodies, I call them."

"You hear music everywhere, don't you, my dear?"

She spoke more to herself than to him. "I have to."

Inspired by the singer, Daniel bought pralines. He downed his quickly, but Maura savored hers in tiny bites which she didn't finish until they reached Basin Street. Knowing Daniel didn't like seeing Storyville in daylight with its tawdriness so blatantly laid bare, she stopped and faced him.

"Please tell me you understand what we discussed earlier, Daniel. It's essential if we're to continue seeing each other."

"I understand."

"I'm glad." She squeezed his arm. "Will I see you tonight?"

"You know how I detest those vulgar Saturday night entertainments."

"I forgot it was Saturday. Tomorrow afternoon then?"

"We'll go for a drive. I'll call for you at three."

"Why so late?"

"I have a great deal of thinking to do, and I have...obligations."

It was an unexpected allusion to Daniel's private life, a subject deliberately avoided since their first night together. Instinct warned Maura not to pry.

"Alright."

"You know I love you, Maura."

"Yes, my dear. I know." She expected a kiss, but Daniel only tipped his hat, bowed curtly and walked away. "And that," she murmured to herself, "is our misfortune."

Maura crossed Basin Street and headed up Iberville, melancholy lifting when she saw Zozo coming out of Windsor House. She considered Zozo one of God's more peculiar souls with conversations to match. She waved and called out.

"How're you doing, Zozo?"

"I'm fine, Miss Maura." She pretended to glance nervously over her shoulder. "It's alright if I don't call you Désirée, ain't it?"

"Of course," Maura laughed. "Between you and me, I seriously doubt if any of those johns believe I'm French Creole."

"It's all about illusion, ain't it, honey?" Zozo leaned down to inspect the stoop for brick dust and clucked with disapproval. "Gotta ride my girls. They're not keeping things up like I showed 'em."

"How many are working for you now?"

"Nine. We in other neighborhoods too. Even got a few houses uptown." She flashed a near toothless smile. "Ain't just black folks believe in voodoo, y'know."

"No, I didn't."

"Color don't make no difference, child. If you're a true believer, the curses and blessings have power. If you don't believe, they don't."

"I'm not sure I understand."

"Cause you ain't a believer."

"No, I'm not."

Voodoo, which some spelled voudou and others called hoodoo, was the unofficial religion of Storyville. Maura didn't buy it any more than the Baptist theology shed when she was damned by her preacher father. A great many Storyville girls were ardent acolytes, however, and gris-gris popped up as regularly as silverfish. Voodoo even found its way into the agenda of the top madams' regular powwows. Only last month, in a proposal spearheaded by Lulu White, the madams had agreed not to use it against each other, but that didn't stop their girls from calling on voudouiennes like Zozo for help and hurt. Zozo could reputedly trigger abortions, cause or cure impotence and even infect people with venereal disease. Zozo's most feared and grotesque gift was her "sealing power" that prevented a prostitute from doing business.

"What're you doing here today?"

"One of the girls needed some goofer dust."

"Oh, my!" Maura had heard enough to know goofer dust was reserved for the most extreme spells. Made of graveyard dust, gunpowder and grease from the bells at St. Roch's chapel, among other things, it invoked a wide range of illnesses and could even bring death. Because Zozo had not named the girl, Maura knew better than to ask. "Someone always seems to be stirring up trouble," she sighed.

"For sure." Zozo nodded good-bye when Omar stepped outside. "I'll see you folks later."

"'Bye, Zozo." Maura turned to Omar. "Madam Charlotte feeling better this afternoon?"

"Nothing wrong with her that a trip to Lin Lee's won't cure." She'd never heard such sadness in his voice. "The truth is, I don't know how much longer this can go on."

"I'm sorry to hear that."

"Yeah. Me too." Omar lit a cigar and sucked noisily until the tip glowed. "By the way, do you know a man named Lewis Hatcher?"

Maura endured a rush of horror when she recalled the man standing over her husband's bloody corpse, and the frantic scramble to hide the hideous crime that brought them together.

"I did," Maura managed. "Once upon a time."

"He was here looking for you a couple of hours ago," Omar reported. "And I

gotta say he's not the kind of man I'd expect you to know."

"What do you mean?"

"He was drunk as a fiddler's bitch and looks like a tramp. Smelled like one too."

"Did he say what he wanted?"

"No, but I'm guessing it's money."

"I wonder how he found—"

"Said he saw your picture in the Blue Book and that you looked a whole lot different than you did in Mississippi."

Not for the first time, Maura berated herself for allowing Madam Charlotte to publish her photo. She had protested, but weakly, because she was so desperate for money, and now that poor decision had come back to haunt her. Then again, judging from Omar's description, maybe Hatcher had fallen on hard times and only needed a handout. Considering he'd kept her from going to prison for murder, she was certainly willing to help.

"Did he say how I could contact him?"

"Said he'd be back." Omar frowned. "You okay, Miss Maura?"

"I'm a little tired. I did quite a bit of walking this afternoon."

"Better get inside and rest up. Lotsa bigwigs coming tonight."

"I know," she sighed. "Tonight and every night."

29

"Ahhh."

Maura leaned against the railing and sighed heavily, filling her lungs with the heavy wet air. As dusk descended, scores of swallows emerged to swoop and dive and gorge themselves on mosquitoes. Down below, Storyville was girding itself for the night. Lamps began winking from windows and doorways, flooding streets and banquettes with oily light. It was a tawdry magnet. Tourists and locals, sports and suckers, dockworkers and swells, all were drawn by its erotic energy, a siren call as old as mankind itself. Directly across Villere Street, Bugling Sam the Waffle Man blasted a trumpet to announce he was open for business. His mule-drawn wagon carried a coal fire beneath an enormous waffle iron, and if the wind was right Maura smelled scorched sugar. She was a loyal customer and waved when she caught Sam's eye. She lingered to watch him stoke his fire before a sound she hadn't heard before drew her to the other end of the gallery. Hattie heard it too and joined her at the rail. Down below, a clutch of spectators gathered around a gang of white street urchins. One wore a sandwich board with crude chalk lettering proclaiming themselves the Razzy Dazzy Spasm Band. One boy played a fiddle fashioned from a cigar box while another sang through a section of rainspout. A harmonica, a home-made drum and a boy playing spoons on the sidewalk completed the ensemble while a sixth danced with zany, jerking motions like someone having an epileptic fit.

"Isn't that the wildest bunch you've ever heard?" Hattie asked.

"Yes, but there's something wonderful about them."

"I know. It's called guts and survival. I 've talked to the one that's dancing. Calls himself Stale Bread. Those poor boys are all homeless orphans and, God bless 'em, they're getting by the best way they can. Treading water until the next gig."

Maura was silent while Hattie's words hit home.

"Stale Bread said that last week they performed for Sarah Bernhardt. She was slumming in Storyville and stopped to watch."

"I hope she was a good tipper."

"Nope. Stale Bread said she tipped below whore scale."

Maura laughed but it was a hollow sound. "Do you ever get tired of it, Hattie?"

"What? Whoring? Sure. All the time." She looked down when the street exploded with applause and cheers. The Razzy Dazzy Spasm Band had finished their number and was decamping to another block. "But I don't let myself think about it too much, or I'll go crazy."

"That's good advice. I wish I could follow it."

"We all feel that way one time or another. Fancy's the only one I never heard complain. 'Course, she's been on her own since she was fourteen, and whoring's the only life she knows." Hattie coughed softly. "This morning, Chloe yammered on and on about how she wasn't gonna become no slave to cocaine or hooked on booze so that she ended up screwing derelicts for penny beers." Maura grew queasy at the thought. "She was all het up because a girl she knew went to work at Maude Rose's joint. It's the nastiest beer brothel in Storyville. Chloe said the girls make themselves up with ground-up chalk mixed with cheap perfume. Anyway, her friend got beaten to death by her pimp, and a fisherman found her body in Bayou Sauvage but not before an alligator had—"

"Stop, Hattie. I don't want to hear any more."

"I'm sorry, honey. Sometimes I can't help running my big mouth."

"It's alright. We'd better get dressed. Omar said we're expecting an especially rich crowd tonight."

"True enough. What are you wearing?"

"My pale-yellow silk, I guess."

"Can I borrow your little blue number with the rosettes?"

"Of course. It looks sweet on you."

"Thanks. Hey, I'm sorry about that ugly talk. Sometimes it gets to me, you know?"

"Of course I know. It gets to me too."

Storyville always put on the dog for an influx of dignitaries because they left the madams flush and the barkeeps and colored professors pocket-heavy. Tonight's party included politicians from both Louisiana and Arkansas, and Maura's mood improved when she lost herself in the festive crush in the parlor. As the establishment's most sought-after girl, she was introduced to one well-heeled gentleman after another. She made use of her much-improved memory skills, filing away each name, profession and promise before making her choice for the evening. She had settled on Arkansas Lieutenant Governor Victor Mathis when Omar directed everyone into the bar for a special entertainment. The crowd eagerly gathered around the stage, thrilled by the piano wizardry of Tony Jackson behind a tall screen. Like Tony, Maura had no interest in the unsavory spectacle to come and whispered to Mathis that she'd like to go upstairs. To her shock, he declined.

"Not now, young lady. I've heard so much about Madam Charlotte's entertainments that I dare not miss one."

"As you wish."

"The show is not to your taste?"

"Frankly, no."

Mathis gave her a censorious look. "Who would've thought you had such delicate sensibilities?"

Maura was stung by his sarcasm. "If you please, sir, I only meant that I've seen it so often that—"

"Suit yourself, miss." He called over his shoulder as he walked away. "You're hardly the only woman here."

It was the first time a client had rebuffed Maura's invitation, and for a moment she didn't know how to react. She knew only that she couldn't stomach the sight of Fancy and Chloe performing the vulgar clodoche and simulating sex in skin-tight body stockings. She fled the room to wait out the show in the parlor. As she took a seat and arranged her skirts, George's voice boomed from the hall.

"You can't go in there, sir!" His warning was followed by loud scuffling. Maura leapt to her feet when she saw the cause of the commotion. Had she not received warning earlier that day, she would never have recognized the pitiful human being in George's fierce grip. Bearded, unkempt and reeking of unwashed flesh, he bore no resemblance to the compassionate soul who had come to her rescue the night of Ronan's murder.

"Mr. Hatcher!"

"So we meet again, eh, Mrs. O'Rourke?"

George gave her a quixotic look. "You know this fool, Miss Lamballe?"

"Miss Lamballe!" Hatcher mimicked horridly. "Got ourself a fancy dress and a fancy new name too, eh?"

"Yes, George. I know him. Bring him in here and—"

"You know I can't do that. Omar would have my hide."

"Then take him outside. I'll follow."

"Yes, miss." George stiff-armed Hatcher into the street and left him leaning against an empty buckboard. "I'll be within earshot if you need me."

"Thank you, George." She took a step forward but Hatcher's stench kept her at bay. "What's happened, Mr. Hatcher. Are you alright?"

"Hell, no, I'm not alright."

"Then please let me help you."

"Oh, you're gonna help alright. You're gonna give me some money. A lot of money."

Maura's heart chilled. "What are you talking about?"

"Oriole." Hatcher lost his balance and grabbed the wagon seat for support. "I ain't told nobody what happened up there, and I'm sure you wanna keep it that way."

So that's it, Maura thought grimly. Blackmail.

"Alright, then. Come by tomorrow afternoon and I'll—"

"A thousand bucks," Hatcher grunted. "I want a thousand bucks."

"A thous—?" Maura reeled. "I don't have that kind of money!"

"Sure you do. I seen your picture in that Blue Book, lady. You're famous. Rich and famous. Look at you in that get-up. Maybe the richest whore in Storyville, huh?"

Maura winced at the coarse accusation. "I assure you I'm not rich, Mr. Hatcher, but I'll see what I can do." When Hatcher continued staring, she indicated her evening gown. "Obviously I don't have any money with me."

"Figured you'd say that," he muttered. "I'll be back alright, but don't be thinking you can put me off or that I'll just disappear."

"I understand. Come by tomorrow at noon."

Hatcher took a moment to register her words before muttering to himself and lurching into the night. Maura watched him weave down Villere and disappear at the corner of Conti Street. She heard movement behind her.

"Everything jake?"

"Yes, George. Thank you. The man's a harmless drunk."

"Begging your pardon, ma'am, but, no, he ain't. He ain't neither harmless or drunk." George held the door as Maura went back inside. "I've seen his kind before. Got all kinds of nerves jumping around in his head. Man's high on something rough, or maybe he's just got the crazies. Whatever it is, you need to stay away from him."

"You really think so?"

"I been at this a long time, miss. I know what I'm talking about."

"I see."

"Were you trying to get rid of him or are you serious about giving him money?"

Realizing the houseman had overheard her conversation, Maura tried to remember if Hatcher had specifically mentioned murder. Deciding he had not, she said, "Our families were friendly back in Mississippi, and the poor man's plainly fallen on hard times. I can't refuse him help, but certainly not to the tune of a thous—"

"Hey!" George grabbed Maura's waist when her knees buckled. "Maybe you better sit down a minute."

"No, no. I promise I'm fine." She patted a powerful bicep until George relaxed his grip. She slipped free and smoothed her skirt as whoops and applause from the bar announced the clodoche was over. "Thanks again, George. Now I'd better get back in there or I'll have Omar to answer to."

"Yes, ma'am."

Maura tried to shove Lewis Hatcher from her mind and concentrate on business. She entered the parlor in time to see Omar remove the screen surrounding the stage. Something unknown propelled her through the crowd, rendering her oblivious of everything and everyone except Tony as she mounted the stage.

"Hello, Tony."

"Hey, Miss Maura. You looking a little peculiar. You alright?"

"Never better, my friend. You want to shake things up a little?"

"Your call, lady. I'm only the piano man."

"And I'm in the mood to sing. How about Some of These Days?"

"Coming right up!"

Tony needed no music. He launched into the opening bars with such flourish that conversations slowed and all eyes turned toward the stage. Talk ceased altogether when Maura began singing, burnishing her soprano with roughness as she belted to the bar. "One of these days, you're gonna miss me, honey!" She not only seized everyone's attention but held it tight as she and Tony segued smoothly from one song to another. Eschewing Nellie's usual smutty patter and bawdy lyrics, Maura instead gave a performance worthy of the finest concert halls. Tony also caught fire and synchronized every step of the way. She was sweating now. Both were. The applause was constant and thunderous. She rode it like a storm, buoyed from the edge of the stage where she felt the crowd's heat, to Tony's side when he finished the last song with his trademark fortissimo.

"Think they're ready for Pretty Baby?" he asked.

"I don't know about them, but I sure am." She blotted her damp forehead. "Shall we make it a duet?"

Tony swigged his drink and made room on the piano bench. "It's your funeral, missy."

Maura laughed off the warning and sat beside him. The room went silent as they began twin duets, singing and playing together as though they'd rehearsed for weeks. Their voices soared, meshing in rich harmony like their hands on the keyboards. The audience response was electrifying, made more so when Hattie, Winifred and Carol Ann gathered alongside the stage and clapped hands in time to the rhythm. Maura and Tony were near breathless as they delivered the final lyric.

"Oh, I want to love a baby and it might as well be you, pretty baby of mine!"

Those few still seated rose to their feet as applause and whistles grew deafening. This, thought Maura, exhilarated, is the gift I was given and what I was born to do. She and Tony also stood, and he, at her urging, bowed alongside her. In a moment of sheer exuberance, she threw her arms around him and hugged him close.

The applause died and the room went quiet as a tomb.

30

Maura remained in her room all day, awaiting the inevitable. It came at two in the afternoon when Omar appeared to say Madam Charlotte wanted to see her. That he was the messenger underscored the gravity of the matter, as was his silence while he escorted Maura downstairs. As before, Charlotte's dark quarters wore the sharp bite of opium smoke, and she was ensconced on the chaise lounge. Omar stood behind her, arms folded across his chest. Charlotte cleared her throat and dabbed her upper lip with a lacy handkerchief.

"You know why you're here, don't you, Maura?"

"Yes, ma'am."

"Then sit down and explain yourself."

"It was a completely spontaneous moment," she began. "Tony and I were singing and playing the piano together, and the audience was applauding and yelling and when we took our bows...oh, I don't know. It seemed like the most natural thing in the world to show my appreciation for a fellow artist."

A weighty silence crawled by. Then, "You embraced a colored man, Maura."

"Yes, I did."

"In public."

Softer, "Yes."

Charlotte coughed again. "Surely you know that such behavior is unacceptable in my house."

"Yes, ma'am, although I don't understand why."

Charlotte ignored the retort. "I'm told this wasn't the first time you and Tony had some sort of...incident."

"We jammed together one afternoon when the place was closed. No customers saw us."

Charlotte picked up a palmetto fan and riled the pungent air. "I also understand you were less than hospitable to the lieutenant-governor last night."

"I invited him upstairs before the show started, but he wanted to stay and see it." She swallowed. "I didn't, so I excused myself."

"Is your job not to put the client's wishes first?"

"Yes. I was wrong."

"I also understand you're being blackmailed."

Dear Lord, Maura thought. Is there anything this woman doesn't know?!

"Whatever you may have heard is my business," she said evenly.

"Not so, Maura. As long as you're living and working under my roof, your business is my business. It's that simple."

"But—"

"Any one of these indiscretions is enough to merit dismissal because they reflect badly on my house. I've no doubt that gossip about you and Tony Jackson spread throughout Storyville before you were asleep last night, and the other top madams will demand to know why I employed a white girl who cavorts with colored men."

"I wasn't cavorting!" Maura shot back. "It was a perfectly innocent, perfectly spontaneous act of gratitude. If you could only have seen and heard us—"

Charlotte waved the fan dismissively. "I believe you, my dear, but others won't because they're eager to think the worst. I grant you it's unfortunate, but it leaves me with no choice. If I am to maintain the high standards I've so carefully cultivated, I must ask you to leave my house."

"I see."

Charlotte's eyebrows rose. "Have you nothing else to say?"

"Only that you were kind to take a chance on me, and that I'm sorry I disappointed you."

"I'm sorry too, Maura. I've not forgotten you and Tony rescued me the day after the hurricane or that you are my best girl. The best, in fact, that we've ever had. Wouldn't you agree, Omar?"

"I would."

"For that reason, I'll allow you to remain until you find employment elsewhere. It will, I regret to say, be with a less prestigious house run by a less discriminating madam, but there you have it."

"Thank you, Madam Charlotte, but I'm leaving Storyville."

"Oh?" For the first time, the inscrutable mask showed emotion. "Where will you go?"

"I don't yet know. I've thought about nothing else all morning and have concluded that all these events were fated to set me on a new course."

"Perhaps they were." There was a scintilla of a smile. "You have a superstitious streak like myself, Maura. Always listen to it."

"I will."

As Maura left Madam Charlotte's darkness for the bright April daylight, she welcomed a sense of relief. It deepened when she spotted Hattie at the end of the hall.

"Did she fire you?"

"She didn't have any choice."

"That's what we figured. It's all the girls talked about at breakfast. Even Chloe thinks it's a stupid rule."

"We don't make the rules," Maura said.

"No, I reckon we don't."

Maura took Hattie's hand as they started upstairs. "In truth, I'm relieved. I told Madam Charlotte I believe all this has happened for a reason. It started with something Daniel said yesterday."

"I'm all ears."

"Remember I told you he asked me to become his mistress the second time we were together?"

"Of course I do. I felt stupid because it went against everything I warned you about."

"I was surprised too, and I've been putting him off ever since. But yesterday when we said good-bye, he told me he loved me in a way I'd not heard before. It quite literally hurt my heart." Hattie squeezed her hand. "Afterwards, when we were outside listening to that idiotic band and you were saying those terrible things about Chloe's friend and—"

"I'm sorry. I shouldn't have—"

"Hush, honey. You had every right to speak your mind, and I'm glad you did. It reinforced what's tormented me since I started whoring. It came up again when the lieutenant governor put me in my place, and it downright exploded after Tony and I had that crazy jam session."

"I'm not sure I follow you."

"I can't turn tricks anymore. I...just...can't!"

Hattie's eyes widened. "Truly?"

"Truly. I plan to tell Daniel when I see him this afternoon." She glanced at the hall clock. "Oh, no! It's almost three. I have to hurry."

Hattie grabbed her arm. "Hold on a minute, girlie! I got something to say."

"What is it?"

"I'm happy for you, Maura. I couldn't be happier unless it was me walking out of this place." She gave her a quick hug. "Now run along before your coach turns into a pumpkin!"

The cathedral bells were chiming three when Maura hurried outside to find Daniel in a duster with driving goggles pushed atop his forehead. He leaned against a sporty red Hupmobile, amid a throng of street Arabs gawking at the scarlet leather upholstery and matching spoked wheels. Daniel shooed them away and opened Maura's door. She gathered her long skirts and slid inside, dazzled by the posh surroundings. She thought of Cinderella's pumpkin and smiled.

"Does my new car amuse you?"

"It's beautiful." Maura said. "If I seem amused, it's because I've never been in an automobile before."

"Then it's time for a change."

You've no idea, Maura thought as he passed her goggles and a long scarf. "What do I do with these?"

"Tie the scarf under your chin and around your bonnet so it doesn't blow off. The goggles will protect those pretty green eyes from the dust."

"Aren't you sweet!"

"Not to mention gallant and rich." Daniel laughed. "High time you realized it, I might add."

Maura rolled her eyes. "Listen to you!"

She blew him a kiss as he bent before the hood and cranked the car until the engine sputtered to life. The chassis shuddered and continued to rock as he climbed into the driver's seat and took the wheel. He pulled the safety goggles back over his eyes.

"Ready?"

"Ready!"

Daniel shouted at the ragamuffins to stand clear and scattered those who refused by blowing his horn. The boys squealed with delight at the loud "Ah-OOH-gah!" and chased the car almost to Canal Street.

"I feel like everyone's staring at us," Maura shouted over the loud engine and street noise.

"They probably are. Hupmobiles are a rarity in New Orleans."

"Do I look like an insect with all this paraphernalia?"

"We both do!"

Maura caught his good spirits and leaned against his shoulder. "I have something important to tell you, my dear. Where are we going?"

"Somewhere I should've taken you a long time ago."

31

During her five years in New Orleans, Maura had seen surprisingly little of the city. She became a child wide-eyed with wonder when Daniel turned onto St. Charles Avenue and drove beneath a double row of massive live oaks arching overhead, a canopy trailing graceful streamers of Spanish moss. The commercial structures of downtown fell behind as they entered a neighborhood of elegant homes with spacious, lavishly landscaped lawns. Maura had no doubt this was the fabled Garden District and marveled at one mansion after another as Daniel drove down Washington Street before turning onto Chestnut. He drew up before an iron fence of entwined morning glories casting shadowy arabesques on the sidewalk. Looming beyond in silent majesty was a two-story Italianate masterpiece with more floral ironwork wrapping deep galleries. When Daniel turned off the engine, Maura lifted her goggles and gazed in amazement.

"You like it?" he asked.

"It's the most beautiful house I've ever seen!"

"This is my home, Maura." She stared, disbelieving. "From the day I was born. Shall we go inside?"

She was so awestruck it took a moment to find her voice. "Not yet." She scanned a lawn dotted with April sunlight and spied a gazebo. "Let's go there."

"Alright." Daniel helped her from the car and escorted her to the gazebo. The setting was so enchanting she was fairly bursting to reveal her news, but he commandeered the moment first. "I brought you here for a reason, Maura. I've thought only of us since yesterday and made a decision I should have made long ago." He slipped to one knee and took her hand. "I love you with all my heart, Maura O'Rourke. Will you be my wife?"

"Oh, no!" she cried. "Not today of all days!"

"What are you talking about?"

"I've also thought of nothing else but us and have been dying to tell you that I'm leaving Storyville so I can live with you." Before he could blurt his elation, she touched his lips with a fingertip. "But not as your wife."

"What?! Why not?"

"You know why not, Daniel. I'm no fool, nor are you. I've met too many men from the Garden District and heard all about their houses and children and daughters' cotillions, more than enough to know I don't belong in this world."

"Nor do I!" he insisted.

Still holding his hand, Maura drew him onto the bench beside her. "But here we would still be living in the middle of it, Daniel. What about our neighbors? We'll hardly be invisible, and what if I encountered one of those men I know from the Windsor?"

"They'd never say anything because it would be an admission that they were there too."

"I wish I could believe that, darling, but I would awake every morning to wonder if that was the day someone recognized me spread the ugly truth."

"You must understand that I don't give a damn about those people, Maura. I was pushed into their world at an early age and nearly forced into marrying a woman I found feckless and spoiled. I was so fearful of drowning in all that emptiness that I walked away. It's a decision I've never regretted."

"You never fell in love?"

"Never. I found contentment with my work and my love of music. I never needed or wanted anyone else in my private world until I met you. Now I'm asking you to join me there, without marriage if you wish, and together we can build a future and bury the past."

The past, Maura mused. A cloud crossed her mind when she thought of Ronan and, then, Lewis Hatcher. She wondered again why he hadn't come looking for her at noon.

"You know nothing of my past, Daniel. You only think you do."

"I know all I need to know."

"No, you don't. If we are to continue together, you must hear the truth about what brought me to New Orleans."

"It won't make any difference," he declared, stubborn to the core.

"Don't be so hasty, my darling." Maura's eyes wandered over the magnificent house before returning to Daniel. "I murdered my husband."

Daniel's mind reeled, but he said nothing as she recounted the horrible years leading up to the final night with Ronan. By the time she finished, Maura had grown magnolia pale.

"I still don't know if I intended to kill him or only wanted to stop the pain, but it scarcely matters. Either way a man is dead by my hand, but it was not my only crime. People always assume it's the boy who seduces the girl, but that wasn't the case with Ronan. It was one of those youthful times when one loses control of one's senses and nothing matters but the immediacy of the moment. It was overwhelming." She sighed wearily. "And it was all my doing."

"I know that feeling, Maura. It's why we're here, on this bench, discussing a future together."

She only half-heard. "With that one careless act, I betrayed myself and Ronan too. I had his baby, my daughter Sloane, and saddled Ronan with a life he was ill-equipped to handle, and in the end, I destroyed him. I betrayed my grandmother too. She taught me to play the piano and write songs and filled my head with magic. I'm forever grateful that she never knew how far I've fallen."

Daniel gently took her hand. "Where is Sloane now?"

"With my cousin in Pascagoula."

"We'll drive up and get her as soon as I find the right house."

"What?!"

"If you won't marry me or live in this house, we'll go elsewhere. For appearances sake, we'll tell your daughter we're married."

"What?!" Maura said again.

"Did I not speak plainly enough?"

"Yes, but—"

"No buts. I love you and my decision is final."

Daniel spoke with such authority and conviction that the last of Maura's reluctance evaporated and she burst into laughter. "You're the craziest man I ever met, Daniel Stafford. Alright, then. I'll live in sin with you." She hugged him tight. "And, yes, yes! I love you too!"

PART SIX

"You can make prostitution illegal,
but you can't make it unpopular."
-New Orleans Mayor Martin Berhman, 1917

32

Two weeks later, Maura's heart raced when Daniel parked the Hupmobile on leafy Baptiste Street. Behind a wrought iron fence she spied a handsome two-story, raised cottage with generous galleries on both floors. A red, orange and yellow stained-glass fanlight window crowned the front door.

"Welcome home," he said.

Maura's grabbed his hand. "It's perfect, Daniel! Absolutely perfect!"

"But you haven't seen inside."

"It doesn't matter. I feel it in my heart." She gave him a quick peck on the cheek. "And I adore that upstairs gallery."

Enthusiasm swelled when Maura entered the empty house, footsteps echoing as she explored every room, upstairs and down, and the kitchen in the rear. She went outside and marveled at the back yard, generously shaded by a great live oak.

"That big tree seems to hug the house, as though it wants to protect it. Sloane will love playing out here. Peter says she's become quite the tomboy."

"I was thinking of you both when I looked at houses," Daniel said, pleased. "This one spoke to me too, and if you're agreeable, I'll buy it and you can move in as soon as it's furnished."

"Wonderful!"

"I'll take you to Maison Blanche tomorrow to look at furniture."

"You're much too generous, darling." She gave him a quick hug. "Will you help me choose the furnishings? It's your home too, after all."

"I'm afraid you must do it alone. I've been so busy looking at houses that I've been negligent at work. I have urgent business that can't be further delayed."

"I understand. There's no real rush, you know. Madam Charlotte said I can stay as long as I keep out of sight." She clucked at the notion "What a peculiar world I live in."

"Not for long." Daniel took her arm and ushered her back to the car. "Not for long."

Maura's first purchase at Maison Blanche was a brass bed. Noting her elegant afternoon dress, the salesman tried to interest her in an extravagant mahogany tester with a carved headboard teeming with putti. She enjoyed shocking him by saying it was better suited for Mahogany Hall. By late November, the cottage on Baptiste Street was complete, draperies hung, carpets down and furniture in place. Daniel offered to buy a new piano, but Maura insisted on having her grandmother's piano shipped from Oriole where the Gunthers had kept it in their garage. When it was safely ensconced in the parlor, he surprised her with a mahogany and brass Canterbury for housing her sheet music. To ensure she had time for composing, he engaged a housekeeper named Lurleen, a no-nonsense black woman who doubled as a cook. A widow with grown children, Lurleen was content to live in the small servant's quarters and took an immediate liking to Maura. Happily, the feeling was mutual.

Daniel adored indulging Maura, but he was less than enthusiastic when she said she wanted Hattie to be their first guest. "I'd hoped that when you moved out of Storyville you'd leave those people behind."

"All except Hattie, darling. She's my closest friend and who could object to a friend making a social call?"

Daniel acquiesced as he often did. "You're right. And it would be hypocritical of me to object after claiming I don't care what people think."

Maura beamed. "Good. You'll adore Hattie. She's pretty and funny, and although I love you dearly, quite frankly I could do with some female companionship." She chuckled. "Lurleen is a treasure, but she and I can hardly gossip about the latest fashions."

"No, I suppose not."

"Then I'll ring Hattie and tell her to come over this afternoon."

Maura hadn't realized how much she'd missed her old friend until they embraced. She thought Hattie delectable in a modest afternoon ensemble of sky-blue silk and matching hat.

"Look at you!" Maura cried. "Dressed like an uptown lady."

"You too. That dark green sets off your hair and skin, but you could sure use some color."

"No, no. My romance with the rouge pot is over."

"Well, you know me. I've always believed it pays to advertise." She shrugged. "Not that I figured on finding a john on the streetcar."

Maura laughed, but was glad Daniel was out of earshot. "You're such a breath of fresh air. Now come along and see the house."

Hattie gushed approval as she trailed Maura, touching everything from tablecloths to lamp shades. "It's all so beautiful. You have such fine taste!"

"All I did was tell the salesman at Maison Blanche that I wanted the latest things but nothing gilded and absolutely no fringe. Charlotte's apartment always gave me the heebie-jeebies."

"Poor Charlotte."

"What do you mean?"

"I haven't seen her in weeks. George has been making more trips to Chinatown, and you know what that means."

Sadly, "Yes, I do."

"Omar's more in charge than ever. Sugar Boy's back. Seems he went somewhere and got dried out, but Nellie thinks it's only a matter of time before he dives back into the Raleigh Rye. Everyone misses you, including that nasty drunk who pestered you right before you left."

Maura had a chill. "Lewis Hatcher?"

"I don't remember his name, but he came back a few times, even after George told him you'd moved out."

"Is he still coming around?"

"No. George finally had enough and gave the guy the heave-ho. You know how he hates noisy drunks."

"Yes, I do." Relieved that her nemesis was vanquished, Maura forgot her foreboding and took Hattie's arm. "We'll sit in the parlor. You take that chair. It's the most comfortable. I'll fetch tea and some of Lurleen's pralines."

"No pralines for this fat lady," Hattie said.

"You're hardly fat, my dear. In fact, I think you could put on a few pounds."

"Omar thinks otherwise. He told me last week, in front of everybody I might add, that my rear end could service two. Imagine!"

"The man has never been celebrated for his tact."

"That's the Lord's truth."

For the next half hour, Maura heard enough news to fill an issue of The Mascot, a muckraking weekly tabloid specializing in the lurid goings-on in Storyville.

"There's been some ugly poaching among the high-level madams," Hattie reported. "Queen Gertie pilfered not one but two of Annie Dechard's girls, and Gertie made a play for Chloe too. Chloe is such a pill I wish she'd taken the bait, but she's still around, bitchy as ever. And of course there's the usual brawls at Florence Reed's place, but Julia Dean's house is even worse. The Mascot said that if the fighting keeps up that Julia will have to move her establishment to the first recorder's court!" Hattie cackled. "It also printed Lulu White's juicy quote about the new Japanese house on Customhouse Street."

"Uh-oh. Speaking of tactless."

"Yes, indeed. Miss Lulu allowed as to how she had checked out the Japanese emporium first-hand and reported that they were a bunch of light-skinned coloreds decked out in kimonos and geisha wigs and wearing rice powder!" The two doubled over with laughter, making so much racket that Lurleen came from the kitchen to see what was the matter. Maura assured her they were fine and asked for more tea.

"She's not an eavesdropper, is she?" Hattie asked.

"Heavens, no. We were making enough noise to wake the dead. Now tell me some serious news."

"The Mascot continues claiming that the biggest property owners in Storyville are uptown businessmen and the Catholic diocese and makes the usual accusations of police and political corruption. An undercover reporter watched Josephine Arlington's maid leave a mail sack on the doorstep in the wee hours and saw it picked up by a policeman. He wrote that the same thing happened at several Basin Street houses."

"The only news there is that they used the front door instead of the back. I remember going out Charlotte's back door and getting a skinned knee when I tripped over a bag of payoff money. I always wondered why it hadn't been stolen."

"Because big, bad George kept an eye on it, no doubt."

"I'm sure you're right."

"There was one item that has everyone yammering, and I admit I've been a little worried myself."

"Oh?"

"There's talk that Storyville's gonna be shut down by somebody real high up."

"Like who? The governor?"

"I don't know, but it's all anyone's talking about. I swear Storyville would dry up and blow away if it wasn't fed a daily dose of juicy gossip."

"Then why are you worried?"

"Zozo, that's why. She's been forecasting doom and gloom ever since you flew the coop. It sure wouldn't be the first time she messed with the future."

"You mean the hurricane?"

"That, too, but I was thinking about Bucktown Billy."

Maura refreshed her tea. "That must've been before my time."

"Bucktown Billy was one of the nastiest thugs in Storyville. Nobody knows how many men he knifed, but things caught up with him when he killed his own brother. There were a slew of eye witnesses, but when time came for their testimony, none of them talked. Or should I say none of them could talk."

"What do you mean?"

"Zozo was in cahoots with another voodoo queen named Echo Papaloos. The two of them went over to Bucktown Billy's shack and took the sheets off his bed and hung them in front of a mirror. That was supposed to confuse the judge. Then they bought beef tongues and stuck needles through them to tongue-tie the witnesses. Zozo swore Bucktown was gonna walk free the day after he was arrested and way before she and Echo Papaloos did anything and sure enough he did. I swear, Zozo knows some scary stuff!" Hattie sipped her tea, eyes twinkling as she remembered something. "My personal news is more important than any of that foolishness."

"Oh?"

"Remember Charlotte's strict policy about no pets?"

"I remember when Fancy got caught with that stray kitten and had to get rid of it."

"Well, I guess the lady's mellowing in her old age because a week ago Omar announced that we could have any kind of animal we wanted. And guess what?"

"Uh-oh. What did you get?"

"An ocelot! I named her Cleo. Short for Cleopatra."

Maura looked dubious. "That's a wild animal, isn't it?"

"Yes, but they can be tamed if you get them when they're little."

"Where in the world did you get her?"

"Where else but Zozo?" Hattie clapped her hands. "I can't wait for you to see her. She's still a kitten but is growing like Topsy." She looked toward the door when she heard a knock. "You expecting more company?"

"Not at all. I'll be right back." Maura opened the door to an unfamiliar face. "Yes?"

"Miss O'Rourke?"

"Yes?"

The man doffed his bowler. "I'm John Stafford."

"Oh!" Maura scarcely knew how to react. Daniel had told her precious little about his brother, but made it clear that they were estranged.

"Forgive me for dropping by unannounced. I hope I haven't come at an inconvenient time."

"Not at all," Maura managed. "Please come in. I have another visitor but—"

Hattie bustled into the vestibule. "I really must be leaving, my dear."

"So soon?"

"I'm afraid so. Thank you for the tea."

"But—" Before Maura could manage introductions, Hattie patted her arm and bustled out the door. Puzzled by her friend's abrupt departure, she turned to John. "Will you join me in the parlor?"

"By all means." John took inventory as he talked. "Your little house is lovely, Miss O'Rourke. I've been most anxious to see it for myself, and meet you too of course, but Daniel has not been very, shall we say, forthcoming about your relationship."

"Oh?"

"May I ask how you met?"

His tone warned Maura that she was being baited. "Through a mutual acquaintance."

"How charming." He looked smug. "We have a number of mutual acquaintances, my brother and I. Perhaps it's someone I know."

"I shouldn't think so?"

"Really? Why not?"

"I suggest you ask Daniel."

"But since Daniel is not here—"

Maura bristled. "Tell me, Mr. Stafford. Are you here to become acquainted or to conduct an interrogation?"

"A bit of both I suppose." He waved a hand in front of his face. "Does your friend always wear so much perfume?"

"I'm sure I don't know. Although," she added, pointedly touching a handkerchief to her nose, "I might make a similar query about the heavy odor of whiskey."

John sat and scowled. "I was merely making an observation."

"An unwelcome one, sir. As unwelcome as you seating yourself while a lady is still standing."

"A lady?" he scoffed. "Let's dispense with the pretense, shall we? You're in no position to set a moral compass."

Maura had reached for the bell pull to summon Lurleen for more tea, but withdrew her hand upon hearing his affront. So there it is, she thought.

"Then you've come here merely to insult me, eh?"

"Not altogether, although I fear some criticism is unavoidable."

"I'm not partial to wordplay, sir. Kindly explain your visit or get out."

"Very well." John rose unsteadily to face her. "I know all about you and your foul little love nest. I was appalled from the moment Daniel told me about you and I prayed that you were an infatuation that would fade and be forgotten. I was very disappointed when that didn't happen, and I decided he had lost his mind when he said he wanted to marry you. I didn't bother reminding him of his social standing because he rejected it years ago, but I will not tolerate our family name being dragged through the mud." John glared with utter disdain. "I don't know how in the hell you convinced him to marry you, but I assure you I will do everything in my power to see that that never happens. Do not dare to doubt the veracity of my warning."

Maura was coolness personified. "As you can see, I am absolutely atremble with fear."

"What brass!"

"Tell me, Mr. Stafford. When did you last speak with Daniel?"

"Some weeks ago, when he told me he intended to propose marriage."

Maura couldn't resist a smirk. "Then let me put your mind at ease. I never wanted to marry your brother and, in fact, refused his proposal without hesitation." She relished John's bewilderment. "I know exactly what and where my place is and am perfectly content to live a quiet life as Daniel's mistress. In case you've forgotten, such liaisons are time-honored here in New Orleans, especially your precious Garden District." She returned his derisive look in equal measure. "You and I have nothing further to discuss, Mr. Stafford, and since you've chosen to dispense with good manners, I will not see you out. Your hat is in the hall, and I suggest you use it as soon as possible. Unless, of course, you're too drunk to find your way."

Maura swept from the room.

33

Hearts were full and hopes were high as the train approached Pascagoula.

"I can't remember when I've been so excited," Maura confessed. "I've prayed for this moment since that awful day I had to leave my little girl and go to New Orleans. These have been the longest five years of my life."

"I'm so happy to be a part of this day." Daniel leaned close. "Bringing Sloane home will make our little family complete."

"It will indeed." Maura smiled when she heard the conductor's announcement.

"Pascagoula in five minutes, ladies and gentlemen. Pascagoula. Five minutes!"

"I think I'm going to jump out of my skin!"

"I'm sure Sloane is just as excited, my dear."

"I do hope so."

Daniel stepped into the aisle to retrieve their belonging from the luggage rack and made room for Maura to join him. The train blasted a final deafening whistle and halted with a rumble of couplings and an expulsion of steam. The next thing Maura knew she was holding Sloane in her arms.

"My darling girl!" she cried. "My darling, baby girl!"

"Mama!" Sloane wailed. "Oh, Mama!"

Daniel stood to the side, quietly enjoying the moment. He sought a resemblance between mother and daughter, but Sloane bore no trace of her Maura's green eyes and red hair. At ten, she was a budding beauty, olive skinned with dark hair and thickly lashed blue eyes. No doubt, Daniel thought, she reflected her father's black Irish lineage with its infusion of Spanish blood.

"Please forgive me everyone." Maura pulled away from Sloane long enough to introduce Daniel. Peter and Dora Byrne and their daughter Nancy greeted him warmly, but Sloane cast a wary eye.

"You're very tall, Mr. Stafford."

Daniel knelt to her level. "Is this better?"

"Yes, thank you. Mama wrote me a letter about you." She cocked her head. "Are you going to be my father?"

"Sloane!" Maura cried. "Where are your manners?"

Daniel smiled. "It's alright, Maura. I'm flattered." Although she was not his child, he experienced a powerful parental rush. "Would you like that, Sloane?"

"I don't know. Maybe if you give me a present."

Maura was exasperated. "For heaven's sake, child! When did you become such a little negotiator."

Sloane feigned confusion. "I don't know what that means, Mama."

"Oh, yes, you do!" Dora declared.

The adults laughed as the ice was broken and everyone piled into Peter's Model T for the short drive home. When they arrived at the Byrne home, the Gunthers' car was waiting in the driveway. Maura had written a letter to Frieda pleading for her and Karl to meet her in Pascagoula for a long-overdue reunion. More embraces were exchanged and introductions made before everyone crowded into the little shotgun cottage where the women gathered in the kitchen to put dinner together. Maura begged a private word with Frieda, and the two stepped into the backyard.

"Did you get my letter about Lewis Hatcher?"

"Yes," Frieda replied edgily. "Karl and I were horrified to hear that he found you. He's crazy, Maura. Even crazier than Ronan. In fact, that's how Karl describes him. Another Ronan."

George's dire warning came rushing back. "What on earth happened to him?"

"Karl says things turned bad when Lewis lost his job at the factory. You remember Oriole. It's as poor as ever, and Lewis couldn't find work anywhere. Finally he stopped looking and, like Ronan, spent his time in the taverns. Karl said he picked fights every night and was rumored to have killed another drunk." She groaned. "How in the world did he find you?"

Maura thought fast. As with Peter and Dora, she had glossed over the facts of her life in New Orleans, reporting only that she was singing in a cabaret. Daniel was explained as her fiancée.

"For such a big city, New Orleans can be a very small town. I'm sure he saw my name and photo on a bill somewhere because he first approached me at the place where I work. He asked for money right away." She lowered her voice to a whisper. "Money to keep quiet about Ronan."

"Dear Lord! What did you do?"

"I told him to come back the next day, but I quit my job and moved uptown so he couldn't find me."

"What if he tracks you down when you go back to work?"

"Thanks to Daniel, I won't be working anymore," Maura replied, embellishing her lie. "I'll devote my time to being a wife and mother, and I'm sure everything will be fine."

"I pray so. You've finally found happiness and I can't think of anyone more deserving." Frieda hugged her close. "And you look wonderful in that beautiful traveling outfit. New Orleans obviously agrees with you."

"I have you and Karl to thank for it, my dear. Were it not for you two, I shudder to think what might have happened to me and my precious child."

"So do I," Frieda confessed. "So do I."

34

1917

Oblivious to the night chill, Sloane was giddy with anticipation. Like thousands of other children, and not a few adults, she stared down the broad, tree-lined boulevard of St. Charles Avenue, waiting anxiously for the telltale glimmer of firelight. She tried to lean further over the curb, but Daniel's hands were firmly on her shoulders lest she fall victim to the restless, heaving crowd. Finally, there it was.

"Mama, look! I can see them! They're coming!"

Excitement mushroomed when blurred flames sharpened into flambeaux, the smoking calcium wicks borne by robed and hooded black men. Their wild gyrations spun bright arcs in the darkness as they lit a path for the Krewe of Proteus, one of the most beloved Mardi Gras parades.

"Hold on to her, Daniel" Maura urged. "You know how keyed-up she gets."

"No one knows better," he grinned.

In the four months since Sloane had come to New Orleans, Daniel and Sloane had become all but inseparable, and she had taken to calling him Papa. Maura was delighted if a bit jealous, joking that her daughter spent more time with him than with her. She enjoyed their constant escapades, but held her breath when Daniel climbed the monstrous oak tree beside the house to rescue Sloane who had gone after a neighbor's cat without a care for her own safety. When the two descended, cat in tow, Maura had tried to berate them but succumbed to tears of relief. That fright was only one instance of their mutual, ongoing mischief.

"She's fine," Daniel said. "Aren't you, pumpkin?"

"I see the horses!" Sloane cried. "Look there, Papa!"

The lead float slowly emerged through the smoke, borne atop a cypress caisson drawn by a mule team with plumed headdresses and ghostly white caparisons. The crowd roared approval for the sea god Proteus, trident in hand, in a gilded chariot drawn by dolphins. The flambeaux bathed him in flickering light, and, as the caisson's wooden wheels rumbled past, the float shimmered with unearthly magic. Behind Proteus, a dozen robed maskers waved to the adoring massess. Sloane was still agog when the second float appeared. She gawked at a massive Pandora's Box of black marble, lid raised to release red and blue cardboard flames, and, a block behind it, came the silvery Temple of Astarte and the Tower of Babel. By the time the King of Proteus appeared on the final float, high atop his bejeweled throne, Sloane was delirious with carnival fever.

"I remember my first Mardi Gras parade," Maura told Daniel when they headed home. Sloane was between them, lost and silent in a child's private world of wonder. "I thought it was the most beautiful thing I'd ever seen. I never imagined artists could do so much with chicken wire and papier mâché."

"I recall mine too. I was much younger than Sloane and was scared silly by an enormous red devil on a mountain of coal. When he emerged from all that smoke, I must've jumped ten feet. I was happy and terrified at the same time, the way boys are."

"Girls too," Maura laughed.

Daniel turned serious. "It's good that Sloane saw the parade. Word at the Exchange is that carnival will be canceled next year if America enters the war."

"Do you believe we will?"

Daniel nodded grimly. "I've expected it since the Germans sank the Lusitania two years ago, and don't know how we can keep ignoring the carnage. That battle in Verdun lasted almost a year and killed a third of a million men. That number is incomprehensible, and so are the German atrocities in Belgium." He tempered his words when Maura's signaled that Sloane was listening. "After that German U-boat sank the Housatonic off Galveston last month, I don't see how President Wilson can avoid declaring war. It's grown too close for comfort."

"Please tell me you won't have to fight!"

"At age thirty there are far more robust soldiers to choose from, but if the war continues—"

"I can't think about it," Maura insisted. "All I cano think about is some hot chocolate when we get home."

"Me too!" Sloane piped up.

"And then straight to bed, young lady. It's way past your bedtime."

As he swung open the gate to the house, Daniel saw something under the glow of the porch gaslights. "Who's there?"

"It's me, Mr. Stafford. Tony Jackson." His baritone laughter rang through the night. "I reckon I'm hard to see."

"Especially in that black suit." Maura laughed too and introduced Sloane. "This is my daughter, Tony."

"What a pretty little thing she is." Sloane thanked him and dropped a quick curtsey. He smiled and bowed back. "And such fine manners!"

"You must be freezing out here," Maura said. "How about some hot chocolate?"

Daniel intervened. "I'm sure we'd like something stronger to warm us up, eh, Tony?"

"Yes, sir!"

While Maura tended to Sloane, Daniel lit a fire and poured bourbons for himself and Tony. It was a scenario he could never have envisioned prior to entering Maura's world, but her respect and genuine affection for the colored musician made him rethink his racial priorities. He took perverse pleasure in imagining how horrified Garden District society would be, particularly his brother, if they knew he was entertaining a Negro in his parlor - and Storyville's most celebrated professor at that! He smiled as he handed Tony the glass.

"Cheers."

"Cheers."   .

They made small talk until Maura reappeared after giving Sloane hot chocolate and tucking her into bed. "It's wonderful to see you, Tony. I apologize for being a stranger all these months."

"No need to apologize. Not many folks wanna come back to Storyville once they get out, and that's the God's truth."

"I suppose, but I do miss some of you folks."

"We miss you too, which brings me to why I'm here. I'm leaving for Chicago next week, Miss Maura, and I wanted to say good-bye."

She was surprised. "I thought you loved New Orleans."

"You're right about that, but love is a two-way street, and lately this old town ain't been loving me back."

"What do you mean?" Daniel asked.

"I mean that I'm mighty tired of being beat on and laughed at and got to thinking there's gotta be a better place for an epileptic sissy who's black as a swamp night. 'Scuse my language, Miss Maura." He took a deep swig of whiskey. "Chicago ain't no safe haven, but there's a neighborhood on the southside supposed to be easy on folks like me."

"I hope so, Tony, and shame on those causing you pain. You were always so generous and patient with me, and I'll never forget what you taught me about composing music."

"Your talent was already there," he insisted. "All I did was scare it up and give it a little push." He nodded at the piano in the corner. "Is that the old upright you told me about? The one your grandmama gave you?"

Maura enjoyed the memory of their shared confidences and the unlikely friendship that bloomed between them. Both were surprised at how much they had in common, from their passion for music to the fact that Tony, like Sloane, had a twin who died in childbirth.

"Indeed, it is. I had it brought down from Mississippi. Poor old thing was a wreck, but I had it repaired and tuned."

"You written any new songs?"

"Nothing new, but I finished a folk song my grandmother started over sixty years ago and like to think of it as a collaboration. The music was wonderful, but the lyrics were confusing, so I rearranged them to tell a story. I also added a last verse and changed the location from Galway to New Orleans." She moved to the piano. "Would you like to hear it?"

Tont grinned. "Need you ask?"

He and Daniel were enrapt as Maura began a cautionary tune about innocence forever lost. Served by her clarion soprano, the lyrics became increasingly personal as her message unfolded, its warning driven home in the concluding stanza.

"There's fool's gold o'er the doorway," she sang, "and sun that rises west. Spurn that place, ye weary, lest you find no rest." Her audience was silent while the tragic tale resonated.

"It's mighty sad," Tony said finally, "but it's catchy and it puts a shiny new spin on an old story. But I don't understand that business about a sun coming up in the west."

"It's a quirk of the neighborhood," Daniel explained. "We're tucked in a bend of the river so that the sun comes up over the West Bank."

"So the song's about this house?"

Maura nodded. "Storyville, too."

"Yeah. I can see how you mixed them together." Tony pursed his lips. "You planning to publish it?"

"Thinking about it."

"Tell her she should." Daniel said refilling Tony's glass. "She thinks it's too personal."

"The best songs always are, Mr. Daniel. They're like dreams, and this is one dream you shouldn't keep to yourself. Especially since the time is so ripe."

"What do you mean?"

"I mean that Storyville's fallen on hard times, and when it's gone folks are gonna forget about it. A lotta houses have shut down, and most of the girls have left town. Except on holidays, half the cribs are empty, and the madams have all cut their prices. Last time I played at Mahogany Hall, Miss Lulu only had four girls working for her, and the place was looking raggedy. Willie Piazza's house too. And poor Tyrella Brown had to close up shop 'cause she couldn't afford to fix the plumbing."

"What's behind all this?" Daniel asked.

Tony chuckled. "If you'll excuse me for being frank again, Madam Lulu says it's 'cause the college girls and debutantes are giving it away these days, and I reckon that's as good an explanation as any." He sipped again. "I ain't the only musician that's bailing.

Jelly Roll's already gone, and King Oliver and Manuel Manetta are right behind him. There's other stuff going on too."

"You mean Storyville being shut down?" Daniel asked.

"Yes, sir, I do. That very thing."

"I've been hearing that for years, but I think it's serious this time."

"Why do you say that?" Maura asked.

"According to the talk at the Exchange, it's the federal government who wants to close it, and if that's the case, nobody can stop them."

"All the more reason for me to jump ship." Tony drained his bourbon and waved away Daniel's offer of another. "I gotta get back downtown. Gonna take me a while with those carnival crowds."

"A moment please first," Maura said. "There's something important I'd like to ask."

"I'll go check on Sloane," Daniel said, ever the diplomat. He shook Tony's hand. "Good luck in Chicago, young man."

"Thank you, sir. I appreciate that." With Daniel gone, Tony gave Maura a curious look. "Well?"

"It's about Charlotte and Zozo. That day after the hurricane, after we got Charlotte out of Hop Alley, you said Zozo was the reason Charlotte was an addict and that—"

"I remember what I said, Miss Maura, and I reckon the truth don't matter now that you're gone from Storyville and I'm leaving town. But why are you asking?"

"Because Charlotte was always kind to me and I worry about her."

"Alright, then. But you can't tell nobody."

"You have my word."

Tony took a deep breath. "To begin with, Zozo and Charlotte are half-sisters."

"What?!"

"Yeah. I grew up across the street from them, and they was always fighting. Charlotte was a lot lighter 'cause they had different daddies. Fact is, Zozo used to call her a white nigger. Anyway, Zozo took up with a white man and was living pretty good up on Rampart Street. Charlotte stole him away and got him to set her up in Storyville. You know what they say about scorned women. Zozo vowed revenge, and that's when she took up the voodoo. She learned all them spells and curses so she could ruin her sister. She picked goofer dust 'cause it can make a person die a long, drawn-out death."

"The opium," Maura breathed.

"Yes, ma'am, and it's finally working. Unless I miss my guess, Madam Charlotte ain't gonna last out the year."

Maura thought of Storyville's racial edicts. "If Charlotte's colored, how can she run a house with white women?"

"Tom Anderson fixed it so the powers that be never knew she was colored and he paid Zozo to keep her mouth shut. He was the big money behind the Windsor and wanted only white girls because Lulu White had cornered the market on octoroons. Charlotte was refined, not vulgar and flashy like Lulu, and with Omar running things, they landed the richest johns."

"What happened to Charlotte's boyfriend, the one she stole from Zozo?"

"That's Mr. Omar. Now you know why he takes such good care of Charlotte. They ain't lovers no more, but he still cares about her."

Maura was reeling. "But I've seen Omar and Zozo together, and they're always civil."

"Zozo blames Charlotte for everything, so she forgave Omar years ago. He financed her brick dust business, which is another reason she don't say nothin'."

"I thought Tom Anderson was her backer."

"So does everybody else. That's how Zozo wanted it. You know we colored folks gotta have our secrets, Miss Maura. It's how we get through life, plain and simple."

"It's all so unbelievable. I'd never have guessed in a million years."

"Remember I told you once most everything in Storyville was smoke and mirrors."

"Zozo said that too. Said it was an illusion, like Starla said all whores are actresses."

"They're both right. And it's sure good that you and me got out before they ring down the curtain that last time."

"Yes, it is." Maura sighed with a touch of nostalgia and opened the front door. "It is indeed."

Tony turned up his collar before stepping into the cold. "It's been a real pleasure knowing you, Miss Maura. Good luck in selling that song."

"Good luck to you, too. I'll never forget you and will always cherish my signed copy of Pretty Baby. Thank you, Tony." To his surprise and her satisfaction, she gave him a heartfelt hug. "Good-bye, professor, and Godspeed."

35

Daniel's suspicions about Storyville were well-founded. In August, 1917, U. S. Secretary of War, Newton D. Baker banned open prostitution within five miles of all American army bases. Secretary of the Navy Josephus Daniels followed suit regarding naval installations, and in September, because Storyville was close by a naval base, a source of much business, Mayor Martin Behrman was instructed to comply. When he resisted, Secretary Daniels warned, "You will close the red-light district or the armed forces will." Hand forced, Behrman ordered the place shut down by midnight, November 12. There was no grand exodus as many expected. The madams and their girls vacated at their leisure, opting for greener pastures in other cities or operating elsewhere in town as they had before Storyville. Ever pragmatic, Mayor Behrman said, "You can make prostitution illegal but you can't make it unpopular."

A year had passed since Maura left Storyville. She'd never had any desire to return, but news of its imminent closure changed her mind. One morning while Daniel was dressing for work, she announced that she was making a final visit.

"Whatever for?"

"Morbid curiosity, I suppose. I also think it might help with those awful dreams about being back at the Windsor. Maybe if I literally see for myself that Storyville is disappearing, my nightmares will disappear, too."

"Like returning to the scene of the crime."

"That's one way to put it." Maura adjusted his tie. "I may also drop by Maison Blanche on the way home and buy you some new ties. These patterns are woefully out of style."

"I appreciate your thoughtfulness, but I'm not sure I want you going back downtown."

"I'll be fine, and besides I want to check on Hattie. She hasn't visited for a couple of weeks, and when I called the Windsor this morning, the telephone had been disconnected. I know Charlotte's been ill and am wondering if Omar has closed up shop."

"Please promise you'll be careful."

"I promise, darling." Maura stood on tiptoes for a quick kiss. "Thanks for understanding."

A sense of doom was near tangible as Maura's taxi turned off Canal Street onto Basin Street. The November sun threw harsh, unforgiving light on the once-grand row of bordellos. With faded awnings, shuttered and broken windows and no signs of life, they looked naked and lifeless. How different, Maura mused, from the lively, colorful spectacle greeting her when she got off the train with Starla six years ago. She was different too, changed in ways she could never have imagined.

"I'll get out there," she told the cabbie. "At the corner of Iberville."

"You sure, lady?" The man eyed his fashionably dressed fare. "You know what this place is, don't you?"

"Yes, I do, sir, and I appreciate your concern."

As Maura got out and began the familiar four-block walk to Villere Street, she witnessed more unsettling change. Anderson's saloon was dark, and the raucous cries of vendors and crib girls and the sweet sounds of jazz were gone too, replaced by a hollow stillness. Her shoes echoed on the wooden banquettes, and she saw no one until she approached Liberty Street. Coming out of Edna Clarke's place was a lone bawd hauling her few possessions in a wheelbarrow. She appeared in a stupor, oblivious to Maura as she passed. Things were also sad at the Windsor, doubly so because Omar was had always been meticulous about maintenance. It was shuttered on all three floors, a cypress tomb closed to the world. Two of the colonettes on the top floor were askew, and the fanlight bearing the gold coronet and initial W was cracked. Maura was further saddened when she ventured inside. A glance in the Gold Parlor revealed furniture draped in sheets and the gasolier swathed in cheesecloth. The floors were in bad need of sweeping, and silverfish, voracious as ever, darted singly and in tiny regiments.

Maura continued through the empty, dusty bar and up the stairs, calling as she went. "Hello! Is anybody here? Hello!!" She had no response until she reached the third floor where she found Hattie and Fancy playing bourré. Cards went flying as both rushed to embrace her.

"I thought I heard someone," Hattie said.

"It's so good to see you!" Fancy cried. She ogled Maura's stylish blue suit with velvet lapels and matching hat. "Goodness, but don't you look like a grand lady!"

"Thank you, honey." Maura hid her shock at finding the girls pale and slovenly. She glanced around the room and tried to make light of the mess. "Place could use a little dusting." Neither girl laughed. "I tried to call this morning, but the telephone's been turned off."

"Omar called it quits day before yesterday," Fancy said. "We didn't have no more business."

"And Madam Charlotte's not gonna last out the week," Hattie added. "Truth be told, I'm surprised the poor thing's hung on this long."

"I'm sorry to hear that. She was always good to me."

"She was good to all of us," Hattie said. "Fair too."

"It's like the end of the world," Fancy whispered.

Maura thought of Tony's story about Charlotte and Omar and wondered if there was still love left between them. "How's Omar?"

"Keeping vigil and making funeral arrangements. Charlotte was very specific about how she's going to glory."

"She was specific about everything," Maura said. "Have you two found work elsewhere?"

"I'm gonna with Hilma Burt," Fancy replied, "but nobody knows where she's reopening."

"What about you, Hattie?"

"Lizette Abadie's been after me. She's opened a place on Annunciation Street, not too far from you in fact, but I don't know. Rumor has it that she cheats her girls." Maura started to sit, but hesitated upon seeing the filthy cushions. Hattie, who missed nothing, stood and took her arm. "Let's go out on the gallery and get some fresh air."

"Y'all go ahead," Fancy said. "I gotta start packing."

Hattie opened the shutters and grabbed a rag to wipe off chairs so she and Maura could sit. "The place is like a tomb, isn't it?"

"It breaks my heart." Maura looked at the city spread out below. "My goodness!"

"What're you thinking about?"

"The day I arrived when Nellie brought me up here. Where is she?"

"Got a gig up in Memphis. Everybody's sorta scattered to the four winds."

"How much longer will you stay?"

"Until Charlotte's funeral, I suspect. Like Fancy said, business has dried up." She leaned close to the railing and peered down onto the street. "My, oh, my! Would you look at that!"

A flashily dressed octoroon carrying a caged canary strutted down Iberville like the Queen of Sheba. Behind her, towing a two-wheeled cart piled high with her mistress's belongings, was her black maid.

"Who is that?"

"The last of Lulu White's girls, I think. Hmmm. Wonder why she's heading for back-o'-town. Nothing over there but shanties and criminals." Hattie scratched her head. "That don't make sense."

"No, but I'll tell you what does make sense. You're coming to stay with Daniel and me until you find work."

Hattie demurred. "You're sweet, Maura, but I can't do that."

"Why not?"

"Let's be honest. Daniel's polite enough, but I know he doesn't approve of me."

"It's not you, darling. It's what you represent. He finally realized that, and said he was glad you were my friend."

"Oh, I don't know."

"Please."

"What about Cleo and Caesar?"

"Caesar?"

"My cockatoo. I inherited him from Winifred when she moved to Biloxi, so now I have a big pink bird to go with my big striped cat."

"Sloane loves animals. She loves you too. She's forever talking about your pretty clothes and how she wants to be like you when she grows up."

"Heaven forbid!" Both laughed, but it was an uneasy sound. "Thanks, Maura, but I'd better not. I'm bound to embarrass you."

"Surely by now you know I don't care about such things. Neither does Daniel."

"That's nice, but—"

"What we do care about are friends in need."

Hattie pulled a face. "You could always get around me, Maura O'Rourke, but I promise I won't stay long."

"Then it's all settled." Hattie chuckled. "What's so funny?"

"I was thinking about that gal walking away with the canary. Wait'll folks get a load of me strutting out of here with my menagerie!"

36

With Hattie in residence, the house on Baptiste Street quickly became an object of curiosity to its neighbors. The woman next door, whose windows overlooked Maura's side yard, screamed and closed her shutters when she saw Sloane and Cleo frolicking on the lawn. Cleo was now full-sized, standing twenty inches at the shoulder and weighing twenty-two pounds. With her enormous paws and innate stealth, she was formidable and frightening, and tormented the neighborhood dogs by perching in the live oak tree and slowly twitching her long tail. Sloane, whose tomboy phase remained in high gear, was often beside her. When she wasn't romping with Cleo, Sloane flounced around with Caesar perched on her shoulder and spent hours learning to play bourré from Hattie. Daniel and Maura were both pleased with the arrangement, and discouraged Hattie from going to work for Lizette Abadie whose house three blocks away was regularly raided by the police.

"I have a much better idea," Maura announced one morning after Sloane had left for school. "Remember Starla Callahan?"

"Sure," Hattie said. "She hooked you up with Tom Anderson."

"We're going to her place for tea this morning. She may have a job for you."

"I thought she quit the business."

"Not that kind of business, goose. She runs a boarding house on North Rampart and recently bought a second place across the street. When she said she needed someone to run it, I told her you might be interested. She knows all about you and said to bring you over."

"That's nice, Maura, but I don't know anything about boarding houses. I never even been in one."

"Starla will explain everything. Now, fetch your hat and let's be off."

A few blocks below Chinatown, North Rampart Street was lined on both sides with raised cottages covered with wood-lap siding or stucco. Dating to antebellum days, they were mostly built by wealthy white men for their free mistresses of color in a time-honored system called plaçage. When the arrangement ended, usually when the man married or died, the woman inherited the house. While some resumed their work as courtesans, most turned their homes into boarding houses. Starla owned one of the largest, a two-story affair with a roof pierced by chimneys at opposite ends. A discreet sign alongside the front door announced Chez Callahan.

It was only a month since Maura and Starla had seen one another but they fell into each other's arms like long lost sisters. After introductions, Starla ushered her visitors into a parlor reminding Hattie of a spinster aunt's house. The smell of fried oysters and pipe smoke lingered, and a calico cat lazed in one corner. Abundant antimacassars made it fussily inviting.

Starla gave Hattie a frank appraisal. "You may be too pretty, dearie. I only rent to men, and I don't want 'em getting ideas. You either, for that matter. I won't have a girl turning tricks behind my back or running off with some sweet talker making wild promises. Do I make myself clear?"

"Yes, ma'am." Hattie winked. "But that might depend on the promises."

Starla looked at Maura. "She's got nerve, like you."

"Afraid so. Stop clowning, Hattie."

"I'm sorry, Starla. I make jokes when I get nervous. What would be my duties?"

"Actually it's a lot like running a brothel, except I provide room and board instead of girls and booze. Guests get two hot meals

236

daily and fresh linens and towels once a week. They can use this room for visitors, but absolutely no women and no alcohol. Your duties include collecting the rent, a little bookkeeping, overseeing a cook and cleaning woman, and getting a repairman when something breaks. You come to me for any other problems. The place is being remodeled and should be finished in a week or two. You'll live in a room in the back and report to me daily until I say otherwise."

"That's it?"

"It's not as simple as it sounds. Every boarder is different. Some men keep to themselves. You'll only see them at meals. Some will talk your arm off and others will complain about every little thing."

"You're right. It sounds like a cathouse."

Easygoing and quick to laugh, Starla and Hattie quickly found common ground, but Starla left no doubt that she was in charge. "We both know whores are lazy by nature. I'm sure as hell not in that camp, and you better not be either. I have a reputation to maintain, and if you tarnish it, you're finished."

"Fair enough."

"Then the job is yours."

"You mean that?"

"As Maura knows, I operate on instinct and I think you'll be fine."

Hattie was thrilled. "Thank you!"

"Dear Starla," Maura said. "You're forever doing favors for me. You're a saint."

Starla roared with laughter, and for the first time Maura heard Africa in her deep voice. "Honey child, I've been called a lotta things in my day, but saint ain't one of 'em!"

Maura and Hattie shared unspoken relief that she wasn't going back to the brothels. They decided to celebrate by shopping at Krauss's department store, dining on trout amandine at Galatoire's, and browsing the specialty shops in the French Quarter. Maura indulged in a two-piece velvet suit in a daringly bold check and treated Hattie to a chambray house dress suitable for her new job. Their gay moods caused them to lose track of time until the cathedral bells struck four and sent them scurrying home. High spirits faded when they turned onto Baptiste Street as a police wagon pulled away from the house. Maura leapt from the cab before it came to a full stop and raced inside. The place was silent except for a soft whimpering in the parlor. Heart pounding, she followed the sound to find Daniel on the sofa with Sloane in his arms. Her little body trembled as she wept.

"Darling!" Maura cried, sitting beside her. "What is it? What's happened?"

"Oh, Mama!" Sloane rushed into Maura's arms and clung tight. "It's Cleo!"

"What about her?" Hattie asked from the hall.

Daniel went to her. "I'm so sorry to tell you, but someone shot her this afternoon."

"What?!"

"She was up in her tree when someone fired from behind the house."

"I'll bet that witch next door was behind it!" Hattie snapped. "She's always yelling at us to get rid of Cleo and...where's my poor kittycat?"

"In the side yard. I covered her with a sheet." Daniel turned to Maura as Hattie dropped her packages and rushed outside. "I hated telling her that."

"When did it happen?"

"Sometime this afternoon. I found out when I got home. Sloane was in the tree and saw the whole thing."

"My God! She could've been shot too!"

"That's why I made a police report. Lurleen heard the shot, which is how we know it came from Felicity Street. I still can't believe someone would do this in broad daylight."

"What did the police say?"

"That they were sorry but that they didn't have time to investigate animal murders with human beings killing each other every day."

"What a world," Maura sighed. Sloane muttered something, unintelligible with her face buried against her mother's throat. "What did you say, darling?"

"Can we have a funeral for Cleo?"

"Of course we can." She drew a handkerchief from her handbag and dabbed Sloane's tears. "We'll bury her by the tree, tomorrow after Daniel gets home from work."

"Will you dig a hole, Papa?"

"Of course, Pumpkin." He kissed her damp cheek and peeled off his jacket as he stood. "Right now. Before it gets dark."

He found Hattie outside and told her about tomorrow's funeral for Cleopatra. "Two in one day," she said.

"Two?"

"They're burying Charlotte Townsend tomorrow morning in St. Roch's Cemetery."

37

Charlotte's service in the chapel at Johnson's Funeral Home gathered the Who's Who of Storyville. Omar and Tom Anderson were on the front row alongside Lulu White, Josephine Arlington and Countess Willie Piazza, with the less stellar madams and their girls seated behind, along with other Storyville denizens whose lives had been touched by Charlotte. Bricktop's hennaed hair and Lulu's enormous wig bloomed like red poppies in a sea of black hats. When she saw Zozo on the back row, Maura wondered if she had recriminations about slowly killing her sister or had come to admire her lethal handiwork. Her gaunt face revealed nothing.

After eulogies, the mourners followed the coffin outside. Parked at the curb was an elaborately carved black hearse drawn by four caparisoned horses. Their black ostrich plumes fluttered in a light morning breeze. Waiting behind them was the Hot Hounds Brass Bass Band.

"What on earth?! Maura whispered.

"Your first jazz funeral?" Hattie asked.

"I've only heard stories."

"You ain't seen nothing yet," Starla said.

The crowd assembled behind the band while Charlotte's casket was slipped into the hearse. The moment the door clicked shut, the coachman slapped the reins, and the procession began the slow, short walk down North Claiborne Avenue to St. Roch's Cemetery. Despite their name, the Hot Hounds played a somber rendition of Just a Closer Walk with Thee, followed by Free as a Bird which everyone knew was Charlotte's favorite. Maura marveled at St. Roch's magnificent iron gates, orderly rows of tombs and a broad campo santo lined with grand mausoleums leading to a Gothic-style chapel dating to 1876.

"It looks like a little town with miniature buildings and streets."

"Which is why our cemeteries are called Cities of the Dead," Starla said.

The walls surrounding the cemetery were blasted white by the subtropical sun and pocked with Resurrection ferns. They contained vaults for single bodies, stacked one atop the other so that they resembled ovens, and were nicknamed as such. Bricktop, who feared death, often said she was "afraid of the ovens." Final words for Charlotte were said before her vault, and the amens that followed were drowned out as the Hot Hounds crashed into Didn't He Ramble. The cloud of gloom hovering overhead was shattered by revelry when mourners hugged and laughed and shed tears of joy. Parasols decorated for the occasion bloomed as everyone began dancing and waving handkerchiefs to signal heaven that someone was coming home.

"Old-timers say the music and dancing cuts the body loose," Starla explained. "It also proves that funerals don't have to be grim affairs with a lot of weeping and wailing."

"It's wonderful. I've never seen anything like it." Maura watched the procession march toward the gates. "Shall we go?"

"You go ahead. Whenever I'm here, I like to visit St. Roch's chapel."

"May I tag along?" Hattie asked.

"Of course. Maura?"

"Alright."

The temperature noticeably dropped as they entered the chapel. Starla led them to a small shrine presided over by a statue of Saint Roch and his faithful dog. Beyond was an even tinier room reeking of mold, dust and time. Flaking walls were all but obscured by a conglomeration of crutches, braces and plaster body parts. There were, Maura noticed, more hearts than anything else.

"What in the world is all this?"

"Tokens of appreciation from believers whose prayers were answered by St. Roch," Starla explained. "They're called miracles."

Hattie inspected a child's wooden leg brace and a plaster eye. She grimaced. "The place gives me the willies."

"It affects a lot of people that way, but I find it comforting." Starla sank onto on a creaky wooden bench. "I've spent many hours here, finding hope when I needed it most."

"Hope?" Maura echoed.

"Let's be honest, ladies. We all know a whore's life isn't the most blessed."

"No," Maura said almost reverently. "It's not."

Hattie went to the wall and inspected a withered baby shoe, rusty with dust. She gave it a tentative touch before joining Starla on the bench. "I think I understand what you said about this place being comforting. About all these things representing miracles, I mean."

Starla squeezed her hand. "I'm glad."

The two fell silent while Maura scanned the shrine in search of similar solace. Instead, she found melancholy and distress when she saw a tiny plaster baby's head that reminded her of Sloane's stillborn twin. It roused a dormant sadness that deepened as the teeming walls began to pulse and close in. She endured it as long as she could.

"I'll wait for you two outside."

"You alright?"

"I'm fine. I just need some fresh air."

"We won't be long."

Back outside, Maura heard the waning blare of the Hot Hounds as poor Charlotte's funeral procession dispersed far down the avenue. The November sun played hide-and-seek with cottony clouds as she wandered the empty campo santo, pausing to read names and dates on the imposing mausoleums. She was saddened by the tomb of an entire family felled by a yellow fever plague, including three children under five years old. A row of red ants at the base of the tomb reminded her of the morning when she and Hattie awaited the hurricane in the Windsor's courtyard. She and Tony had rescued poor Charlotte from the opium den the next morning. Another lifetime, Maura thought, as she found a seat by the chapel and settled in to wait for the others. Passing clouds cast chiaroscuro over the cemetery. She smiled at the otherworldly beauty before closing her eyes and drifting with the sound of a lone seagull mewing high overhead. Maura thought she might drowse, but she had never felt so wide awake. It was a beguiling moment until her heightened senses brought the scent of something foul and the crunch of footsteps on the oyster shell path..

"Whore!"

Maura's eyes flew open to find herself confronted by a raggedy figure more feral than human. The filthy face was hideously contorted, but she knew the man. He lurched closer, seeming to move in slow motion as he withdrew something from inside his raggedy shirt. Maura was blinded by the flash of sunlight on metal as the knife arced high before plunging into her breast. Her final breath escaped in one long, piercing cry

"No!!!"

Maura's agonized scream pierced the chapel like a thunderbolt, shocking Starla and Hattie from their reverie. They rushed from the chapel and burst into the blinding sunlight to see Maura slumped to the ground with a man looming over her lifeless body. The knife, its sheen dulled by Maura's blood, still hung in his hand. Time froze, and no one moved until gunfire exploded the stony silence, and her killer was dispatched with a single shot to the head.

"Dear God!" Hattie cried in confusion. "What's happened?"

"Stay with Maura!" Starla ordered. She dropped the smoking derringer back into her purse and made for the cemetery gates. "I'm going for Tom Anderson."

PART SEVEN

"If I am pressed to say why I loved him,
I feel it can be explained only by replying:
'Because it was he; because it was me.'"
-Michel de Montaigne

38

Daniel held Sloane in his arms until she fell asleep, exhausted by tears, sorrow and the unfathomable. He put her to bed and remained at her side until Hattie begged him to let her keep vigil.

"Perhaps you could rest a little," she whispered. Hattie wasn't certain he heard until he looked up at her, ashen face an unreadable mask. "Please, Daniel."

He frowned, struggling to sort his thoughts. "Is…is Miss Callahan still here?"

"She's downstairs."

He cast a parting look at Sloane. "Don't leave her alone, Hattie."

"I promise."

Starla's eyebrows rose when Daniel entered the parlor. "How's Sloane?"

"She cried herself to sleep. Hattie is with her." He sat heavily. "God help me. What am I to do now?"

Starla's heart ached for him. They had never met until she arrived with the terrible news, but she and Daniel knew each other's histories. Because he was estranged from his only family and had built his life around Maura, she could not imagine his loss.

"If you will trust a total stranger, Mr. Stafford, I will gladly make the necessary funeral arrangements."

"Thank you, but that's not what I meant. I…I don't know how to live without Maura."

"I wish I had an answer, sir. I can only say that when things like this happen that we must pick up the pieces of our lives and go on. There's no other choice."

"What about you, Miss Callahan?"

"Sir?"

"You killed a man today. Why have the police not come for you?"

"The father of my child is a man with considerable influence. He will ensure that the incident will be recorded as justifiable homicide." She shrugged with remarkable cool. "Which, of course, it was."

"Did you know the man you shot?"

Starla had explained both deaths when she and Hattie arrived, but Daniel was in such shock that he comprehended little. She patiently recounted details.

"No, but Hattie did. His name is Lewis Hatcher, and he'd been trying to blackmail Maura. Something to do with her late husband. Hattie said he came to the Windsor a number of times until they ran him off."

"Did Maura tell you about her husband?"

"She didn't have to. Someone in my line of work, former line of work, that is, sees a lot of girls who've been beaten by family members or boyfriends or pimps. Some talk openly. Others, like Maura, say nothing but their demeanor offers subtle signs."

"Did any of these girls kill their tormentors?"

"Some did. More justifiable homicide, to my way of thinking."

"Then you won't be shocked to know that Maura's husband...that he—"

Starla quickly interrupted to save Daniel the pain of verbalizing Maura's deed. "There's little that shocks me, Mr. Stafford, and I've no doubt whatsoever that Maura was in the right."

Daniel studied his hands. "This Hatcher character and a neighbor helped cover up the crime. Maura described him as a good Samaritan, so why would he want to hurt her?"

"I know only that Hatcher had fallen on tough times and that desperation can wear a person down to the point of insanity. It's something I've personally witnessed. More than once I regret to say," she added heavily.

Daniel paced the parlor before pausing at the window. Outside loomed the great oak and the hole he dug the night before, for the poor animal Sloane had seen killed.

"Sloane was five when Ronan died but she wasn't home that night. Maura said she always tried to shield her from the beatings, but I worry that over the years Sloane saw or heard something. She must have."

"Children have the knack of blanking out bad memories," Starla offered "We can only hope."

Daniel looked at the ceiling, as though he could see into Sloane's bedroom. "What's much more troubling, Miss Callahan, is that I don't know what to do about the child now. I have no legal claim, and with Maura gone—" He threw up his hands. "I'm completely lost."

"What do you know of Maura's family?"

"She's estranged except from everyone except her cousin Peter Byrne in Mississippi. Sloane lived with him and his wife before we brought her to New Orleans."

"Would they want her back once they learn what happened?"

"I'm sure they would. They're very decent people, and have a daughter Sloane's age. Nancy and Sloane are best friends. They write each other all the time, and there were a good many tears when they said good-bye." He sighed tiredly. "I know the Byrnes want what's best for Sloane, as do I, but I...I don't know if I'm prepared to give her up. Then again, what do I know about raising a child alone? Dear God! I'm talking in circles."

"Maura told me how good you were with Sloane and how much you loved each other. I saw it myself earlier today. I'm sure she's been happy living in this house."

"That's another thing. I'm not certain I want to stay here. I bought this house for Maura, and there are so many memories—"

"Please, Mr. Stafford," Starla urged. "Nothing must be decided today. You need time to rest and organize your thoughts."

"You're right. I honestly don't know if…what was that?"

Both heard footsteps flying down the stairs and a slammed door. Seconds later, Hattie appeared in the doorway. "Sloane ran outside before I could stop her."

Everyone, including Lurleen, hurried outside to witness Sloane, dry-eyed and determined, wrap Cleo in a sheet torn from her bed. She slid her gently into the hole Daniel had dug at the base of the tree. She tucked her doll inside the sheet and said, "Riley will keep you company." That done, her small hands began pushing dirt into the hole. Daniel and Hattie tried to help, but she waved them away.

"No!" she cried. "I want to do this by myself."

Once the double burial was finished, Sloane patted the earth flat and stepped back to observe her work. Satisfied, she climbed into the oak and perched on the broad limb she often shared with Cleopatra.

Daniel stepped beneath her. "Do you want to be by yourself, Sloane?" She nodded. "Alright, but come back inside before it gets dark."

"I promise."

"That's my girl."

"I love you, Papa."

Daniel gave a bare foot an affectionate squeeze. "I love you too, Pumpkin."

All three women wept upon witnessing such an intimate moment..

39

Daniel scanned the platform as the train pulled into the Pascagoula Station. He turned to Sloane. "Are you excited about seeing everyone?"

"I guess so."

"I'm sure Nancy's looking forward to having you back. Your Uncle Peter and Aunt Dora too."

Sloane stared at her lap and fidgeted with the holly corsage. It was a farewell gift from Hattie who pinned it in her lapel when she saw her off at the train station. "They're nice."

Daniel had discussed Sloane's future with Peter when he called with the news of Maura's death. They agreed to maintain the status quo for the time being, but Daniel grew distressed when Sloane underwent a distressing metamorphosis. Her laughter, which once echoed through the house, was gone, along with her tomboyish behavior. She attended school as usual and appeared at family meals, but had little to say and mostly remained sequestered in her room. Hattie and Lurleen were equally alarmed and tried their best to help. Hattie even offered to give Sloane the cockatoo, only to have Sloane refuse with the caustic observation that pets always die. By Thanksgiving, with no change, Peter and Daniel decided that the only solution was bringing Sloane back to Mississippi. Peter assured him that they would be happy to have her again, and, with his struggling new printing business, welcomed Daniel's offer of a generous monthly allowance for Sloane's room and board. Daniel planned to bring her in time for Christmas and, having nowhere else to go, was pleased when Peter and Dora asked him to stay for the holidays.

The train whistled, hissed and rumbled to a stop. "Here we are, Pumpkin. Come along."

Daniel flagged a porter to fetch their belongings before taking Sloane's hand and heading for the far end of the platform. Peter, Dora and Nancy waved and called greetings, and to Daniel's immeasurable relief, Sloane smiled when she saw them. The smile bloomed when Nancy ran toward her with a funny-looking dog on a leash. When the girls hugged, the animal barked excitedly and reared up on its hind legs, begging Sloane to be petted.

"What on earth is that?" she cried.

"A dachshund," Nancy replied. "I got him as an early Christmas present. I call him Schatzi."

"What a funny name?"

"It means treasure in German."

Sloane dropped to her knees. "Hello, Schatzi. I'm Sloane."

She scratched the dog behind the ears and giggled when he lapped at her chin. Daniel considered her shift in behavior miraculous, especially considering her icy remark to Hattie about pets, but when they got to the Byrnes' house, she again became subdued. Over the holidays, however, thanks largely to Nancy's company and Schatzi's endless antics, Sloane began to thaw, and by New Year's Day, when they took Daniel to the depot, she was almost her old self. She took his arm as they approached his train car and spoke in her best grown-up voice.

"I'll miss you something awful, Papa."

"I'll miss you too, Pumpkin."

"May I come visit?"

"I'm counting on it. How about Easter? We'll go on the egg hunt in the park like last year."

"Heavens, no! That's for children."

"And what are you, pray tell?"

"I'm nearly twelve, and Aunt Hattie said I was a young lady. Well, almost anyway."

"I see. So when would you like to come?"

"Mardi Gras!"

"I should have known." Daniel chuckled. "Alright then. Mardi Gras it is. We'll go to all the big parades."

"And will you take me to Commander's Palace for lunch? It's my favorite, you know."

"Maybe so. In fact, we might even be able to walk there."

"What do you mean?"

"I mean that I'm going to sell the house and move into the one where I grew up. I think you'll like it. There are lots and lots of rooms and a big yard with a fountain and—"

"No, Papa!" Sloane yanked her arm away and spun to face him, eyes brimming. "You can't sell the house! Not ever! It's Mama's house!"

Alarmed by the transformation, Daniel dropped to his knees and gathered her in his arms. "Hush, now, and don't cry. I won't sell the house. You can stay in your old bedroom when you visit and eat Lurleen's pralines to your heart's content."

"Promise?" she snuffled.

"Cross my heart."

"Will Aunt Hattie visit?"

"I'm sure she will."

She hugged him tight. "Thank you, Papa!"

"You're welcome." The conductor's shout brought Daniel to his feet. "Now I must hurry or I'll miss my train."

"Good-bye, Papa. I love you!"

"I love you too." He kissed her forehead. "Good-bye, Pumpkin."

Daniel settled into his seat and weighed the past few days, gratified that what began as a voyage unto the unknown became a tribute to the resilience of youth. As he hoped, Sloane responded well to the familiarity of the Byrne household and emerged from her cocoon of grief. Her eagerness to stay and burst of affection at the train station assured him that he and Peter had made the right choice. With Sloane's life in order, Daniel realized it was time to turn attention to himself. He made plans to sell the house on Chestnut Street and sever his last connection to the uptown world he abjured. The decision brought a warm rush of relief, and as he listened to the rhythmic clickety-clack of the rails, he eased into the new year and his first comforting moment since Maura died.

40

Because his English father was a firm believer in primogeniture, upon his parents' deaths from yellow fever death in 1911, Daniel inherited the Stafford home and the bulk of the estate, while younger brother John received a much smaller bequest. Upon the reading of the will, John rented an apartment on fashionable St. Charles Avenue, took a bank job, married his childhood sweetheart, Belinda Thomas, and embraced the uptown social world Daniel loathed. The brothers remained civil, but over the years their relationship grew tenuous. Despite knowing Daniel had nothing to do with their father's will, John's resentment festered. Matters worsened when Daniel's star soared at the Cotton Exchange while John's banking career faltered. John was a lackluster businessman with little acumen, and his insistence on living beyond his means, coupled with a fondness for gambling, steadily eroded his meager inheritance. Daniel's offer of help only antagonized John further, and when John learned of the liaison with Maura, his condemnation destroyed what little remained of their relationship. Despite their estrangement, when Daniel scored a hefty price for the sale of the house, he felt obliged to share the profits with his brother. He didn't anticipate full reconciliation, but hoped his gift would at least make their affiliation less acrimonious.

Daniel drove to John's apartment to present his offer, but found Belinda alone. She was a small, thin woman, very shy and self-effacing. He liked her well enough, but considered her a bit of a pudding. She invited him in, although clearly uneased by his presence.

"I'm afraid John's not home."

"I tried calling, but the operator said the number wasn't working."

"There were problems with the telephone, so John had it taken out."

"I see."

"Would you like some coffee or tea?"

"Nothing, thank you." He followed her into the parlor. "When does John usually get home."

"I…I really can't say. He's looking for work, and I never know when to expect him."

"What happened to the job at the bank?"

"Something about a merger, I think. John doesn't discuss his job."

"Is he talking to other banks?"

"I don't know."

Clearly, Daniel thought, John isn't telling this poor woman anything. "Are you two doing well?"

"I caught a terrible cold before Christmas and a cough still lingers, but I'm otherwise well. And yourself?"

"It'd been difficult, but things are slowly getting better."

She looked lost. "Better? What has happened?"

Daniel was stunned. Was it possible she didn't know?

"Maura's death, of course."

Belinda's brow wrinkled. "Maura?"

"Dear Lord!" Daniel gasped. "I know John didn't approve of her, but I never suspected he would keep her a secret."

"Forgive my ignorance, Daniel. Is…was she your wife?"

"She wouldn't marry me, so we lived together."

"Oh, dear."

"I'm sorry if that shocks you, Belinda, but it's the truth."

She was foundering. "Is that why you and John have been at odds these past couple of years?"

"Since I told him about Maura to be exact."

"I don't understand. Why did she upset him so much?"

"Because, unlike us, she was not to the manor born. She was a poor Mississippi girl struggling to survive the best way she knew." Daniel was weighing how much more he should tell this fragile soul when Belinda burst into tears and buried her face in her hands. He hastened to join her on the settee. "My dear, what is it? What's wrong?"

"Everything, Daniel!" she cried. "Everything!"

"Tell me. Please."

"I can't."

"You must."

He listened with a discordant mix of pity and anger when Belinda revealed John's ugly downward spiral. She didn't know why he lost his position at the bank, only that he left every morning with promises that he would return with a job. Instead he brought home more bitterness and was, Belinda tearfully confessed, more often than not drunk.

"We're living on much reduced circumstances, you see. The phone wasn't taken out. The telephone company shut it off because John couldn't pay the bill. We owe everyone in town. Grocers. Butchers. I live in fear that I'll wake up one morning without electricity."

"I wish I had known."

"I suggested he tell you, but he flew into a rage unlike anything I'd ever seen. He said such terrible things that I've since kept still."

"Where does John keep his bills?"

"That secretary in the corner. Why?"

"I'll take care of them, Belinda. I can't have you two living like this. I'm also going to leave you some cash."

"That's very generous, but John won't take it."

"Let me worry about that." As Daniel gathered the stack of bills, Belinda began weeping again. Unable to face more tears, he sat beside her and thrust a roll of dollar bills in her hand. "Take this, Belinda. I won't hear otherwise." She dropped the money in her lap and grabbed his hand with a strength belying her frail appearance. His cheeks burned when she kissed his hand. "Please, my dear. You mustn't—"

She touched his lips with a fingertip. "You've saved our lives, Daniel. I thank you from the bottom of my heart."

"We'll speak of it no more. Now I must go."

"Yes," Belinda breathed. "Before John gets home. I…I don't know what he'll do if he finds you here."

"I'm sorry for you both." He kissed her cheek and rose. "Good-bye, Belinda."

The St. Charles streetcar clanged down the avenue as Daniel walked to his car. He remained so immersed in Belinda's tragedy that he didn't notice someone stepping from the shadows.

"Why the devil were you in my apartment?"

"John!"

"Yes. John. Answer my question."

"The more important question is what you're doing here."

"I saw your car and decided not to come inside and say things Belinda shouldn't hear."

"Such as?"

"Don't play me for a fool, Daniel. I've taken great care to keep my wife from learning about your abominable behavior. She hardly needs to know how deeply you've dragged the family name through the mud."

Heat knifed down Daniel's spine. "You'd better watch your mouth, little brother."

"Alright. Alright." John waved a hand as though shooing a fly. "I'm sorry the woman's dead."

"Is that all you can say?"

"You told me to watch my mouth," John shot back. "Now, for the second time, what are you doing here?"

"To give you money."

"What? Why?"

"I sold the house on Chestnut Street. I thought you should share in the profits."

"A little late, isn't it? Where was your generosity the day the will was read?"

"Good God, man! Will you never stop carrying that idiotic grudge? You know damned well that I've repeatedly offered you money over the years."

"I also know you cheated me out of my inheritance!"

"I didn't create primogeniture nor did I write the damned will, John, so stop being a horse's ass and let me help. According to Belinda, you can certainly use it."

John's face darkened. "What did that fool tell you?"

"She's no fool, John, and she isn't to blame for any of this. It's all your doing."

"She had no right to tell you—"

"Belinda didn't volunteer anything except that you lost your job. I began intuiting the rest when I learned your telephone had been disconnected. Either way, she had every right to share troubles with a family member, and I have every right to help."

"That's all I need!" John snapped. "For everyone to know you're bailing out your ne'er-do-well brother. That my wife and I are living on your charity."

Daniel's patience was fast-fading. "I'm merely offering your half from the sale of the family house, John. No one could possibly think ill of that."

"You've been gone too long to remember how the Garden District thinks."

"Hardly, which is why I want nothing to do with it."

"So she dragged you down to her level, eh?"

Daniel's fingers curled into a fist, but instead of smashing his brother's face, he reached inside his jacket and shoved a fistful of bills at John. "Then pay the damned things yourself!"

"What's this?"

"Just giving the devil his due." Daniel laughed when John fumbled the bills and the wind caught them and scattered them across St. Charles Avenue like confetti. "Uh-oh. Looks like everyone will know you're a deadbeat now."

"You bastard!"

"Good-bye, John."

41

1922

The June heat bore down on Daniel and Hattie at the New Orleans depot. Across Basin Street, the phalanx of once-lavish bagnios loomed like tombstones for Storyville. They'd been shuttered for five years, and only one building, Willie Piazza's place at No. 317, showed any signs of life. The phony countess lived alone and occasionally threw lavish parties, but sex was no longer included in the entertainment. Daniel gave the vista a cursory glance before turning to Hattie.

"I'm so pleased you could meet Sloane's train with me. I know she'll be thrilled to see you."

"Her visits are always a joy," Hattie said.

"Especially when they're long overdue. I hated not seeing her for a year, but with Peter being ill, Dora needed Sloane's help. Thank goodness he's back at work, and she'll be here two weeks instead of one. The house will be so much livelier."

"May I say something frank?"

Daniel chuckled. "Dear Hattie! I've never known you to be otherwise. It's one of the things Maura loved about you."

"Then she'd want me to say that I worry about your being alone so much."

"I appreciate your concern, but I assure you I'm fine. I have my work and my gramophone recordings and I still go downtown to hear jazz. Lurleen takes good care of me, and Sloane's visits are aways something to look forward to."

"I see." Hattie didn't remind him that Sloane was growing up and wouldn't always be around. "Did you know she and I have been corresponding?"

"Yes, I did. She writes beautiful letters, don't you think?"

"They're lovely. Her penmanship too. My letters are an embarrassment because Sloane knows so many grand words. I don't have much education, you know. Maura was aways helping with my spelling."

"She would've made a good teacher."

Further conversation stopped when they heard a distant whistle. Both watched the tracks, excitement swelling when they spotted the locomotive's twinkling headlight. It seemed to crawl before finally coming to a halt, and they retreated when the platform exploded with the chaos of disembarking passengers and redcaps wrangling luggage. The noisy crowds slowly dwindled with Sloane nowhere in sight.

"Oh, no!" Daniel groaned. "How could she miss the train?"

"She didn't." Hattie pointed. "Look there!"

The conductor swung down from a railcar, turned and extended his arm. A gloved hand took his and a fashionable vision stepped from the train. She wore a cobalt blue cotton jacket over a white silk blouse and a blue-and-red plaid skirt that rose to mid-calf. A straw cloche covered her forehead but did not conceal dark hair reaching her shoulders. Sloane waved, but unlike other visits, she didn't run to her party. She approached at a pace far too stately for someone newly turned sixteen.

"My goodness!" Hattie cried. "Our little girl is growing up!"

"I can't believe she—" Daniel grinned when Sloane suddenly waved, hiked her skirts and made a childish dash to embrace him.

"Darling Papa!" she cried.

"Hello, Pumpkin."

"I've missed you so." She turned to hug Hattie. "And you too, Aunt Hattie!"

"You look wonderful," Hattie said. "I love that outfit."

"Oh, thank you! I saw it when Aunt Dora took Nancy and me shopping in Mobile. She thought it looked too old for me, but she let me have it when she realized how hard I'd worked to save money from my allowance."

A trait inherited from your mother, Daniel thought. "I'm proud of you."

"Thank you, Papa!" Sloane dropped a playful curtsey. "There's so much to catch up on. I hope you've both set aside lots of time for me."

"Of course we have."

"Sure enough," Hattie said. "That old boarding house doesn't need me all day."

"Oh, good!"

Sloane positioned herself between them and took their arms as they walked through the cavernous train station. The porter followed them onto Canal Street, and Sloane's eyes widened when Daniel directed the man to load the luggage into a sleek touring car parked at the curb. In gray over black with a canary leather interior, it had matching yellow artillery wheels and a second windshield with wind wings for driving with the top down. Gracing its hood was the sleek archer ornament giving the automobile its name.

"Goodness, Papa! What is that?"

"A Pierce Arrow four-seater. That old Hupmobile wasn't big enough for the three of us."

"May we drive with the top down?"

Daniel laughed. "If we did, you two would lose your hats. Now hop in. After we get you settled at the house, I'm taking you two pretty ladies to Commander's Palace for lunch."

"You remembered!"

Sloane hopped onto the running board and pecked his cheek before scrambling into the car alongside Hattie. On the drive uptown, she entertained everyone with tales about school, what subjects and teachers she liked and didn't like and a senior boy who'd been calling on her. He was handsome and fun and all the other girls were after him, but she insisted it wasn't serious.

"In fact," she declared, "I don't think I shall ever marry."

The adults exchanged knowing looks. "Why on earth would you say that?" Hattie asked. "Don't you want a husband and children?"

"Why should I? You seem to be doing fine without them."

Hattie stifled a laugh. "Oh, honey. I promise you don't want to pattern your life after mine."

Sloane considered. "Didn't you have lots of beaux when you were young?"

"Sloane!" Daniel chided. "You're being disrespectful."

"It's alright," Hattie insisted. "I turned a few heads in my day, but that was then and this is now. I'm content with what I have and consider myself very lucky. Life rarely give us what we want, you know."

"It's all so bewildering," Sloane groaned with classic adolescent angst. "Sometimes I don't know how I can bear it."

"Considering you're wearing those fine glad rags and riding down St. Charles Avenue in a fancy car, I'd say you're bearing it just fine," Hattie teased.

Sloane laughed and hugged her. "Oh, Aunt Hattie! You're the cat's meow!"

Hattie feigned horror. "I hope that's a good thing!"

As he drew up before the house on Baptiste Street, Daniel honked the horn to alert Lurleen. She opened the door as everyone got out of the car and looked up and down the street, pretending not to recognize Sloane.

"Where's that pretty little girl who used to live here?"

Sloane giggled and ran to the front porch. "Here I am, you big silly!"

"I'm only playing with you, lamb." Lurleen gave her a hug. "It's good to have you back."

"Thank you." Sloane lifted her head and sniffed. "Do I smell pralines?"

"Right out of the oven. They cooling on the counter."

"Don't spoil your appetite," Daniel called from the car. "We're going to Commander's for lunch, remember?"

"I remember!"

Everyone laughed as Sloane raced to the kitchen, skirts flying, but as soon as she was gone, Lurleen turned serious and sought Daniel while he was unloading Sloane's luggage. "Your brother came by right after you left for the train station, Mr. Daniel. He was drunk as could be and downright ugly."

"What did he want?"

"I ain't sure. When I told him you weren't here, he demanded to know when you was coming back. I figured that was none of his business so I said I didn't know. He said he'd be back and stormed out of here."

"You did the right thing, Lurleen."

"Alright then. I better see what that child's gotten into."

As Lurleen headed back up the sidewalk, Daniel pulled Sloane's portmanteau from the boot of the car and muttered to Hattie. "Why am I surprised? Whenever things are going well, my brother turns up like a bad penny."

"I saw him the first day I visited Maura here. He was so nasty she threw him out of the house."

"What are you talking about?"

Hattie realized her mistake too late. "I'm sorry, Daniel. I shouldn't have said anything."

"It doesn't matter now. Just tell me what happened." Hattie repeated what Maura said about John's insults and demeaning behavior. Daniel's face went red with rage as he continued retrieving Sloane's luggage. "Goddamned bastard! How dare he come here and insult her!"

Hattie had never heard him swear and apologized again. "Maura always said I had a big mouth." She retrieved Sloane's valise and followed Daniel into the house. Sloane was in the hallway, munching contentedly on a praline.

"Goodness me, Papa! Your face looks like a thundercloud. What happened?"

"I dropped your suitcase on my foot, that's all. Are you ready for lunch?"

42

"You know what, Aunt Hattie? People who live outside New Orleans don't know what good food is." Sloane finished hanging her dresses in the armoire and plopped onto her bed. "I didn't either until Mama brought me here."

Hattie tucked the empty suitcase atop the armoire and sat beside Sloane. "What made you think of that?"

"The bread pudding at Commander's. It absolutely melted in my mouth."

"Was it the cat's meow?" Hattie teased.

Sloane laughed. "Maybe the bee's knees." She propped pillows against the headboard and leaned against them. "All that rich food made me think about how poor Mama and I were, and how much I hated going to bed hungry."

"I didn't know."

"Mama usually managed to come up with something to eat, and the neighbors helped out, but things got bad right before daddy went away."

Hattie, like Daniel, wondered how much Sloane remembered about her father. She proceeded carefully. "Went away?"

"Mama said he went to work one day and never came home. After that we went to live with Uncle Peter and Aunt Dora, and then Mama had to come to New Orleans to find work. I hated it and there were times when I thought she'd never come back for me, but she did."

"Of course, she did. I remember those times, honey. Your mother missed you something awful and worked real hard to get you here."

"I know. Seems like I'd barely gotten here when Mama died, and back I went to Mississippi. You were right when you said life rarely give us what we want."

"I'm sorry you've had so much disappointment, Sloane, but you're young and much loved by people who will always care for you."

"I appreciate you saying that, Aunt Hattie. I truly do. But I wish I had better memories of Mama in Oriole. I only remember bits and pieces, mostly about sleeping on a pallet in my parent's bedroom and the smell of fatback."

"That's normal. You don't remember much because you were little."

"I suppose." Sloane brightened as she looked at the feminine frills on lamp shades, curtains and chairs. "I love this room."

"Me too. Did you know I gave your mama that vase?"

"No." Sloane propped herself on an elbow. "You were her best friend when she came to New Orleans, weren't you?"

"I sure was."

"How did that happen?"

Hattie had a ready answer for a question she'd anticipated for years. "Your mother got a job singing in a cabaret. They had Vaudeville acts too, the best in town. I was working there, so we met."

"Were you a singer?"

"Heavens no. I couldn't carry a tune in a bucket. I was a jack-of-all-trades. I mended costumes. Ran errands for the performers. Saw that the acts were ready and got on at the proper time. Collected tickets. All kinds of things."

"Is the cabaret still there?"

"No, honey. It burned down a long time ago."

Sloane was silent for a long moment. Then, "You were with her the day she died, weren't you, Aunt Hattie?"

Hattie had also anticipated this and swallowed hard. "Yes."

"What happened?"

"What did your papa tell you?"

"That some crazy man killed her in a cemetery."

"Is that all?" Sloane nodded. "He's right. We had gone to the funeral of old friend, and the man came out of nowhere. I was in a chapel, so I didn't actually see anything."

"Did he know Mama?"

"No," she lied.

"And nobody knows why he did it?"

"Like Papa said. He was crazy."

"Did he go to prison?"

Hattie started to claim she didn't remember, but the pain in Sloane's eyes prompted the truth. "Someone else was with us that day. Starla Callahan is her name. She owns the boarding house where I work. She met your mother on the train that brought her to New Orleans that first time and helped get her the singing job. Miss Callahan had a gun in her purse, and when she saw what had happened, she shot the man dead."

Sloane's voice was barely audible. "Oh."

Hattie brushed a wayward strand of dark hair from Sloane's forehead. "I told you because I think you're old enough to know the truth. I'm not sure Papa would approve, so we'll make it our secret."

"Alright."

"Good. Now I'd better get downtown. I told Miss Starla I'd be back by late afternoon. Papa's taking you to the zoo tomorrow but I'll see you the day after that."

"Aunt Hattie?"

"Yes, darling?"

"I want to meet Miss Callahan."

"Why?"

"I want to thank her for shooting the man who killed my mother."

"Goodness!" Hattie gasped. "What a thing to say!"

"Will you introduce us?" Before Hattie could insist that Daniel wouldn't approve, Sloane said, "It can be another secret."

"Alright." Hattie shook her head. "You know something, Sloane? You sure inherited your mother's determination." She said good-bye and went downstairs to find Daniel in the parlor. He looked at her over the top of the Times-Picayune.

"Did you two have a nice girl-to-girl talk?"

"I'd say it was more woman-to-woman. Sloane is growing up and fast. You'd better prepare yourself for some changes, Daniel. Questions, too."

"About?"

"Everything. She's going to surprise you."

"Thanks for the warning. I've value your advice, you know."

"Happy to oblige." She adjusted her hat. "Now I must get back to work."

"I'll drive you."

"No, no. You've done enough driving for one day. St. Charles is only a few blocks away and I enjoy riding the streetcar."

"Are you sure?"

"Absolutely. Thank you for a lovely day, Daniel. I'll see you both day after tomorrow."

"Fine."

Hattie was closing the gate when a car sped down Baptiste Street and braked hard in front of the house. It came within a foot of crashing into the Pierce-Arrow and stirred a cloud of dust that made her grab her handkerchief. She was about to upbraid the driver when John Stafford leapt out of the car and barreled down the sidewalk.

"My, my," Hattie said to herself. "Who says history doesn't repeat itself?!" She was tempted to linger, but discretion kept her on her way. She did not, however, miss hearing John's shout as he pounded the front door.

"Open up, Daniel! Your fancy new car's here so I know you're home!"

Daniel threw open the door and glowered. "What the devil's wrong with you?"

"You, goddammit! You're what's wrong with me!"

His disheveled appearance and slurred accusation told the story. "You're drunk!"

"Damn right I am!" John lurched past him and into the parlor. "Get in here!"

Daniel hissed at Lurleen, drawn to the hall when she heard yelling. "Keep Sloane in her room!" When she fled upstairs, Daniel confronted his brother. "Look at you! Tie askew. Stained shirt and trousers. You're a disgrace!"

"That's a laugh!" John snarled. "You're the one who—!"

"Watch your mouth, little brother!" Daniel took a menacing step forward. "Now tell me what the hell you want."

"Money!" John spat. "That stuff you've got to burn. What did that new car cost? A couple thousand?"

"I already tried giving you money, but your nastiness changed my mind. Nothing else has changed except that I learned you came here and insulted Maura."

John ignored the accusation. "Are you gonna give me some money, or not?"

"More money to keep from your poor wife and throw away on the gaming tables?"

"What?"

"Don't look so surprised. I don't move in your circles, but I hear plenty about your escapades at the Exchange. Men gossip too, you know. You can't imagine how many have extended their sympathy for my brother's reprehensible behavior."

"You're one to talk!"

"Get the hell out of my house!" Daniel growled.

"You and your damned whore!"

John's fist shot out, but he was off balance and barely grazed Daniel's shoulder. The lunge spun his body around, enabling Daniel to grab his brother's arm and shove it behind his back. John yelped with pain as he was pushed into the hall where Daniel struggled to open the front door while keeping John under control. A slender hand reached out to help.

"Sloane!"

"Well, looky who's here!" John leered." One big happy family, are we?"

Daniel's clamped his free hand over John's mouth to keep him silent as he propelled him down the walk. Anger grew with every step as he marched John to an overgrown lot two blocks away where he gave him a final, powerful shove that sent him sprawling onto the muddy ground. John rolled onto his back to see Daniel looming over him, fists clenched.

"Listen to me, you son of a bitch. If you ever come to my house again, I will kill you. Do you understand? I will kill you!!"

"Go to hell!" John staggered to his feet and lurched forward, but Daniel had only to sidestep the drunken lunge and watch him crash to the ground again. John lay face-down, mumbling into the muck before passing out cold.

Daniel nodded with satisfaction. "Wonder what your fine friends will say when the police find you here." He turned to leave and discovered he had an audience. "Sloane!"

"Don't blame Lurleen. She told me to stay home, but after what happened, I had to follow you."

"It's alright. I'm glad you did."

"Who is that man, Papa?"

"I'm sorry to say he's my very drunk and disorderly brother, and why he behaved like that is a very long story."

Speaking with wisdom beyond her years, Sloane said, "I'll be here two weeks."

"Alright then. Let's go home."

43

The zoo in Audubon Park was carved from an antebellum sugar and indigo plantation and sprawled from St. Charles Avenue to the Mississippi River. It was a favorite of locals, especially on Sundays when people in their finest came to gawk at the animals, picnic on the grounds or to simply see and be seen. Sloane, whose discerning eye continually entertained Daniel, remarked that the fashionable crowd was almost as colorful as the animals. She insisted on seeing every creature in the zoo, even the reptiles, and lingered longest at the newly installed flight cage. It teemed with all manner of feathery exotica, parrots, cockatoos, toucans and enormous Amazonian macaws which occasionally unleashed near-deafening screeches. Sloane was especially taken with the flamingoes.

"How can something be beautiful and silly-looking at the same time?"

"Perhaps because God has a sense of humor." After a while, they left the aviary and wandered alongside a lotus pond stocked with fat koi. When Daniel spotted an empty gazebo on the far side of the pond, he suggested ducking out of the sun and cooling off with some ice cream. "There's a lovely spot."

"It's perfect, Papa."

After getting her situated in the gazebo, Daniel went in search of ice cream. When he returned, he found her engaged in conversation with three well-dressed young men. Paternal instinct roused, he quickened his step and called a warning. "The young lady doesn't talk to strangers."

"We're not strangers," one of them quipped. "We're Tulane students!" He and his companions laughed heartily, but Daniel's glower warned that he meant business. "Sorry, sir. C'mon, boys."

Flattered and amused, Sloane waved good-bye. "They were only being friendly."

"Maybe so, but remember you're not in Pascagoula." Daniel handed her the ice cream and sat beside her. "New Orleans is a big city. Danger can come out of nowhere."

"So I've heard. Even cemeteries."

"Sloane!"

"It's alright, Papa. I know you still see me as a little girl, but I'm not and you must stop shielding me from things."

"What things?"

"Things I've overheard from Uncle Peter and Aunt Dora. From you and Mama and Aunt Hattie, too. I need to know the truth about the family, yours as well as mine. That fight with your brother yesterday gave me nightmares. I pretended I wasn't frightened, but I was."

"I'm sorry you saw that, Pumpkin. On your first day back, too. John is a very sad, bitter man who tries to drown his troubles with liquor. He came to the house looking for money. I refused because he'll gamble it away like the last time."

"That's not what bothered me."

"Oh?"

"What did he mean about 'one big happy family' and why did you put a hand over his mouth?"

"Because he has a filthy mouth when he drinks, and I didn't want you hearing ugly words. He's never forgiven me for falling in love with your mother, you see. He never approved of her, always looked down on her because she came from Mississippi and not the Garden District."

"What's that?"

"A wealthy neighborhood a few blocks above us." Daniel grabbed his handkerchief when the ice cream melted onto his hand. "I grew up there."

"Did your parents disapprove of Mama too?"

"They died long before I met her."

"Why didn't you marry her?"

Her boldness struck like lightning. Thank goodness Hattie warned me, he thought.

"Who said we weren't married?"

"That was one of the things I overheard from Uncle Peter and Aunt Dora."

"Your mother refused to marry me."

"But why?" When Daniel hesitated, she said, "The truth, Papa. Please."

"She had several reasons, all very personal."

"Was one of them my father?"

So there it is, he thought. The question that had most plagued him for years. Did she remember her mother's beatings or had she buried that horror deep in what psychiatrists now called the subconscious?

"Yes."

"Oh." Sloane rose a bit unsteadily, oblivious when her ice cream slipped away and splattered on the ground. "Could we walk a little?"

"Of course."

Sloane steadied herself on his arm as they passed the last cages and approached the high levee marking the zoo's border. To

Daniel's surprise, she insisted on climbing it to see the river. He reached the crest first and extended a hand to help her the rest of the way. She squinted at the watery sun-dazzle, wishing she'd worn a brimmed hat instead of a cloche.

"Look," Daniel said, pointing. "Down there."

"What in the world—?"

Sprawled along the river's edge for several blocks in both directions was a motley collection of shantyboats, cabins and stilt houses. A few hugged the base of the levee, while others perched over the Mississippi. Some were accessible by rickety catwalks that looked as though they might collapse in a good wind.

"It's called the batture," Daniel explained. "Nobody owns it, and it's almost as old as the city itself."

"Who lives there?"

"I don't know. Poor folks who can't afford to live elsewhere, I suppose. Probably some hooligans hiding from the law. Riffraff."

"Then it's dangerous."

"To be sure, but not just from outlaws. Those people are living on borrowed time, or at least at the whim of the river. Their little shanties are like matchbooks, forever collapsing or being swept away by floodwaters."

"How awful!"

"Your mother didn't think so." Sloane gave him an odd look. "She admired those people, called them modern-day pioneers. She'd sit on that old wooden bench over there and watch them. She said they inspired her."

"You mean she wrote songs about them?"

"Several, in fact. Artists find inspiration in the oddest places. Beauty too. I don't have much imagination, so I never understood it."

"Me either. I loved listening to Mama sing and play the piano when I was little. She wanted to give me piano lessons, but we moved away and left the piano behind." She watched some children scavenging driftwood along the river's edge. While two older boys fought over an especially big piece, a young girl grabbed it and ran away. The boys whooped with laughter and ran after her. "I like knowing Mama was here. Could we sit on that bench awhile?"

"Of course."

They took their seats and watched the Walnut Street Ferry depart for Westwego across the river. Moments later, she passed her sister ship heading in the opposite direction. Smoke from their stacks blended into an acrid black cloud which Sloane watched until it was shattered by the wind.

"Will you tell me about the neighborhood where you grew up?"

"Of course, my dear. It's very pretty with lots of big houses and yards, but it has a lot of rules I never liked. I first learned them when I was a page at a Mardi Gras ball. The costumes and pageantry were fun at first but became tedious as I got older. I grew tired of seeing the same faces at the same functions, year after year, and realized what I'd been missing when my father sent me north to college. To Princeton. I had a great many new and exciting experiences there, and when I came home after graduation, I found myself more bored than ever. I didn't particularly want to follow in my father's footsteps as a cotton broker, but nor did I want to be ungrateful for his generosity. I also tried to please him by attending the usual cotillions and dinners, but when he and mama died, I stopped going. I was content to live alone and went nowhere except the Exchange and downtown to listen to music. While I was at Princeton, I'd fallen in love with jazz on trips to New York and was surprised to learn it had been born in my own back yard. I knew people were talking about me, calling me a traitor to my class and my family. Maybe they're right, but I knew what I wanted and what I didn't want too."

"What about the ladies, Papa? You must've wooed some of them."

Dear God, he thought. Maura had asked the very same question.

"One or two, but my heart was never in it. I began writing it off as dead until one night when I heard your mother perform. After that...well, you know the rest."

"And it's all I need to know." Sloane took her handkerchief and blotted his sweaty brow. "Thank you for telling me these things and for talking to me like a grown-up."

"You were right, Sloane. It was time." He checked his pocket watch. We'd better get home. Lurleen is preparing a special welcoming dinner."

"Alright, Papa."

Lurleen outdid herself with a lavish supper of redfish bouillabaisse and chicken Pontalba with rice, macque choux and mirliton. The grand finale was a fragrant peach melba still warm from the oven. As Lurleen was setting it on the table, the doorbell rang. She answered it and returned with an envelope.

"For you, Miss Sloane."

"Who delivered it?" Daniel asked.

"Some little colored boy, sir."

"In a uniform?"

"No, sir."

Daniel leapt to his feet and stuck out his hand. "Give it to me, Sloane!"

It was too late. Sloane had already read the short message. She turned to Daniel, face leached of color, and chilled his heart with two words.

"What's Storyville?"

44

1924

"Your mother was a Storyville whore!"

John's damning words were intended to destroy his brother's family but instead generated unity. Exposure of Maura's last, most deeply buried secret brought tears of shock and disbelief, but ultimately of relief as Sloane accepted the news with remarkable grace for one so young. She was helped enormously by Hattie's revelations about a woman who, despite selling her body, had integrity and compassion, and she came to understand that Maura's desperate acts were those of a mother driven by love for her only child. When Daniel and Hattie had answered all her questions, Sloane asked to visit St. Roch's cemetery. It was not to see where Maura died, she explained, but to pray for her mother's soul and leave a miracle. She bought a carved wooden heart from a Choctaw vendor on Jackson Square and added it to the collection in the tiny chapel. The experience lifted her soul, and when she returned to Pascagoula, Peter and Dora welcomed someone much-changed.

Sloane immersed herself in schoolwork, and for the next two years enjoyed a lively social life with her peers, including a string of suitor. Her greatest pleasure, however, came from correspondence. She regularly wrote Hattie and occasionally Lurleen, but saved her most heartfelt letters for Daniel. He cherished them, but grew uneasy when they began assuming an intimate tone. Her boyfriends, she insisted, bored her with their naivete and could not compare with his worldliness and maturity. When he shared his concern with Hattie, she dismissed it as a phase and he put it out of his thoughts until he received a letter written on the train after Sloane's last visit. His hands began trembling as he began reading.

"Darling Papa,

"Please forgive the wobbly handwriting as I am writing on the train while I still feel your parting embrace. I had hoped to say what I am about to write while we were together, but could not find the courage. Since we have learned to be honest with each other and harbor no secrets, I must confess, my dearest Papa, that I have fallen in love with you."

Daniel continued reading but comprehended little beyond the first paragraph. He'd never been given to strong drink, but poured himself two fingers of whiskey and downed them in a single shot. He sat in the parlor with the letter in his lap. He stared at it. He picked it up and turned it over and weighed its lightness. He wondered how something so fragile could be so portentous. He was a ghost at dinner, afterwards apologizing to Lurleen for being unresponsive when she expressed concern for his silence. After a sleepless night and an inability to focus on work, he telephoned Hattie from the Exchange and asked to see her that afternoon. Hearing urgency in his voice, she told him to come right away. She was horrified when he arrived at the boarding house looking abysmal and forlorn

"What on earth has happened, Daniel! You're white as a sheet."

He thrust the letter in her hand. "Read this." He sank into a chair and fidgeted with the antimacassar on the arm. "It explains everything."

Hattie's reaction was only slightly less than his. "My God, Daniel! We both knew she was flirtatious, but this! No wonder you're in shock." She sat and reread the damning words. "Did you have any idea Sloane's feelings ran this deep?"

"No. Never!" he cried. Then, "I don't know. Yes. Maybe."

"What are you saying?"

"That maybe I thought about a certain look or a touch or perhaps an embrace that lasted too long. Such things frightened me, so I told myself I misread them or was flattering myself. Why would a girl her age be attracted to an old man?"

"You're thirty-seven, Daniel. That's hardly old."

"It is when the girl is eighteen."

"Age differences like that aren't all that uncommon. Wives are always younger than their husbands."

"Who said anything about wives and husbands?!" Daniel cried.

"I'm sorry, Daniel. My big mouth again.." Seeing that he was frightened and distraught, she sought to smooth the moment. "I have fresh coffee. Would you like a cup?"

"Please," he said, voice barely a whisper. He listened to Hattie's footsteps echoing down the hall and was lost in their wake. The small room, wallpapered with pink cabbage roses and emerald green leaves, started to shrink and close in. He began sweating and tugged at his collar when the hideous roses grew ever larger and more menacing. He was on the verge of flight when Hattie returned. "I'm sorry, Hattie. Coming here was a mistake."

"Nonsense. It's the smartest thing you could do."

"Why do you say that?"

"Because I'm the only one who understands your predicament." Hattie set down the coffee service and poured cups for both. She gave him a searching look. "I want you to look deep in your heart and tell me the truth. Have you ever had feelings for Sloane?"

There was no hesitation. "No. Never."

"Are you sure?"

"I never allowed myself, Hattie. She's Maura's daughter."

"Like it or not, dear friend, that's proof that you thought about it."

"Oh, God!" Daniel buried his head in his hands. "How can this be?"

"It simply happened, that's all. Sloane looks nothing like Maura, but something about her obviously reached you. It doesn't matter what, only that it's there."

Daniel lifted his eyes. "Then why does it seem so wrong?"

"Because when Maura was alive, the two of you lived as husband and wife, and, with Sloane calling you Papa, you naturally thought of her as your daughter. Even though she's another man's child, any sort of attraction was bound to stir unspeakable…notions. I'm sure I don't have to spell it out."

"No, of course not. I understand intellectually, but emotionally it's not so easy."

"Because it came without warning, and you need time to sort through things and put them in perspective."

He scarcely heard. "She's still a child, Hattie!"

"You may want to believe that, Daniel, but you must accept the fact that she's a young woman." Hattie sipped her coffee. "Right now, you believe that Sloane has crossed some type of forbidden line, but she hasn't. She's just being honest about her feelings and now you must be honest with yours."

"How can I do that when I don't know what they are? This whole blasted business has knocked me senseless!"

"Knocked you senseless or shaken you awake?" He gave no answer as he unfolded Sloane's letter and read it yet again. "You're going to answer it, aren't you?"

"I have to, but I don't know what to say."

"Sequester yourself somewhere and study the letter. The words will come, I promise."

"How can you be so sure?"

"Because you're a man who will fight hard and risk everything for what you believe in. I know because I've seen it. Call on that strength to learn the truth about your feelings for Sloane. You'd best prepare yourself because you may love her and you may not."

"You're right." Daniel tucked the letter away and gave Hattie a curious look. "Where on earth did you acquire such wisdom?"

Hattie winked. "We all have secrets, my friend."

45

Daniel took Hattie's advice and devoted the better part of a week to composing the most important letter of his life. He acknowledged Sloane's love and confessed to feelings, albeit lesser, of his own. A brisk exchange of letters followed, each more intimate than the last, until Daniel found the mettle to recognize and return her love. Despite an urge to take the first train to Pascagoula, Daniel chose to wait until Sloane's graduation. He planned to be circumspect, but discretion disintegrated the moment he spied her through the train window. He was suddenly on his feet, pushing for a clear path to the exit. While Dora and Peter watched, bewildered, Daniel swung down from the train car and drew Sloane into his arms with an embrace that was anything but avuncular.

"Will you not kiss me?" she whispered.

"Soon enough," Daniel promised, mindful of watching eyes. "I'm afraid we've already shocked your uncle and aunt."

"Then we must explain ourselves right away," she insisted.

"Agreed." Daniel tucked her arm inside his and approached the others with as much confidence as he could muster. He'd rehearsed this speech a dozen times, but as fate played out, it was Nancy who broke the news. Sloane had not only confided the truth about the newfound liaison but shared a few of Daniel's letters too. Bursting with excitement, she hugged Daniel and said, "I want to be the first to offer congratulations."

"Congratulations for what?" Dora asked.

Nancy's hand flew to her mouth. "Oh, no! I forgot it was a secret!"

"Secret?" Peter asked. Over the years, he and Dora had come to think of Sloane as a second daughter and he gave Daniel a stern look. "What're these girls talking about?"

"I'd hoped to better prepare you," Daniel said, "but the truth is that Sloane and I have fallen in love. After graduation, we are to be married in New Orleans."

"You'll do no such thing!" Dora declared. Daniel and Sloane exchanged anxious looks until they caught the twinkle in her eye. "You'll be married here in Pascagoula, and that's final!"

"But—" Daniel faltered.

"Peter and I aren't fools, Sloane." Dora took her arm as they walked to the car. "It would be hard to miss the profound change in your behavior and the excitement in your voice whenever Daniel's name came up. In fact, we were both wondering how long it would be before you broke the news."

"So you're happy for us?"

"Of course. We both are."

"I apologize for not coming to you privately," Daniel told Peter. "It would've been the proper thing to do since you're Sloane's legal guardian."

"Please don't concern yourself. This is a day for congratulations all around. Look there." Peter pointed with pride at a gleaming new Studebaker. "I bought it last week. My print shop is booming with this insane 'roaring twenties' economy, and Dora and I are looking to build a new house."

"That's wonderful!" Daniel squeezed Peter's shoulder. "It couldn't happen to more deserving people."

The remainder of Daniel's visit was a blur of excitement, especially for Sloane. As she told Daniel on the train back to New Orleans, one moment she was receiving a high school diploma and the next he was sliding a ring on her finger in the Byrne's cozy living room. Her status as a wife became a reality when Daniel carried her across the threshold of the house on Baptiste Street. Sloane burst into tears of joy when she found Lurleen waiting with a plate of pralines.

"Welcome home, Miss Sloane."

"Dear Lurleen!" she cried, embracing her so heartily she almost toppled the plate. "I've missed your pralines almost as much as I missed you!"

The household settled quickly and easily into a routine. Sloane shared her mother's taste in décor, but now that she was mistress of the house, she decided the vestibule needed freshening up. She was contemplating wallpaper samples when she noticed cracks in the fanlight. When Daniel climbed a ladder for a better look, he discovered the damage much worse than he thought.

"I'm afraid the whole window will have to be replaced. Would you like something different? Blue perhaps? I know that's your favorite color."

"No, no. Mama loved the fanlight the way it is and, besides, it reminds me of her song."

Daniel feigned horror. "Not the Waffle Man I hope."

"No, silly. The one about the sun."

"Of course, my dear. And, luckily, I know just the man to make a new window."

"Oh?"

"He designed the stained glass windows in the new Exchange building and his work is beautiful. We had a little ceremony when the windows were unveiled, and I got to meet him. Nice fellow but a little rough around the edges. Oddly enough, I can't think of his name but I recall that he lives on the batture. Remember the day I took you there? We'd gone to the zoo and—"

"Of course I remember it. That was the same day you told me about falling in love with Mama, and your brother John sent me that horrible note."

"Yes, I suppose it was."

"Did you ever see him again?"

"Never. His wife Belinda almost died from la grippe last spring, and his life continues to be in turmoil."

"How do you know?"

"Some men I work with move in John's circles. I know he's still struggling to make ends meet because he's tried to borrow money from them."

"I've never known more different brothers."

"Nor I. We've never had anything in common, and I marvel that we shared the same parents."

Sloane changed the subject. "I'm going to look through Mama's music. That silly song is in my head and I can't remember the lyrics"

Daniel followed her into the parlor where she bent over the canterbury and rifled through the sheet music. He chuckled softly.

"What's so funny?"

"Your skirt."

Sloane straightened and looked down. "Did I spill something?"

"No, dearest, but I remain astonished at how short skirts are these days. I can only wonder what your mother would've thought."

"But all the girls are wearing them. It's the latest fashion."

"I know, my darling, and you wear it very well, but I hope those hemlines don't get any shorter."

"That reminds me of something Hattie told me the other day."

"Oh?"

"It seems that some little boy ended up at lost-and-found at Maison Blanche after getting separated from his mother. When someone asked why he didn't grab his mother's skirt to keep from getting lost, he said he couldn't reach it."

Both enjoyed a laugh before Sloane found the sheet music she wanted. She frowned.

"This is strange. The lyrics aren't as I remember."

"That's no surprise. Your mother was constantly rewriting her songs. Maybe the version you're remembering is somewhere else."

Sloane looked some more. "You're right. Here's another version I've never seen. I can hardly read it because it's all marked up."

"Marked up," Daniel muttered. "Marked up. Mark. Marcus. That's it. The man who made the stained glass is named Marcus. Marcus Gentry."

46

1939

"It's been far too long, Aunt Hattie." Sloane slipped an arm around Hattie's waist as they entered the parlor. "What on earth has kept you so busy and what's that big secret you mentioned on the telephone?"

"Let me catch my breath, and I'll tell you." Hattie sank into the couch, took off her hat and smoothed her hair. "First tell me how you like my perm."

Sloane settled in beside her. "Very much. It suits you."

"Thanks. It's something new called a cold wave. You should try it if you ever cut those long locks. It takes half a day, but they don't hook you up to any hot machines." She smiled impishly. "The beautician also lightened things up a bit."

"I thought there was something different."

"It's the clothes too. I know this outfit's a bit showy for a woman pushing fifty, but that's part of what I've come to tell you."

"Oh?"

"I always appreciated your mama getting me work with Starla, and Starla's been more than fair, but I've wanted to be my own boss for years, and last fall I finally got the chance."

"That's wonderful, but why did you wait so long to tell me?"

"Because even though you're a married lady of thirty-three with a twelve-year old son, sometimes I still think of you as a little girl." Hattie peeled off her gloves and rummaged in her purse for a cigarette. "And I guess I was a little embarrassed."

Sloane had a riffle of apprehension. "Don't tell me you've gone back to the life."

A smile played on Hattie's lips when she looked up from her purse. "You sly minx! How did you guess?"

"Because I've heard you say a dozen times that no self-respecting prostitute ever leaves the profession. Not completely, anyway."

Hattie chuckled and wedged a cigarette into an ivory holder. "That sounds a heap better than me saying, once a whore, always a whore. I swear, your sweet mama and Starla were the only gals I ever knew who got out and stayed out. I always wondered where they got their courage or gumption or whatever it was because it just ain't in me." She lit her cigarette and exhaled a pale stream of smoke. "Poor Starla. I'd only been there a few months when I started fooling around with her boarders. I was very discreet, mind you, and they were sworn to secrecy, so it worked out fine. Starla paid a fair wage, but I never could get ahead, never had money for the kind of clothes I wanted or the occasional frippery. I solved that problem by spending my free time at Carlota Higgins' place on Canal Street. At least I did until I got too old."

"Starla didn't know?"

"I'm sure she suspected, but she never said anything because there were never any complaints. Plus, I was very good at my job." She grinned. "Both of them."

Both enjoyed the joke while Sloane's maid Zephyr delivered a tea service and disappeared. "Why are you telling me now?"

"Because Carlota's almost seventy, and last October she asked if I'd be interested in taking over her business. The idea of being ringmaster instead of performer was very appealing, so I start as madam next week." Her shoulders rose and fell. "So now you know my secret."

Sloane said, "If you're happy, I'm happy, but promise me you'll be careful. I read something in the Times-Picayune just last week about a police raid across the lake."

292

"Nothing to worry about, honey. Carlotta's had the cops in her pocket for years."

"Have you told Starla you're leaving?"

"Told her yesterday. She didn't mind. She's got herself a steady boyfriend and is all the time talking about them moving up to Jackson to be near Katherine and all those grandchildren. There must be seven or eight by now. I swear, that dame drops them like a brood sow."

Sloane laughed, warmed as always by Hattie's candid humor. "Is Starla going to sell the boarding houses?"

"She didn't say, but I wouldn't be surprised. She's tired of running them, and I don't blame her. The woman works like a fiend. Always has."

"I haven't seen her in years," Sloane lamented. "I must pay a call before she leaves for Mississippi."

"She'd love to see you." Hattie watched Sloane pour and served from an elegant silver service. "I wish your mama could see you right now. You're such a grand lady." A shadow passed over Sloane's face. "What's wrong, honey?"

"Do you think she's forgiven me?"

Hattie took Sloane's hands. "We've been over this a thousand times, Sloane. There's nothing to forgive. Your mama wanted nothing more in this world than for you and Daniel to be happy, and the fact that you found happiness together and had that precious child is surely making her smile down from heaven." She squeezed Sloane's hands. "Now why in the world would you bring that up again?"

"She's been on my mind a lot lately. I don't know why, and I'm sorry I mentioned it."

"Don't apologize. Just tell me how Daniel and Robert are doing."

Sloane managed a smile. "They're fine. They spend every waking moment together. I've never known a boy who was more his father's son."

"Where are they now?"

"Where they are every weekend. Sailing Lake Pontchartrain. Daniel's determined to make Robert a good sailor, and Robert's determined to please his father by becoming one."

"That's wonderful. Will I not see them today?"

"When I told Daniel you were coming, he promised to be back in time." She glanced at the hall clock. "Which should be most any minute."

"I'd hate to miss them."

Sloane brightened. "In that case, you'll stay for dinner."

"I'd love to, only I promised Carlota to be there at five to interview some new girls."

"Couldn't you telephone and tell her…hold on. I think I heard a car."

A few seconds later, Robert bounded into the house with his usual explosion of energy. He dangled a string of fresh redfish. "Hey, Mama. Hey, Aunt Hattie! Look what I caught!"

"I thought you were going sailing," Sloane said.

"We did, but everyone said the fish were biting like crazy so we—" He stopped and looked sheepish. "Papa bought these on the dock. He tossed me the package and said it would be fun to tell you I caught them."

Hattie chuckled. "Somebody's got a sense of humor."

"Now you know what my life is like with those two clowns," Sloane said. "Alright, young man. Take those fish to Zephyr and tell her we'll have them for dinner." She shook her head as Robert raced from the room like his feet were on fire. "I love that boy to pieces, but some days he wears me out."

"I can see why."

"Hello, Hattie."

"Captain Stafford, I presume." She pretended to swoon when Daniel kissed her hand. "Good to see you, Daniel. It's been much too long."

"And whose fault is that?"

"Mine of course."

Sloane stood. "You look a little worse for wear, darling. Was the lake rough today?"

"Very choppy and whitecaps everywhere. I actually felt a little queasy, and you know that's not like me."

"How was Robert?"

"Fine. The boy's indestructible." He drew a handkerchief from his jacket and wiped his forehead. "Excuse me, but I can't seem to stop sweating."

"Maybe you should have a rest before dinner." Daniel nodded and excused himself. "That's odd. I've never seen him seasick."

"I'm sure he'll be fine after he rests." Hattie watched Robert race upstairs after his father. "I swear, he makes more noise on those old stairs than you did at his age, and that's saying something."

"Was I really that rambunctious?"

"I'll only say that you and Cleopatra ran me ragged when I stayed here. I remember one time we were in the side yard and that fool cat was chasing something and…what was that?!"

A loud thump overhead was followed by a cry that froze Sloane's heart. An agonized groan drove her upstairs to find Robert kneeling over his father. Daniel lay on his back, face ashen, lips taut with pain. She dropped beside him and gathered him in her arms. When Daniel remained unresponsive to her pleas, she turned to Robert, pale as his father and shaking with fear.

"Tell Aunt Hattie to call Dr. Robicheaux!" she ordered. "Hurry!"

Hattie was still in the parlor, darkening now with the descent of dusk. Robert was beside her, head in her lap, drowsing intermittently. He had been there since the doctor arrived over an hour ago. Zephyr had been up and down the stairs several times and poked her head into the parlor once to ask if Hattie needed anything.

"Nothing," Hattie replied.

"Want me to turn on some lights?"

"Not yet." Hattie stroked Robert's dark curls. "Just leave us be."

Zephyr scurried back upstairs, leaving Hattie along with deepening dread. Although far from a religious woman, she found herself praying that Daniel was alright. Shortly before dark, she heard heavy footsteps on the stairs and saw the physician's silhouette materialize in the doorway to the hall. He addressed the dimness in a low voice.

"Miss Hattie?"

"Yes, doctor?"

"Is Robert asleep?"

Robert abruptly sat up. "No, sir, I'm not."

"Then you must be a big man for us." He came into the parlor and knelt beside the couch. A shadow obscured his face, but the ache in his voice could not be concealed. "I'm afraid there was nothing I could do for your father, Robert. His heart simply gave out."

"Oh." Robert's voice was faint but surprisingly steady. "Where's my mother?"

Dr. Robicheaux glanced at Hattie's face where horror announced she knew what was coming. He rested a hand lightly on Robert's shoulder. "I'm sorry to have to tell you this, son, but your mother has quietly joined your father in heaven."

PART EIGHT

"If you're open to it, New Orleans will
teach you about yourself.
But if you want to hide who you really are,
The city will help you do that too."
-Laurell K. Hamilton

47

2023

Gemma opened the front door and threw her arms wide. "Darling!" she cried. "Your dearest friend is now officially a madam!"

Maddie grimaced. "Isn't ten in the morning it a little early for cocktails?"

"Don't be gauche, dear. The only thing I'm high on is news from your boyfriend. Come along and I'll tell you all about it. We'll have coffee outside. Crullers too." She wore an elfin grin. "Got them myself at Croissant d'Or this morning."

"Where's Tyrone?"

"It's his day off, so I suspect he's sleeping in. Now go make yourself comfy, and I'll be right back."

Gemma's lush courtyard was Maddie's favorite retreat, an exotic oasis of palms, banana plants and citrus trees. Orange trumpet vines blazed atop brick walls lined with hibiscus, camellia and bougainvillea. The fragrance of lemon blossoms was interrupted by the smell of strong coffee and freshly baked crullers when Gemma returned, burnishing the pure French Quarter moment.

"Dig in!" Gemma chirped.

"So tell me about this 'madam' business," Maddie said.

"It started when Henri dug up all those rouge pots and broken perfume bottles. His suspicions that the place had been a bordello were pretty much confirmed when he found the ocelot skull, but you know what a research nerd he is, bless his heart. He trotted over to city hall and got busy in the records department and tracked down the original owners. The man who built the house was a sea captain named Eric Kennedy. He lived there until eighteen ninety-seven when it was bought by one Mabel Perkins who ran girls out of there before selling it to my grandfather in nineteen-sixteen."

"So it really was a bordello?"

"Ain't that a kick?"

"Does this mean I have to call you Madam Gemma?"

"Only in private, dearie." Gemma dunked her cruller and took a bite. "It's even more fun when you know something about Ms. Perkins. After Henri established ownership of the house, he hit the library for old newspaper files. It seems Ms. Perkins had a serious dust-up with the law, and not for running a bawdy house. She found her boyfriend in bed with one of her girls and took a knife to his privates."

"Oh, my God! Just like Lorena Bobbit!"

"Except this gent didn't live to get put back together."

"What happened to Madam Mable?"

"Not a thing. The old gal either paid people off or had something big on somebody bigger. What's more, the hooker she caught in flagrante delicto went back to work for her as though nothing happened."

"You're kidding!"

"That's not all, honey lamb. Help yourself to another cruller and I'll be right back." Gemma returned with a large mailer which she emptied onto the patio table. "This came yesterday from Peter Brooks."

"Sheet music?"

"There must be thirty songs in here. Brooks found them in an old piano bench that belonged to my great-grandmother, Maura Traver O'Rourke."

"So you finally learned her name, eh?"

"Believe me, missy, it wasn't easy. Back in January, Brooks enclosed a letter written to my grandfather Daniel Stafford by somebody named Sloane dated nineteen twenty-four. When I asked who she was and why he sent it, that old rumpot couldn't remember. I badgered him for months, but all he recalled was that Maura was my great-grandmother and that she wrote these songs. I was sitting out here going through this music when I found one dedicated to Maura's daughter whose name is, drumroll please, Sloane!" Gemma beamed. "I let out such a whoop when I made the connection that Ty came running to see what was wrong."

"That's wonderful, Gemma. I know you're thrilled."

"Thrilled and relieved, although the mystery isn't completely solved. I'm assuming my grandparents were Daniel and Sloane, but I can find no record of their marriage. Either they got hitched somewhere else or they lived in sin. I'm dying to know more." She riffled further into the sheet music. "Good heavens! Some of these lyrics are scribbled on a page from a Sears & Roebuck catalogue. Great-grandma must've really been poor."

"Looks like."

"One things for sure. I didn't get her music gene, but I'd love to hear these songs."

"Me too. You should get someone to play and sing them for you." Maddie picked up more sheet music. "Oh, my God! Look at this title!"

Gemma squinted. "I can't read it without my glasses."

"In the Pines!" Maddie cried. "It's one of the most famous folk songs ever, and no one knew who wrote it. Henri and I saw a documentary on Appalachian folk music at NOMA, and if this is what I think, it's one of folk music's holy grails. Henri's going to flip!" Maddie looked at the next page and found an earlier version of the song, signed by Cara Traver and dated 1863. She scanned both copies. "This must be the original. Maura changed some of the lyrics."

"So now I have to find out who this Cara Traver was."

"Logic suggests she was Maura's mother or maybe grandmother."

"That's my thinking too, but since when does logic have anything to do with my wacky family?"

"Looks to me like your little trip down memory lane is going to have a happy ending."

"Sure does. And you know what else? I'm still fascinated by how the house on Baptiste Street found me, and not the other way around."

"And how it steered you to your ancestors."

"Exactly. By the way, Cane's almost finished with the restoration work and wants me to take a look this afternoon. Want to come with?"

"I wish I could, darn it. Henri's got some faculty party over in Algiers, and I promised to keep him company. I'm dying to see the house though."

"Of course you are, darling. You'll be living there after all."

"I know and I can't wait. I'm sure Cane's doing a great job."

"He really has. The poor guy's practically lived there since he started work. His attention to detail is amazing."

"Sounds like a true artist."

"I never thought about it, but, yes, I suppose he is."

"And everyone knows how you like collecting authors and artists for your salons."

"Yes, I do but...hey! What's that supposed to mean?"

"Not a thing, Madam Gemma. Not a thing."

Gemma called out when she found the front door of the Baptiste Street house ajar. "Hands in the air! This is a raid!"

"Up here, Mrs. Clark!"

Her hand glided smoothly along the gleaming banister as she climbed the stairs. She found Cane installing a brass floor register. "Good afternoon."

He didn't look up. "Hey."

"That staircase is gorgeous."

"All I did was sand and finish the work of a master craftsman. You won't believe what I discovered about the stairs."

"Oh?"

"The treads are fitted seamlessly on the risers. Someone drilled tiny holes by hand and pegged the wood together really tight so the stairs won't squeak." Cane stood and stretched. "It's like they turned all that wood back into a tree."

"That's a poetic way of putting it." She thought of Maddie's comment about Cane's artistry. "Whatever it is, it feels like satin."

"It's supposed to, and the walls are supposed to feel like silk. In fact, the best nineteenth-century builders tested them with silk stockings."

"What do you mean?"

"They put a woman's stocking on their hand and ran it along the wall to make sure there were no snags." He caressed the wall with his fingertips and seemed satisfied. "Ready for the tour?"

"Absolutely."

Gemma marveled at one achievement after another. The original hardware had been cleaned and re-installed, and the cypress doors stripped and repainted. The upstairs bathroom had a heavy makeover incorporating the original black, white and green tiles, and the renovated kitchen gleamed with new appliances. The smell of fresh paint and plaster hovered throughout.

"Very impressive, Mr. Gentry. I don't think you've missed a thing."

"Thanks, but I'll need another week for final tweaks before your friends can move in."

She stroked the banister when they returned to the foyer. "This beauty is a real showstopper."

"Yeah. I wonder how it compared to the one in Mahogany Hall."

"That was a Storyville brothel, wasn't it?"

"The most famous one, I think."

"Then they're comparable in more ways than one. This place was a brothel before my grandfather bought in in nineteen-sixteen."

"I figured that when Henri found the ocelot skull. A lot of these old houses were bordellos at one point or another. The reason they built Storyville was because prostitution was so rampant in New Orleans. They figured it would at least keep the working girls in one place."

"Storyville must've really been something."

"Yeah. It's a shame they tore it down. It would've made a great tourist attraction."

"No doubt. Maddie works at the Wilkins Research Center and said people still come here looking for it."

"That's where I've seen her! I knew she looked familiar."

"You've been to the Center?"

"Lots of times. When I was researching the batture and nineteenth century architecture."

"I see." Her eye wandered to the boards above the front door. "No fanlight?"

"Not yet. That's a major project by itself."

"How badly is it damaged?"

"I tried to keep it together when I took it down, but it came apart in my hands. Good thing I was wearing gloves."

"How many pieces?"

Cane shrugged. "Couple hundred maybe."

"But they're all there, like a jigsaw puzzle?"

"Yeah, but—"

"I've been looking for a new project, and this sounds ideal."

"You can't be serious."

"Why not?"

"Because restoring that fanlight is a job for professionals. Jigsaw puzzles have soft, neatly cut pieces with pictures to help you fit them together. They're not chunks of broken glass with uneven sides that can cut your fingers to smithereens."

"Is the glass all one color?"

"Looked like a lot or red and orange. Some yellow too."

"What do you mean 'looked like'?"

"The glass was filthy, almost black. I didn't notice the colors until I was boxing the pieces."

"So you don't know the design?"

"Sorry."

"May I see the box?"

"After what I just said?"

"Absolutely. I never could resist a challenge."

48

Despite his misgivings, Cane agreed to bring over the shattered fanlight. He was due at four, but didn't show until almost five. Gemma met him at the door with a scowl, but his quick apology defused her anger.

"Sorry I'm late, Ms. Clark. My neighbor Poppy fell, and I had to take her to urgent care. I told you about her."

"I remember. Is she alright?"

"As alright as someone her age can be after tumbling off a catwalk."

"How old is she?"

"Late seventies, I think. She gets prickly if I mention age." Gemma motioned him inside. "Then, when I finally got to the Quarter, it took me twenty minutes to find a parking space."

"That's my fault. I forgot to tell you I have two parking spaces."

"Lucky you." He looked around the foyer. "This box is pretty heavy. Where do you want it?"

"I thought I'd use the dining room table as a workspace. It's right through there."

If Cane was awed by the opulence of Gemma's house, he gave no indication. Noting the sheen on the table when she turned on the chandelier, he hesitated. "We're dealing with chunks of metal and broken glass, lady. You got a pad for this thing?"

"Sorry. I should've thought of that." She retrieved a pad from the buffet and unfolded it onto the table. "Did you say 'we're' dealing with broken glass?"

"Yeah. You've no idea what you're getting yourself into."

"I don't know whether to thank you or throw you out."

"I'm familiar with both." Before Gemma could explore that comment, he reached into the box and tossed her a pair of gloves. "These should fit. I washed everything so you can see the colors now."

"Thank you. How do we get started?"

"The wooden frame is still in one piece, so I'll set it aside for reference. The glass was held together with strips of leading. They fell apart too."

"Those metal pieces?"

"Correct. Glass is still attached to some of them. I'll put those at the end of the table along with the larger glass pieces. You can help me arrange the smaller ones according to color. After that, we start looking for pieces that fit together."

When Cane spread out the shards of broken glass, Gemma realized that he hadn't exaggerated in calling it a daunting task. She picked up a chunk of amber glass and held it up to the chandelier. She did the same with the reds and yellows.

"They're so beautiful. I wonder how they get the different colors."

"They add different metallic oxides to the molten glass. Copper for red. Antimony for yellow and so forth." Like Gemma, he admired a piece before adding it to a growing pile. "I know that because my grandfather worked with stained glass. He died when I was little but my daddy told me about him."

"Really? Could this be one of his pieces?"

"I wondered about that the first time I saw the house. It's possible since it looks to date from his time."

"That would be so cool."

"There's no sure way of knowing since stained glass artists didn't sign their work. They didn't make the glass either."

"I don't understand. When I was in Venice, I watched those guys on Murano heat up the glass and blow it into all sorts of shapes."

"Glassblowing is totally different. With stained glass, the artist creates a design and shows it to the glassmaker. Glass is made to those specifications, and then the artist puts it all together."

"Hmmm. Learn something every day." Gemma lucked out and quickly found a fit between two orange shards, but after an hour of failure, she conceded the challenge was much greater than she anticipated. "I have new respect for archeologists. Those guys must have the patience of Job."

"I warned you." Cane began putting pieces back into the box. "I'll locate some restorers and take it over tomorrow."

"You'll do no such thing. I was commenting, not conceding."

Cane's shoulders rose and fell. "You're the boss, Ms. Clark."

"That's right, I am. And my newest order is that we stop being so damned formal and drop the last names."

A smile flickered and faded. "Okay."

"Good. Now then, Cane. What would you like to drink?"

"This water's fine."

Gemma glanced at her watch. "At five-thirty?"

"Got a beer?"

"I imagine Tyrone does. I'll go look."

"That your husband?"

"No. He works for me. Lives in the guest house."

Well, well, Gemma thought as she retrieved beer from Tyrone's refrigerator. That's the first time Cane Gentry has asked anything remotely personal. Maybe he's reachable after all.

By seven o'clock, Cane had matched three small yellow pieces to a large one, but Gemma was still struggling. After a second bourbon, she decided to call it quits.

"If I don't eat something, I'm going to get snarky," she announced. "You hungry?"

"I could eat something."

"How about some leftover pasta Bolognese?"

"Sure."

"Good. Come out to the kitchen and keep me company." Cane sat at the granite island while Gemma refreshed her drink. "Another beer?"

"No, thanks."

Gemma was taken aback. "Did I detect a note of disapproval?"

"Nope. None of my business."

"No, it isn't." Gemma pulled the pasta from the refrigerator and dumped it into a large pot. She turned on the heat and faced Cane across the island. "I'm sorry. That was rude of me."

"Don't worry about it."

She studied him over the rim of her glass. "You disapprove of me, don't you?"

"I don't judge people."

"Oh, but you do. The first day we met, you pegged me as someone living in the Garden District or, worse, the suburbs."

"That didn't mean I disapproved."

"Alright. Let's just say you labeled me."

Cane considered. "I did, and that was wrong."

"Now we're getting somewhere."

"And where is that?"

"On the road to being friends, I hope. You're an interesting man, Cane Gentry, and I'm drawn to interesting people. If you ever came to one of my parties, you'd find all manner of humanity. Rich, poor, black, white, Latino, gay, straight. If I wanted to live in some kind of homogenized ivory tower, I sure as shit wouldn't be in the French Quarter!" To her shock, Cane burst out laughing. "What's so funny?"

"I never expected to hear you say 'shit.'"

"Believe me, I know all the words." Gemma simpered. "And then some."

"I'll bet you do, and I'm glad to know you're not what I was afraid of."

"Which is?"

"What I often run into when I do restoration work. Overprivileged, entitled types who don't give a damn about a place's provenance, or are only interested in flipping houses. You took a real interest in your house, even to helping Mr. Chabrol with the dig and trying to put the fanlight back together. I was wrong about you and I apologize."

"In fairness, it works both ways. When I heard you lived on the batture, I figured you for an impoverished, uneducated, ne'er-do-well who ended up there because it was the end of the line. I was wrong too."

"Nor entirely. I ran away from home when I was sixteen and kept running until I ended up on the batture."

"Was that the baptism of fire you mentioned?"

"My whole life's been a baptism by fire. Always learning by doing. Like that old song says. Fools rush in where angels fear to tread. I was too young to know how stupid I was." He drained his beer. "Think I might have some of that bourbon?"

"Coming right up." Gemma poured his drink and gave the pasta a stir on her way back to the island. "If you don't mind my asking, what's the most foolish thing you rushed into?"

"Probably logging up in Oregon. I was twenty, and since I had no family and was responsible to nobody except myself, I became a timber faller. That job has all sorts of ways to kill you. A tree can 'barber chair,' meaning come it comes back on you, or you can step on dead limbs called 'widow-makers. You do all this with a live chain saw strapped onto your belt. It's pretty insane."

"You say you had no family?"

"None to speak of. My father got killed when I was twelve, and Mama died when I was sixteen. My older brother got mixed up with the law, and I'm not sure where my sister is."

Gemma filed that away. "And your other jobs?"

"Let's see. Circus roustabout. Short order cook. Boxer, which where I got this." He pointed to his broken nose. "They all taught me something, but the best life lesson I ever got was in Key West. I dated a stripper who hung out with this wild fringe group. Some small-time gangsters, a black transvestite, boozehounds and stoners. Freaks by most standards, I guess, but they welcomed me into their loony little universe and taught me it was okay to be an outsider."

"A valuable lesson."

"For sure. Anyway, all that rambling led me back to the batture when my car broke down. As Poppy said, I was broke and broke down."

"Do you ever regret coming back?"

"Not for a second."

"Good for you." Gemma checked the simmering pasta and unwrapped a loaf of ciabatta. "With the dining table otherwise occupied, do you mind eating at the breakfast table?"

"Fine with me."

Gemma began setting out plates and flatware. "I know what it's like to grow up without a father. Mine was gone all the time and cold as ice when he was home. I was eleven when he died of a stroke, and the sad truth is that I hardly missed him. I never learned how to relate to men, which no doubt contributed to my three failed marriages." She sipped her drink. "The first was a narcissist, which I didn't discover until it was too late. The second was a total workaholic whom I saw at breakfast, the occasional dinner and holidays. At least he left me this house. The third was an alcoholic which is why I drink like I do. I keep reminding myself that he's gone and I no longer have to keep up." She sipped again and leveled her gaze. "Do you mind if I ask what happened to your father?"

"Another long story, I'm afraid."

"Maybe you could tell me while you slice the ciabatta."

49

1980

Dean Gentry blamed his insomnia on pure loneliness. Alicia had taken the kids to Tennessee to visit her parents, leaving him in an empty bed for the first time since their marriage. Even after thirteen years and three children, they still slept spoon-fashion with his arms cocooning Alicia's back against his chest. In her absence, Dean clutched her pillow, but her faint scent only made him more restless. After an hour listening to the river's rhythmic slap-slap on the pilings below, he got out of bed and went into the kids' room. He looked at the bed shared by Cane and Luke and the pallet in the corner where Temple slept. Dean loved his sons, but had a special affinity for his daughter. At age four, Temple already reminded him of Alicia with her mother's eyes and innate sweetness, and she never failed to rush him when he came for work, arms outstretched, begging to be picked up and tossed into the air. Her joyous squeals pierced his heart.

Wearing only shorts and an undershirt, Dean went onto the back porch, hoping the cool night air would drive him back to his warm bed and invite sleep. He sensed it before he saw it, a fog so pungent and thick that it crept under his skin, the overripe breath of the Mississippi. He shivered, but instead of fog, the chill came from sentience born from years of living on the batture. Dean knew what was coming and waited for the ship's horn. After a few anxious seconds, there it was, distant but coming fast, the unmistakable bleat of a vessel in distress. It was underscored by shouts when his neighbors rushed outside, drawn by the familiar magnet of dread. The dense fog cloaked everything, but while it limited visibility, it magnified sound. The horn grew louder, closer, a cry for help heard by those who could only huddle below the levee and wait.

The Mississippi was deeper than it had been in years, gravid with spring rains and northern snowmelt. It was almost a mile wide there at the batture and lapped beneath the camps, high and hungry as it seized the towboat Miranda D and the empty barge lashed to her bow and propelled them toward shore. Dean watched, muscles tensing, as the enormous barge materialized. It seemed to hover for a moment before plowing through the mooring dolphins designed to deflect wayward ships. They were smashed like cardboard when the barge careened to port, ever closer to the batture. The towboat's horn grew deafening, and, between its plaintive moans, Dean heard his neighbors' collective screams and the shriek of metal as the barge finally ran aground. He was engulfed in the acrid stink of fuel and rusted steel.

"Sweet Jesus!"

Miraculously, the barge had missed the batture camps and wallowed like a beached whale with the Miranda D riding high behind, flat prow still lashed to the barge's stern. The towboat was just off Dean's porch, turning the night white with blinding deck floodlights. He shaded his eyes and watched with horror when the engorged river tore at the floundering barge and threatened to rip it from the towboat. The towboat's engines revved helplessly, fighting the river for the upper hand. After a moment, Dean's military training kicked in, and he cupped a hand to his mouth. Between blasts of the horn, he shouted orders to the crew of the towboat.

"Throw me a line and I'll secure you to those trees." After more shouts back and forth, Dean was hit and held by a floodlight, and a line splashed into the water short of his camp. "Again!" he yelled. "Throw it again!" A few more tries and he snagged the rope when it thudded on his porch. He jumped into the frigid water and swam toward the thick grove of willows a few yards away. They were deep-rooted and sturdy and held fast when Dean looped the rope around the thickest trunk and tied it tight. The line tautened as the towboat swayed to starboard, loosened as it tilted to port and grew rigid again.

"Hold, damn you!" he grunted.

Dean clambered back onto his porch to watch the hastily-tied lines stiffen and sag, stiffen and sag. As the seconds crawled by, the ropes seemed to hold. Chilled to the bone by river water, he began shaking when his adrenaline wore off, and his ears hurt when the Miranda D killed her thundering engines and left behind a vacuum of silence. He rushed inside to dry off and get into warm clothing, reassured by the loud distress call as the captain radioed for assistance. Relief was short-lived. The wake of a passing tanker unleashed a wave that rocked the towboat enough to threaten its lifeline to the big willow. With each sway and lurch, the tree bent further toward the river, making Dean fear that the willow might be uprooted. It held fast but, with a loud crackle, the loop slipped up the tree and stripped off the upper branches, as though the trunk had been whittled by a giant. The telltale noise drove him back outside in time to see the rope fly over the top of the tree, and the denuded trunk spring straight again.

"Damn!"

Dean plunged back into the water and swam toward the loose rope. He dove under time and again in an effort to snag it. Those watching from both towboat and batture were relieved when he burst to the surface with the line in hand. As he swam back toward the grove of willows, another wake, much bigger than the last, rocked the barge hard enough to tear it from shore. Still lashed to the barge, the towboat captain revved the engines and fought to steer the barge back to midriver, unaware that the man trying to secure the barge was tangled in the line. As the Miranda D and her barge were buoyed by the current and rode free, Dean Gentry was dragged to a watery death.

50

Cane brushed aside a low-slung willow branch as he led Gemma down the catwalk to Poppy's camp. He pointed toward the Mississippi where a towboat muscled container barges half the length of a football field. "I think about Daddy whenever I see those."

"I can understand why." She had been moved to tears last night with Cane's terrible story about his father's drowning.

"It used to make me sad, so I changed my way of thinking. Now it reminds me that he died a hero."

"It's quite a story, Cane, and I'm flattered that you shared something so personal."

"Must've been the bourbon because it's not something I talk about. I wasn't here when it happened and never knew the details until I moved back. A dude named Wino filled me in because he witnessed the whole thing." Cane yanked his hand off the railing. "Watch out for splinters. I love Poppy, but she doesn't take care of things like she used to."

"How is she since the fall?"

"Using a cane, but otherwise ornery as usual." When they reached the rusty screened door, Cane cupped his hand and yelled. "Hey, old lady! You got company!"

"Hold your water!" Gemma heard the thump-thump of a cane as Poppy approached in her trademark red and gold dragon robe and fluffy alligator slippers. The screen creaked open, and she smiled. "Come on in, honey. I know you're Gemma. Cane's told me all about you."

"He told me about you too, and I did a little homework. You were quite the chanteuse."

"Oh, that's way too fancy. I was just another saloon singer in the Quarter."

"I hope you'll tell me about it."

Poppy cackled. "You just try and stop me!" She took Gemma's arm and steered her through two small rooms jammed with a mishmash of furniture and a scattering of memorabilia from her heyday on Bourbon Street. Gemma didn't miss a faded poster advertising Poppy's appearance at the Hotel Monteleone and made a mental note to ask about her gig there. "It's a pretty day so we might as well enjoy it on the back porch. I've got some sweet tea if you're interested. Fresh-made."

"I'd love some."

Cane opened the door. "You two sit, and I'll get the tea."

"You go right ahead. Lord knows, you know your way around the place." She winked at Gemma. "Boy slept in that old hammock when he first moved here."

"So he told me."

"Did he also tell you that getting him to rebuild his folks' camp was like pulling teeth?"

"Not in so many words."

"Well, never mind about him." Poppy cackled. "Let's talk about me."

Gemma laughed too. "You're my kinda gal, Poppy!"

"Thanks. Now Cane tells me you wanted to know about some songs your grandmama wrote."

"Yes, I do. Her name was Maura O'Rourke, and there are some songs by her grandmother too. At least I think that's who she was. Her name is Cara Traver. These songs date back to the eighteen sixties. Some were Irish ballads and some were, well, you can see for yourself. I brought works by both women."

"Alright." Poppy dug thick reading glasses from her robe and began shuffling through the music. She occasionally paused to hum and sing a few lyrics. "Pretty." She was almost at the bottom of the stack when she paused. "I've sung Cass the Lass With Sass, but not with these lyrics."

"What do you mean?"

"When I first started out, I worked dives that wanted me to spice up the songs like they did in Storyville. You know. The old red-light district. Contrary to what some might think, that was way before my time." She winked. "Anyway, I only sang the bawdy version of Cass the Lass." Poppy thumbed through more songs. "What in the world is this doing in here?"

"What is it?"

"Tony Jackson's old song. Pretty Baby. I sang that one so often it was almost my signature number."

"Who's Tony Jackson?"

"A local cat and the finest piano man to ever come out of Storyville, that's who. Some people say he was Mahalia's cousin. You now, she grew up a few blocks from here and was baptized right in that old river. Her family was so poor she used to scavenge coal from parked train cars. Of course, scavenging is a time-honored tradition here." Poppy took a closer look at the sheet music. "Good Lord! Tony signed it to your great-grandma. Did you see this? Here at the bottom. It's almost faded."

"No, I didn't." Gemma leaned down and read aloud. "'To Maura. Sorry my song got you fired. Tony Jackson.' How on earth did I miss that?!"

"A signed copy like that belongs in the Jazz Museum here. That's a real treasure."

319

Cane reappeared with tea and orange bread. "Tell her about In the Pines, Gemma."

When Gemma explained her find, Poppy said, "Child, if that can be authenticated, you've got another treasure on your hands. A big one! Musicologists have argued over that song for years. What do you know about this Cara lady?"

"Not much. Irish, obviously, but I knew nothing about my family until I bought the house Cane's working on. There was a trash pit in the back, and we unearthed some stuff and one thing led to another. The place used to be a bordello, and Tony Jackson's message makes me wonder if Maura had a connection to Storyville."

"I wouldn't be surprised." Poppy squeezed lemon in her tea and stirred. "In those days, Storyville was about the only place where black musicians could play. It wasn't the birthplace of jazz like most people think, but plenty of greats got their starts in the cat houses. Tony Jackson, Jelly Roll Morton. Sidney Bechet. Buddy Bolden, too, but that dude was bughouse crazy. Maybe Maura sang somewhere in Storyville, and Tony accompanied her."

Gemma reread Tony's inscription. "This is the kind of thing that really makes me wish I could time travel!"

"Me too," Poppy said. "I'd sure love to hear Tony Jackson play, to find out first-hand what made him so great. By all accounts, the man was a genius."

"I'd like to see Lulu White's Mahogany Hall," Cane said. "I heard that some people tried to turn it into a jazz museum, but the city fathers said no. At least Pete Fountain got Lulu's fancy fanlight before they tore the place down."

"And replaced it with another damned housing project," Poppy grumbled. She flipped through more music and turned a page over and back again. "Interesting lyrics but the rest of the song is missing. Or maybe that's all she wrote."

"What are they?"

"'There's fool's gold o'er the doorway, and a sun that rises west. Spurn that place, ye weary, lest you find no rest.' Wonder what the heck that's about."

"Sounds like a warning to miners out west," Cane suggested. "They worked from dawn to dusk and never saw the sun. It was backbreaking work, so they were always tired. And there's the line about Fool's gold."

"But some of these songs are definitely about Appalachia," Gemma offered. "A lot of Irish and Scots-Irish settled there."

"True enough." Poppy continued browsing. "This one looks sweet. It's called The Mislaid Shawl."

"Would you sing it for us?"

"Sure." The song followed an Irish shawl worn by three generations of Galway women, and Poppy's husky contralto brought Gemma close to tears. "That Cara lady was quite a talent."

"So are you, Poppy. Thank you for the song."

"It was good for me too. My voice needed some attention, and lord knows that keyboard inside's been collecting dust way too long. Tell you what, honey. Come back anytime you're in the mood for a tune and bring your music. I'd love to try that one about the Praline Woman."

"I'll take you up on that."

"Good. Now I hate to throw you kids out, but my hip's giving me a fit after that stupid tumble, and I need to lie down."

"You need me to make some groceries?" Cane asked.

"Thanks, but I'm good for a few more days." She offered her cheek for a kiss. "Stay tuned."

Back at Cane's camp, Gemma said, "I understand why you're so fond of Poppy."

"She's my oldest friend and the best neighbor anyone could have."

"I'm also beginning to understand why you love the batture so much. It's like no place I've ever seen."

"I love it because it constantly changes and never waits for anyone or anything. It plays outside the rules and gives me the power that comes only from being alone." He grew solemn, voice reverential. "It's where the river breathes."

"That's beautifully put. You should write a book. In fact, there's your title. Where the river breathes."

Cane chuckled. "I'm a plagiarist, not a writer. I read all that stuff somewhere."

"Oh!" Gemma was distracted by a flash of feathers when a pelican swooped low and scooped a shiny fish from the river. Something beyond caught her eye. "What's that cement thing propped against that piling? There. On the other side of Poppy's camp." She squinted. "It looks like a naked woman."

"That's Our Lady of the River. I remember her as a kid. She's so old even Wino doesn't know who put her there." He threw her a comic salute. "She's a home-made river gauge, and I can still hear Daddy explaining how she worked. Things are copacetic if she's totally exposed, like she is now. If the water reaches her thighs, we move everything in the yard to higher ground. If it reaches her breasts, better batten down the hatches. If she goes underwater, it's time to get the hell out of Dodge."

"Seriously?" He nodded. "And you're truly reconciled to this precarious existence?"

"Otherwise, I wouldn't be here."

Gemma inhaled the wet air, riddled today with the tang of creosote. "I love my creature comforts too much to be a convert, but I admit it would be something special to wake up here and, as you say, feel the river breathe."

"I suspect there's only one way to find out."

Gemma smiled. "Are you flirting with me, Mr. Gentry?"

"Am I doing it so badly that you have to ask?"

51

While Cane was put the finishing touches on the house, Gemma continued working on the fanlight by herself, devoting every free moment to the pieces of broken glass and twisted metal strewn across her dining table. Tyrone worried that she was becoming obsessed, and, although he said nothing, Gemma sensed his concern.

"I'm fine," she assured him. "I've just come too far to turn back. That's all."

"I know what you mean 'cause I'm doing the same thing."

"How so?"

"I'm still keeping my eye on that pretty gal who joined our church last summer. She hasn't given me much encouragement, but I ain't quitting until I'm down for the count."

"Good for you."

One morning, the week before Christmas, Gemma surveyed the groups of red, yellow and orange shards and wondered if the design might incorporate stripes radiating from the center. Because there was far more red and orange than yellow, she centered the yellow and arranged the rest in a sunburst. When that didn't balance, she pushed the yellow to the bottom of the frame, rearranged the top and stepped back to study the whole. She remembered Cane's advice that squinting could reveal shapes invisible to the focused eye and was rewarded when the blurred colors coalesced into a pattern.

"I see it!" she cried. "I see the design!" She grabbed her phone and left Cane a one-word message when he didn't pick up.

"Eureka!"

He called back within minutes. "What've you found?"

"A design in the fanlight!" she cried. "I finally see a design!"

"Send me a photo."

Gemma grabbed her phone and sent an image. "Did you get it?"

"Yeah."

"And?" she urged.

After a long pause. "Sorry. I'm not seeing anything."

"Look at the reds and oranges. Don't they look like they're flowing up and out from the yellow?"

"It's hard to tell in this photo." Another disappointing pause. "I don't know, Gemma. Maybe if I see it in person—"

"And maybe it's just more wishful thinking," Gemma groaned.

"Don't give up so fast. I plan on knocking off here at four-thirty. I'll swing by your house on the way home."

"Never mind. You'll be wasting your time."

"I'll be the judge of that. See you later."

Cane clicked off before Gemma could protest further. She gave the shattered fanlight a long stare, wondering if she had imagined the design out of desperation. Annoyed and frustrated, she went to the kitchen for a coffee break to find Tyrone sorting the day's mail. She was surprised to find an envelope from Philip Brooks, whom she hadn't heard from since she closed on the house. Inside was more sheet music and a note saying that this was the last of the family memorabilia. She thumbed listlessly through the stack and, when nothing caught her eye, took it into the dining room and tossed it atop the buffet. She picked up a piece of yellow glass and held it until it grew warm in her hand.

"Give up your secret, damn you!" she hissed.

Gemma was still studying it when Tyrone appeared. "This must've fallen out of that mail envelope. It was on the kitchen floor."

Gemma didn't look up. "Please put it with that stuff on the buffet, Ty. I'll go through it later."

"I think you better take a look. I didn't mean to snoop but I couldn't help reading it when I picked it up. Be careful. It's been folded so many times it's about to fall apart." He held out a fragile piece of sheet music. "Is this for real?"

Gemma's eyes widened, and a frisson rippled down her spine when she saw the song title. "Sweet Baby Jesus! It can't be!"

"You mean it's fake?"

"No, no. I mean I can't believe it!" Her hands trembled when she examined the page more closely. "But there's my grandmother's name's plain as day. Maura Traver O'Rourke, and a date. Nineteen-seventeen." She noted scribblings in the margins and found another signature among the crossed-out, rewritten lyrics. "Look there!" She pointed. "Cara Walton Traver. That one's dated eighteen seventy-four. That's got to be Maura's grandmother." Gemma's insides turned to jelly. "They wrote it together, Ty! My relatives wrote this song together!!"

Tyrone drew back. "You okay? You look a little freaked out."

"Who wouldn't be?" Her hand shook so hard she put the fragile paper on the buffet and stared as though it were a mirage. "My God, man! It's one of the most famous folk songs ever written!"

Tyrone had never seen Gemma so rattled. "Want some water?"

326

"Please!" Left alone, Gemma took a series of deep breaths and recouped enough calm to sort her thoughts. "Sweet Jesus! Why on earth didn't I think of this before?!" Heart racing again, she scrambled to the top of the ladder for a bird's eye view of the fanlight. She experienced another, even stronger frisson when she saw what she hoped for, and her lips curled into a smile. "It's there in plain sight, right where the song said it was." Gemma was all but hypnotized as the shape sharpened and blurred and sharpened again. Finally she heard Tyrone's voice.

"What're you doing up there?"

"Looking at the solution to New Orleans oldest mystery, that's what!" She barely felt Tyrone's hands as he helped her down. She chugged the water, so excited that she dribbled it on her chin. "Look at me! I'm out of control."

"You gonna tell me what's going on?"

Gemma was lost in her discovery. "First the house and then the song and now the fanlight. The key to the whole thing was in the fanlight!"

"You talking serious crazy, you know that?"

"What?"

"I said you're talking crazy."

She grinned and squeezed Tyrone's shoulder. "We'll see, my friend. We'll see!!"

Gemma was bursting to call Cane again but decided to wait until he got there. She went into the library and rifled through Maura's sheet music until she found the page she needed. She set it on the buffet alongside the other piece and put her newfound knowledge to work on the fanlight. The pieces didn't fit exactly, but the colors and shapes told the story. She called Tyrone back to take a look.

"See anything?"

"Looks kinda like the Arizona flag," he said. "With a sun instead of a star."

"Bingo!" Gemma beamed triumphant. "Speaking of the sun, I do believe it's under the yardarm."

"What's your pleasure?"

"Champagne, my good man. When Mr. Gentry gets here, we are going to do some serious celebrating, and you're welcome to join the party."

"Now I know you've gone off the rails."

"To the contrary. For the first time since we started this project, I know what I'm doing."

Ty left, shaking his head, and when Cane arrived, Gemma shocked him with an exuberant hug.

"Whoa! What's going on?"

"The thrill of the hunt and a mission accomplished, that's what."

"I'm guessing you found something else since our phone call."

"That, my friend, is the understatement of the century. Follow me." Gemma grabbed his hand and led him to the dining room. "Climb up that ladder and tell me what you see."

Cane did as she asked and studied the cluster of glass pieces. "It looks like the orange and red are streaking out of that cluster of yellow."

"Blur your vision and keep looking."

After a long moment, "Is that a sunset?"

"A sun*rise!* Remember those strange lyrics Poppy mentioned in my grandmother's song?"

"About the sun rising in the west?"

"Exactly." She picked up the music sheet and read aloud. "There's fool's gold o'er the doorway, and a sun that rises west. Spurn that place, ye weary, O God, lest you find no rest."

Cane leapt down from the ladder. "I get it now! The fool's gold is that yellow in the fanlight, and the sun is rising over the West Bank. My God, Gemma! She was writing about your house!"

"Warning about it, too. And like she did with In the Pines, Maura changed some lyrics and finished a song started by her grandmother, Cara."

"You mean?"

Gemma held out the page Tyrone found. "Look at the dates and signatures."

"Man, oh, man!" Cane sank onto a dining chair when his knees gave out. "I never in a million years imagined that old song was about a real place."

"Me either, but Maddie says people at the research center ask about it all the time."

"She'll sure have something to tell them now that she'll be living there."

"Indeed she will." Gemma took the page back to the buffet and laid it beside the sheet music. "Come look, Cane. It's all together for the first time. Music, lyrics, history, my family, everything."

Cane joined her, scanned the pages and began reading aloud. "There is a house in New Orleans, they call the Rising Sun. It's been the ruin of many a poor girl, and me, O God, for one. If I had listened to what my mama said, I'd 'a-been at home today. But I was young and foolish, and let a rambler lead me astray. Go tell my baby sister, never do like I have done. To shun that house in New Orleans, they call the Rising Sun. There's fool's gold o'er the doorway, and a sun that rises west. Spurn that place, ye weary, O God, lest you find no rest. I'm going back to New Orleans, my race is almost run. Going back to spend the rest of my days, beneath that Rising Sun." He shook his head. "Wow!"

"Is that all you have to say?" Maura's eyebrows rose when he didn't respond. "Well?"

"Well—"

"Well, what?"

Cane grinned. "Well, I'll be damned!"

Author's Notes

I first heard The House of the Rising on Joan Baez's debut album in 1960, and its evocative mythos remained powerful enough to inspire this novel 64 years later. With prostitution the suspected theme, I devoured Al Rose's 1974 Storyville New Orleans, the definitive book on the subject. Tom Anderson, Lulu White, Josie Arlington, Willie Piazza, Zozo La Brique, and Tony Jackson were real personages. Jackson left New Orleans for Chicago around 1913, but he was such an intriguing character I massaged the dates. Charlotte Townsend is loosely based on Madam Gypsy Shafer, whose three-story house sat at the corner of Iberville and Villere Streets. According to Jelly Roll Morton, "The girls would walk into the parlor, dressed in their fine evening gowns and ask the customer if he would care to drink wine. They would call for the 'professor,' and while champagne was being served all around, Tony would play a couple of numbers."

If a naïve Mississippi country girl like Maura O'Rourke could be lured into "the life," I found this the most plausible setting. Things were very different for the vast majority of Storyville prostitutes. Alcoholism, drug addiction, crime and violence were commonplace, and the everyday speech was far coarser than depicted in my story. Obscene language has its place, but it wearies readers and loses impact with overuse. The Fancy character is my way of thanking Bobbie Gentry for her eponymous song and, of course, her haunting Ode to Billie Joe.

The origins of "The House of the Rising Sun," like a great many folk songs, are lost in the mists of time. Musicologists say it resembles sixteenth-century ballads and is rooted in traditional English folk tunes. In the United States, the song was known to Appalachian miners as early as 1905, and the first published version appeared in 1925 in an *Adventure* magazine story entitled "Old Songs That Men Have Sung." The lyrics of that version begin: "There is a house in New Orleans, it's called the Rising Sun. It's been the ruin of many poor girl, great God, and I for one." The oldest recorded version, under the title "Rising Sun Blues," was made by Clarence "Tom" Ashley and Gwen Foster in 1933. Ashley said he learned the song from his grandfather, which suggests it was written well before 1900. In Ashley's version, the narrator is male. "There is a house in New Orleans, they call the Rising Sun. Where many poor boys to destruction has gone. And me, oh God, are one."

In 1953, folk song collector Alan Lomax found a bawdy house called the Rising Sun in two traditional English folk songs. English folk singer Harry Cox included an old tune called "She Was a Rum One" in his repertoire. The opening verse was "If you go to Lowestoft and ask for The Rising Sun, there you'll find two old whores, and my old woman is one." The coastal town of Lowestoft is the easternmost settlement in the United Kingdom, hence the rising sun reference, and once had a pub called The Rising Sun. When and by whom the song's location was changed to New Orleans is unknown.

In 1938, Roy Acuff became the first singer of note to record it, and Woody Guthrie followed in 1941. A year later, Josh White released a version purportedly learned from a "white hillbilly singer." A widely diverse group of artists followed: Libby Holman (1942), blues legend Lead Belly (1944 and 1948), Glenn Yarbrough (1957), Pete Seeger (1958), Andy Griffith (1959), Miriam Makeba (1960), Joan Baez (1960) and Bob Dylan (1961). All were popular, but in 1964 a blockbuster version by the British group, The Animals, ensured its immortality. Lead singer Eric Burdon first heard it in an English club, sung by Northumbrian folk singer Johnny Handle. On tour with Chuck Berry in 1964, The Animals sought something to close their act distinctive from the expected rock number. From its first performance, "House of the Rising Sun" repeatedly brought crowds to their feet. It was so successful that, between tour stops, the group slipped into a small London studio and recorded it in a single take! The song ran four and a half minutes, much too long for a pop single, but the gamble paid off, and it rocketed to the top of the charts in both England and America. It was the first British Invasion number to knock the Beatles from the top spot, something they graciously acknowledged in a congratulatory telegram to The

Animals. Musicologists have called "House of the Rising Sun" the first folk-rock hit. It ranks 122 on *Rolling Stone*'s "500 Greatest Songs of All Time" and is one of the Rock and Roll Hall of Fame's "500 Songs That Shaped Rock and Roll." In 1999 it received a Grammy Hall of Fame Award and continues to be a staple of oldies and classic rock radio formats.

Theories about possible locations and purpose of the House of the Rising Sun are as varied as the song's origins are obscure. Most consider it a cautionary tale about prostitution being a life of "sin and misery." Others believe it was a prison, due to a version referencing "a ball and chain." Lyrics also suggest a gambling den or saloon, and all interpretations work whether the narrator is a man or a woman. Historically, the name Rising Sun appears several times in New Orleans. When I lived in the French Quarter, I was intrigued by the Rising Sun Hotel on Conti Street which burned in 1822. In excavations years later, the unusually large quantity of cosmetic items and wine bottles suggested it was a bordello. This theory is enhanced by advertisements with provocative copy suggesting prostitution was available in the small hotel. During the Civil War, advertisements for another Rising Sun on Decatur Street in the Quarter variously described a restaurant, coffee house and beer salon. Sometime around 1870, a French Creole named Marianne LeSoleil Levant ("rising sun") may have operated a brothel on Esplanade Avenue. There was also the Rising Sun Hall in the Carrollton neighborhood of New Orleans. According to late nineteenth-century city directories, the place rented out for dances and civic functions but had no connection to prostitution or gambling.

Pamela Arceneaux, senior reference librarian at the Historic New Orleans Collection and author of *Guidebooks to Sin: The Blue Books of Storyville*, made a study of prostitution in the city and found no evidence that the House of the Rising Sun existed. Her conclusion: "To paraphrase Sigmund Freud, sometimes lyrics are just lyrics." No one conducted a more thorough search than Ted Anthony in his seminal book, *Chasing the Rising Sun: The Journey of an American Song*. "Reality provides the raw material for legend, and legend repays it by bleeding back into reality," he wrote. "After a long and winding journey of discovery, it turns out that we are better for not knowing."

Acknowledgments

I met Pamela Arcenaux shortly after moving to New Orleans in 1992 and discovering the extraordinary Historic New Orleans Collection, an author's absolute dream for researching. She was endlessly helpful and resourceful and gave me some sage advice when I was obsessing over finding some obscure historical minutia. Writers of historical fiction often become our worst enemies, something Ms. Arcenaux put into perspective when she politely asked whether I was writing a novel or a dissertation. Over 30 years later, she deserves a note of gratitude for that and her patience when I became one of the legions pestering her about the location of the House of the Rising Sun.

About The Author

Michael Llewellyn is the author of twenty-four books in historical fiction, adventure, true crime, contemporary fiction, mystery, time travel, Southern humor and nonfiction travel. He is a 10th generation Virginian and lives in Fredericksburg.

Made in the USA
Columbia, SC
06 November 2024

45674387R10185